THE BASTARD LAIRD'S BRIDE

Highland Bodyguards, Book 6

EMMA PRINCE

Books by Emma Prince

Highland Bodyguards Series:

The Lady's Protector (Book 1)

Heart's Thief (Book 2)

A Warrior's Pledge (Book 3)

Claimed by the Bounty Hunter (Book 4)

A Highland Betrothal (Novella, Book 4.5)

The Promise of a Highlander (Book 5)

The Bastard Laird's Bride (Book 6)

Surrender to the Scot (Jerome and Elaine's story, Book 7)—coming early 2018!

The Sinclair Brothers Trilogy:

Highlander's Ransom (Book 1)

Highlander's Redemption (Book 2)

Highlander's Return (Bonus Novella, Book 2.5)

Highlander's Reckoning (Book 3)

Viking Lore Series:

Enthralled (Viking Lore, Book 1)

Shieldmaiden's Revenge (Viking Lore, Book 2)

The Bride Prize (Viking Lore, Book 2.5)

Desire's Hostage (Viking Lore, Book 3)

Thor's Wolf (Viking Lore, Book 3.5)—a Kindle Worlds novella

Other Books:

Wish upon a Winter Solstice (A Highland Holiday Novella)

To Kiss a Governess (A Highland Christmas Novella)—*coming soon!*

The Bastard Laird's Bride

HIGHLAND BODYGUARDS, BOOK 6

By
Emma Prince

The Bastard Laird's Bride (**Highland Bodyguards, Book 6**)
Copyright © 2017 by Emma Prince

For Scott. Always.

Chapter One

Late September, 1319
Outside York, England

"Ye asked to speak with me, Sire?" Reid Mackenzie let the wet canvas flap fall closed behind him.

Robert the Bruce, King of Scotland, stood bent over a wooden desk, quickly scrawling something on a scrap of parchment. "Please, Laird Mackenzie, call me Robert when we are alone," he said without looking up.

The King wanted Reid to call him by his Christian name? Reid shifted, spreading his feet to distribute the weight of his dripping chainmail. He'd heard that the Bruce allowed such familiarity with the men of his inner circle—of which Reid wasn't a part. Or mayhap he was now.

The Bruce scribbled a final word on the parchment and set aside his quill, straightening. He met Reid's gaze

I

with a wry smile. "Ye've fought at my side enough times to forego such formalities."

That was true enough. Reid had led the Mackenzies behind the Bruce at the Battle of Bannockburn five years past, and for the siege on Craigmoor Castle a year ago—not to mention a dozen skirmishes in between. Their victory in the Battle of Myton yesterday had only further proven Reid's loyalty to the King and his cause.

"I must thank ye yet again for yer clan's aid yesterday, Laird," the Bruce said, coming around the desk.

Reid dipped his head in acknowledgement of the praise, but felt his mouth quirk. "If I must call ye Robert, Sire, ye must call me Reid."

When he lifted his gaze to the King's face once more, he found the Bruce grinning. "Fair enough. Come," he said, motioning toward two plain wooden chairs against one of the tent's walls. "Let us sit and share a drink as friends."

Reid's brows itched to lift in surprise, but he schooled his features and lowered himself into one of the chairs. He repressed a grunt of relief as the chainmail's weight eased. He'd been standing, riding, and fighting in the damned stuff for a full day and night, and at four and thirty years of age, his body protested more than it used to.

The Bruce lifted a pitcher from a small table between the chairs and poured wine into two goblets, then sat.

"To another victory."

Reid let the sweet warmth of the wine slide down his throat, savoring the way it began to melt the knots in his body. The Bruce, too, took a long draught, leaning back in his chair with a sigh.

The King had already removed his battle armor and washed away the mud and blood, yet he had been with the men for every moment of their fierce siege on York, despite having more than ten years on Reid. The liberal streaks of gray in his russet hair and beard, along with the deeply etched lines in his sun-bronzed face, spoke of the hard-earned victories Scotland's warrior-King had wrested from the English. Reid could think of no other man more worthy to lead their cause for freedom.

After another deep pull of wine, the Bruce set aside his goblet. "Edward's Queen Isabella is in the wind. We will return north tomorrow, or the day after if this rain keeps up."

Reid's brows shot up. "Ye dinnae mean to pursue her?" He'd been told when the Bruce had called him down from the Highlands that the purpose of laying siege to York was to capture and ransom Isabella, Queen of England, who was rumored to be in the city. The second part of what the Bruce had said sank in. "And ye dinnae mean to remain in York."

Another wry grin made the edges of the Bruce's beard lift. "Nay, though I am pleased with today's outcome. I wouldnae have imagined it possible to penetrate so deeply into the heart of England. The failed siege on Berwick Castle and the obvious weakness of York will be a double blow to Edward."

"*Failed* siege? Last I'd heard, Edward's men were still bombarding Berwick's walls relentlessly."

The Bruce chuckled softly. "Just after we claimed

victory yesterday, I got word from one of my messengers —Edward has abandoned Berwick and is now rushing to York, leaving Lancaster floundering and my castle safe."

Reid slowly set his own goblet down and settled back into his chair, awed yet again by the Bruce's shrewdness. "Let me see if I understand. King Edward's forces have been laying siege to Berwick Castle for months now."

"Aye," the Bruce said placidly. The Bruce had only managed to recapture Berwick from the English last year, and Reid knew how dearly the King cherished the Borderland stronghold.

"Edward wanted to retake the castle badly enough that he reconciled with the Earl of Lancaster, the bastard trying to dethrone him practically right under his nose, to lay siege to Berwick with their combined forces."

"Aye," the Bruce repeated.

"But even as the castle's defenses weakened, ye decided to launch an attack on York under the pretense of kidnapping the King's wife."

It was an arrogant and bold plan—and bloody risky. Yet when the Bruce had asked for Reid's help in sieging York, he'd agreed immediately. It wasn't Reid's place to question the King of Scotland, though he'd privately thought it was mad to send men and resources deeper into England rather than use them to defend the Bruce's prized Berwick Castle.

"Ye have the right of it so far," the Bruce replied, clearly amused.

"Yet ye never intended to take York. This—our

attack on the city, the battle, our victory—was all to scare the shite out of Edward—and force him to choose between taking Berwick and protecting his Queen."

"That is *almost* the whole of it." The Bruce took another swig of wine, his dark eyes glittering with clear pride. "The divide between King Edward and the Earl of Lancaster has served me quite well over the years. There was once a time I even let Lancaster believe he and I were allies."

Reid stilled. "What?" If Lancaster had indeed tried to ally with the Bruce, it was an act of treason against the Earl's English King.

"Oh, aye," the Bruce replied. "And I have the letters to prove it."

"Why havenae ye exposed Lancaster, then? Surely ye could have put a stop to the siege on Berwick with the information that Edward's newest ally is actually a traitor."

The Bruce lifted a brow at Reid. "Ye are a direct sort of man, arenae ye?"

Aye, he was. Reid would rather punch his way out of a bind than plot moves and countermoves, but as the Laird of a large and powerful Highland clan, he'd been forced to learn to control that urge. He leaned forward, propping his elbows on the chair's arms. "Ye are playing some longer game, I take it."

The King nodded, a pleased smile touching his lips. "Indeed. Lancaster's reckoning will come soon enough. As it is, chaos and discord are far more valuable to me than exposing the bald truth."

He spread his hands wide. "Queen Isabella has fled

south. Edward is barreling toward York, desperate to save his Queen and a city he no doubt thought too far deep into England to be in any danger from me. And Lancaster is scrambling back to his own lands, once again at odds with his King and obliged to explain himself for his role in all this."

As Reid worked to digest the King's words, the Bruce lifted a finger. "Ah, that was the piece ye didnae ken. There are already rumors swirling that Lancaster has betrayed Edward. In fact, many are asking how I learned that Isabella would be in York at all."

"Lancaster would act so boldly?" Reid asked.

"Nay," the Bruce said with a dismissive wave. Yet the mischievous grin lingered on his mouth. "That's what my spies are for. But those rumors didnae come from thin air, now did they?"

Reid drew in an incredulous breath. "Ye started them." At the King's single nod, Reid put the last few pieces in place. "The rumors will cast suspicion on Lancaster. It will drive a wedge between him and Edward. And Berwick is safe now that the siege has dissolved—all from a single victory on the battlefield yesterday."

At last, the Bruce's face broke into a full, wide smile. "It willnae help Lancaster's cause that I have instructed our men to leave his lands untouched as we return to Scotland. When his lands go unplundered, it will look like a reciprocal favor in exchange for the information about Isabella's location."

Reid couldn't help but chuckle at the audacity of the man.

"Did ye ever intend to kidnap the Queen, or was that all part of the ruse?" he asked.

The Bruce's smile dimmed slightly. "In truth, I dinnae like bringing women and children into warfare."

Reid sobered. It was well known that the Bruce's wife, daughter, and two of his sisters had been held captive by King Edward's father for years. Some of the women had even been held in cages suspended in the air to make their helplessness a humiliatingly public display.

"However," the Bruce said, forcefully smoothing his features, "times being what they are, we cannae always pick and choose who will bear the cost of war." He leaned back in his chair. "Ultimately, it didnae matter whether I intended to capture the Queen or no'. The threat of doing so was enough to accomplish my aims."

Reid shook his head, letting a soft chuckle puff past his lips. "I can say this—I'm grateful to hear that ye werenae planning on lingering overlong in York. Now that this battle is won, I'll be glad to return to Scottish soil once again. We travel tomorrow, ye say?"

"Most of us will be, aye," the Bruce said evenly. "Ye willnae, however."

Reid froze. "What?"

"Dinnae glower so, man," the Bruce said, holding up a hand. "I'm no' punishing ye. Since ye are already in England, I simply have an errand for ye to run on my behalf."

Reid narrowed his gaze on the King. The man had just proven that he had a mind as sharp as a blade and thought a dozen moves ahead like the skilled chess player he was. Where did he plan to place Reid on the ever-shifting board?

"What sort of errand?" he asked cautiously.

"My network of eyes and ears tells me that two lords in Cumbria have arranged an alliance. Edgar de Reymont is sending his only daughter to marry Halbert de Perroy, in part so that they can join forces to protect their borders—against me."

The Bruce's smile turned wolfish. Reid shifted, his chainmail scraping against the wood of his chair.

"And ye want me to—what? Join yer men along the western Borderlands to give them hell?"

"Nay, something far simpler than that," the Bruce replied. "I want ye to kidnap the intended bride and bring her to me."

Simple? Reid nearly snorted, but he managed to repress the urge. "The lords—de Reymont and de Perroy, ye said—if they truly wish for this alliance, won't they find another way even if the lass isnae used for the union?"

The Bruce ran a hand over his russet and gray beard. "Mayhap, though there is much to be said for delaying them. The alliance may collapse without the lass to unite them, or better yet, their lands could fall under my control before they have a chance to sort things out. Besides, de Reymont cannae pass the lass's dowry to de Perroy if they arenae married."

The reasoning was sound. After all, the Bruce had won victory after victory in the last several years using just such tactics—a swift strike to introduce chaos, then a fierce blow just when his enemy was off balance. Bloody hell, it was why they'd won the battle yesterday.

Reid raked his dark hair back as he considered it. "And ye want me to fetch the lass? That is all?" he asked warily.

"Aye," the King said with an easy nod. "I've gotten word that a small party has just left de Reymont's holding headed west. Send the majority of yer men back to Eilean Donan, but take a few with ye into Cumbria to capture the lass."

"And then?"

"I am returning to my camp in Lochmaben. Bring the lass to me there."

"After which I will return to the Highlands." Reid had no place making such a flat statement to the King of Scotland. As a loyal Laird, he was the Bruce's to command. Yet he took his responsibility to his clan just as seriously as his pledge to serve his King.

Though Reid prided himself on keeping a stony countenance, the Bruce seemed to read all his thoughts on his face. "Ye are a man of fierce loyalty, Laird Reid Mackenzie," he said, watching Reid with keen, assessing eyes. "The welfare of yer clan no doubt weighs on ye."

"Aye," Reid said without hesitation.

The Bruce tilted his head pensively. "Ye have never failed to answer my summons when I needed yer help," he went on. "Yet serving me has taken ye away from yer people. And from yer responsibilities."

Despite himself, Reid flinched slightly. Aye, the King was all too astute in his assessment. The duties of Lairdship sat like the heavy chainmail around Reid's shoulders.

Keep the Mackenzies safe.

Build alliances with neighboring clans.

Produce an heir.

Reid's hands clenched around the chair's arms. Aye, he needed to get back to the Highlands. He'd neglected his duty to his people and their future for too long.

"See this errand done, and I promise to reward ye for yer dedication to me and the cause—and to yer clan." The Bruce met Reid's gaze evenly, yet a prickle of unease left Reid wondering just what the King schemed behind his dark eyes.

But it was not his place to ask. He rose, squaring his shoulders against the weight of his armor.

"I'll see it done," he said, dipping his head in a curt bow. "Ye can depend upon it."

Chapter Two

Relinquishing her worldly possessions would be easy. It was cutting her hair that was creating a problem.

Corinne de Reymont stared down at the shears in her sewing basket. The basket was tucked into one of her two trunks. It was no great bounty of goods. She had a few personal items—soap, combs, stockings—and a handful of gowns, one of which was even made of silk for her wedding day. And she had her sewing supplies, which she rarely used.

No quill.

No ink.

No parchment.

She'd been forced to leave those behind. Though it chafed, she willed herself to be grateful for small mercies, for if she'd been allowed to pack her scribing supplies, she would be hard-pressed now to leave them behind along with everything else.

As it was, she would not allow herself to mourn a few lost gowns and a sewing basket, for they weren't truly hers. They belonged to her father, and soon enough, they would belong to Lord Halbert de Perroy. Besides, everything of value—linens, silver, and even coin—would be sent to de Perroy after the marriage was consummated.

Corinne swallowed the bile that rose in her throat at the thought. She lifted a trembling, gloved hand in front of her face, as if she could will it with her stare to cease throbbing. Aye, she would do this despite the injuries on her hands. She could cut her hair if it meant escaping a future as de Perroy's property.

Gritting her teeth against the pain, she reached inside the sewing basket and wrapped her fingers around the shears. The wounds on the backs and palms of her hands scraped against the gloves' lining. She sucked in a breath, squeezing her eyes shut. She could only pray that none of her father's guards could hear her anguish. The wagon's canvas siding was thin, and they slept on the ground only a few feet away.

Biting her lip to stop another pained cry, she lifted the shears. With her other hand, she clenched a hank of her red, unruly hair, pulling it taut despite the throbbing in both her beaten hands.

With a deep breath, she slid the shears around the clump of hair. She closed her eyes and snapped the blades shut. The tension on the strands went slack, and she opened her eyes to find a long clump of the hated orange stuff resting lightly in her palm.

The wild, insane urge to giggle suddenly rose in

Corinne's chest. Oh, how she despised her hair! Cutting it didn't change the color, of course, but she suddenly felt free—free of her responsibility to marry de Perroy, free of her father's control, and free to write her own future as a scribe. Now she could go to a nunnery unencumbered by her worldly possessions—including her hair.

Normally an abbess would cut a novice's hair herself in a ceremony to purify the nunnery's newest member of the outer world's impediments. Corinne assured herself that wherever she took sanctuary, the nuns would forgive her for completing the step herself. Besides, being rid of her long tresses would make it easier to pass herself off as a boy if she were questioned before she could find and reach the nearest convent.

Buoyed by hope, she made quick work of the rest of her locks, cutting along the line of her jaw. She hardly noticed the pain in her hands as she worked, so giddy was she.

Yet as she snipped the last of her hair and let it fall to the wagon's wooden floorboards, the knot returned to her stomach. This had been the easy part. Now she had to find a way to slip from the wagon and past her sleeping guards into the night-dark woods surrounding them.

As quietly as possible, she dropped the shears back into the basket and drew the hood of her cloak over her head. With a stiff, shaking hand, she drew back the wagon's covering an inch, letting in the cold night air. Corinne peered into the darkness, searching for signs of movement from the guards, who lay wrapped in their cloaks nearby.

She gnawed on her lip. Mayhap if she woke one of them and claimed to need to seek privacy, he would let her go without suspicion. Or mayhap—

A twig snapped somewhere off in the woods. Corinne nearly leapt out of her skin. She clapped a hand over her mouth to stifle a startled gasp, remembering too late the welts and bruises beneath her gloves. Moaning into her palm, she closed her eyes until the pain had receded enough for her to think clearly once more.

Only an animal, she told herself. None of the guards had stirred.

She pulled back the covering even farther, leaning her head out into the crisp night. Aye, she would pretend to need to relieve herself, then—

An explosion of shouts erupted all around. Shadows seemed to spring from the surrounding trees and take the form of men on horseback.

A shocked scream rose in her throat. The riders swarmed into their little camp, their already-drawn swords catching the weak light of the crescent moon overhead.

Her father's men scrambled to their feet, reaching for their weapons even as the riders descended upon them.

Now! some distant, primal voice screamed in her head. This was her chance to escape. Her guards were distracted and overwhelmed by the unknown attackers. She could slip away and no one would notice.

Without another moment to waste, Corinne threw herself from the back of the wagon, stumbling upon the ground before finding her feet. Ducking her head, she scrambled toward the trees lining the clearing the men had chosen for their camp. The screams of battle and death sliced through the night air behind her, but she didn't look back until she reached the safety of the trees.

She darted behind a large oak and swept her gaze over the camp. It was a roiling sea of men, horses, and weapons. Death cries ripped from men's throats. Dark blood dulled raised steel. For the first time, she noticed that the men on horseback wore kilts.

Corinne's mind numbed and her blood went cold. Scotsmen were known to be ruthless and savage. If they found her—

She had to focus. None of the Scotsmen had seen her, else they would have already come barreling after her.

The camp sat in a little clearing in a valley that ran east-west. She would be able to move faster if she stayed on the flat, straight path created by the valley. But she would also be easier to run down on horseback. She currently stood at the base of the southern slope protecting the valley. That left her little choice. She had to go up.

Pushing away from the oak, she scrambled uphill, darting between shadows. But before she'd gone far, a booming voice coming from the camp froze her feet.

"Where is she? Where is the de Reymont lass?"

Corinne's heart stuttered and her stomach dropped

to the forest floor. They were after *her*? The deep Scottish voice crashed through her thoughts.

"Tell me now, man, or answer to my sword."

Over the pounding of her own blood in her ears, Corinne hadn't noticed that the sounds of battle had ceased almost as quickly as they'd begun. And judging from the Scotsman demanding answers, the barbarians had been victorious.

She dared a glance back into the valley below. Someone had lit several torches. Even from ·a long stone's throw away, Corinne could see that her father's men lay bloodied and wounded—or dead—all around the wagon. The wagon's canvas cover had been completely yanked off.

In the middle of a circle of mounted men stood a savage-looking warrior. His back was turned to her, his black hair reflecting the torchlight. He spoke to one of her guards, who was on his knees with the Scot's blade to his throat.

"Tell me where the lass is," the warrior demanded again. And then he raised his free hand, and the light caught what he held.

It was a clump of Corinne's discarded hair.

The man on the ground before the Scot blubbered something incomprehensible, his wide, terrified eyes locked on the sword pointed at his throat. The Scot muttered something and turned away, lowering the blade. Then he began to sweep the surrounding forest with his gaze.

Panic spiked hard in Corinne's veins. They were after her, but her fear-addled mind could not comprehend why. All she knew was that the dark Scotsman would hunt her down like a wolf after a fawn if she did not move now.

She flung herself into motion, forcing her legs to drive her higher up the hillside, but only a few steps in, her foot slid out from under her, sending dried leaves, pine needles, and a handful of stones tumbling downhill. Her hood fell back, yet she managed to catch herself before she could slide farther.

But it had been enough. Her head whipped to the torch-lit camp, her gaze colliding with the dark-headed warrior's through the trees. His eyes flicked to the hank of red-orange hair in his hand, then back to her, clearly making out her uncovered head in the low light. He pointed directly at her, murmuring some order to his men.

And then he came after her.

Chapter Three

Their surprise attack had worked without a hitch. De Reymont's men had scrambled like a flock of startled chickens as Reid and his warriors descended upon them. Mayhap Reid had been wrong to be so wary of the Bruce's "errand." It had taken mere moments to subdue the English. Reid was all but home free.

He dismounted as the battle died around him and strode to the wagon. The English lass must be holed up inside.

"Alain, light torches," he called over his shoulder as he reached the wagon. He pulled open the canvas flap at the back. The interior was dim and empty except for a few trunks. The lass must be hiding behind—or inside—one of them.

Without hesitation, he tore the entire covering off the wagon so that the torchlight would reveal every corner. Tossing the canvas sheet to the ground, Reid hoisted himself into the wagon's bed.

The wagon creaked and rocked slightly under his weight, but no other movement or sound came. Muttering a curse, he strode to one of the trunks and flung it open. A few folded dresses lay inside. He moved them aside, but there was no false bottom in the trunk. He gave the other chest the same inspection, finding only a few trinkets and a sewing basket.

Where in damnation was the lass? Just as he stepped toward the back of the wagon once more, a little pile of something orange caught his eye. He crouched, lifting the strands into the light of the torches.

Was that…*hair*?

"What the bloody hell is going on?" he snapped to no one in particular.

Reid leapt from the wagon and stormed over to one of the Englishmen, who cowered on his knees before the mounted Mackenzie warriors.

"Spare me!" the man cried. "Take the girl if you wish, but let me live."

"Bloody coward," one of the Mackenzies muttered. Reid had to agree.

He halted in front of the crouching Englishman, lifting his sword slowly before him to ensure he had his attention.

"Where is she?" he demanded in a loud, cold voice. "Where is the de Reymont lass?"

The man's eyes widened on Reid's bloodied blade. "I-I…she is in the wagon, milord."

"Nay, she isnae," Reid snapped. "I'll ask ye again— where is she? Tell me now, man, or answer to my sword."

The man moaned in terror, his eyes nearly bulging from his head. Reid resisted the urge to spit. *This* was the sort of man Lord de Reymont had sent to protect his only daughter?

"I-I-I swear, milord," the man stuttered. "Last I saw her, she was in the wagon."

"I'll give ye one last chance," Reid managed through gritted teeth. "Tell me where the lass is." He held up a handful of wavy red hair, staring hard at the man before him.

When the Englishman's gaze locked on the hair, then shifted back to Reid's blade, his eyes rolled back in his head as if he were about to faint. Reid lowered his sword with a frustrated exhale. "Bloody Englishmen," he muttered as he turned his back on the spineless guard. "Ye men, search the northern slope," he said, letting his gaze sweep the dark forest. "And ye lot, take the southern side. The damned lass is somewhere."

Just as he was about to turn and remount his horse, a rustling of leaves and a clattering of pebbles had him snapping his head toward the hill enclosing the southern side of the valley.

A little tumble of leaves and rocks was sliding down the hillside. A flicker of movement higher up snagged his eye. Through the trees, a shadowy figure stood frozen—and staring right at Reid. The weak light of the moon caught on the figure's head, illuminating the thatch of cropped orange hair there.

Was that a lad staring back at him? Reid's mind still couldn't make sense of the hair in his hand, but it matched the figure's. The lad was slight and narrow-shouldered beneath his cloak, yet there was no mistaking that cropped flame-orange hair. He let the hair fall to the ground. Now was not the time for puzzling that mystery. He let his body take over, bolting directly for the base of the hill.

"Follow me," he ordered his men. He pointed first to the left and then to the right, indicating that his men should fan out to flank him. They spurred their horses, instantly following his command as he charged straight for the fleeing lad.

He didn't bother remounting—a horse would move just as slowly as a man over that steep, rocky, densely forested terrain. Besides, the surge of battle lust still ran in his veins, now transforming into the thrill of a hunt. Whoever the lad was, there would be no escaping Reid. And he would be made to answer for the de Reymont lass's whereabouts.

Reid drove himself up the hillside at a sprint. His legs devoured the distance between him and his quarry, who still scrambled upward ahead of him. At the edges of his vision, he saw his men urging their horses over the uneven ground. This wee fish would not escape his net.

In another three heartbeats, he was nearly within an arm's length of his prey. Reid dove forward, snagging his hand around the lad's ankle. A high scream cut the night as the lad tumbled forward and landed hard on the sloping forest floor. Before the wee fish could wriggle away, Reid yanked forcefully on the ankle in his grasp, dragging the figure toward him.

But the lad was lighter than he'd expected. Instead

of simply pulling him to a halt, Reid dragged the wee lad straight into his arms.

The lad screamed again, high and piercing, as Reid tightened his hold to keep him from escaping.

But as the lad writhed in his grasp, Reid began to notice things. The tangle of skirts beneath the lad's cloak as he tried to lash out and kick Reid. The faint softness of the lad's chest against his. And the distinct fragrance of lemon.

Just as Reid was about to abruptly release the lad—or rather, lass—the little hellion sank her teeth into his shoulder.

Reid roared as her teeth broke the skin. Before she could do more damage, he rolled on top of her and sprang up so that he straddled her hips, pinning her to the ground. With one hand around each wrist, he held her down. She thrashed wildly, screaming and bucking against him even though he had her completely restrained.

Just then, the yellow glow of torchlight fell on him and his struggling quarry.

"What in the bloody…" Alain mused, reining his horse beside Reid.

"This," Reid said, tightening his grip on the writhing lass, "is de Reymont's daughter. Isnae it, lass?"

She thrashed again beneath him, but then when her gaze caught on the mounted warriors drawing into a tight circle around them, her eyes rounded. She looked at Reid and began to tremble, recoiling as if she could sink into the rocky hillside to escape him.

He used her sudden terror-stricken stillness to

examine her more closely. *This* was the daughter of an English nobleman? Her cropped hair was a wild nest of orange atop her head. Twigs and leaves stuck out from the riotous waves. Her skin was the palest white, except for several smudges of dirt and a few random scratches marring her cheeks.

Her wide eyes gave him pause for a moment. In the flickering torchlight, their exact color was hard to discern, but Reid was struck with the impression of a stormy blue-green ocean. His gaze dipped to her berry-red, trembling lips, and behind them a flash of white teeth—the teeth she'd used to bite him.

She was slight and only faintly soft beneath him, more bone than lush woman's flesh, yet Reid's traitorous body warmed now that he knew she was in fact a lass and not a lad.

He jerked himself abruptly off her, pulling her up to sitting by her wrists.

"What the bloody hell did ye do to yer hair?" he demanded. "And why were ye in the woods instead of inside the wagon?"

Belatedly, Reid realized that neither question was worth asking, for her answers didn't matter. He had an assignment to complete: deliver the lass to the Bruce—naught else. Why should he care to know more about his charge?

"Touch me and I'll...I'll..." she sputtered, staring at him with a combination of fierceness and terror. "I'll gouge your eyes out and bite your tongue off and—"

A soft chuckle rippled through the Mackenzie warriors. Reid only cocked an eyebrow at her. "Dinnae fash, lass. I dinnae wish to touch ye. Until a moment ago, I thought ye were a lad."

A suffusion of red seeped over the lass's face. She once more pulled against his hold on her wrists, but her gloved hands remained trapped.

A twinge of regret at the callousness of the remark niggled at Reid. She was completely under his power now, his captive. There was no need to insult her. For some reason, though, he needed to remind himself of what he was about. This was an errand for the Bruce, a simple delivery of this English lass. There was no room in Reid's life for even a passing softness, a flicker of interest, toward her.

"What do you want with me, then?" she demanded, though her voice wavered with fear.

"King Robert the Bruce cordially requests the honor of yer presence," he said dryly, causing another faint chuckle from his men.

He stood, pulling her to her feet after him.

"You...you are kidnapping me?" the lass breathed. "Taking me to Scotland?"

"Aye."

Like a startled cat, she turned wild once more, attempting to bolt away from him. A few of his men's horses nickered and stepped back as she fought once more for her freedom.

Good God, the lass was a fierce wee thing. She struggled against him as if her life depended on it—which he supposed it did. After this, naught would be the same for her. The Bruce would see her marriage arrangement dissolved. Assuming the King released her back to

England at some point, her family might send her to a nunnery to shield themselves from rumors about her kidnapping by barbarian Scotsmen.

Once again, guilt tugged at Reid. The lass's future was none of his concern, he reminded himself harshly. He was doing his duty to his King, and once he'd delivered the wee hellion, he could return to the Highlands and see to his responsibilities there.

To put an end to the lass's wild struggles, he hoisted her up and folded her over his shoulder like a sack of grain. She screamed and kicked and pounded his back, but he ignored her.

"To the camp," he commanded his men. "We'll take aught of value then ride north."

As they descended into the valley, he let the others pull ahead.

"Ye willnae be harmed," he murmured to the lass.

Her thrashing slowed, but Reid wasn't sure if it was because she'd accepted what he'd said or if she was merely exhausted from her struggles.

When they reached the camp, he glanced at the wagon. "Leave it," he said, "but take the contents of the trunks. The lass may have need of her things."

It was a small mercy, but at least she would have a few gowns for the time the Bruce planned to hold her in Lochmaben, however long that might be.

As a handful of his men began passing the lass's gowns out to be tucked into their saddlebags, Alain brought Reid's horse to him.

"Do ye need rope to bind the wee thing, Laird?" Alain asked, a faint note of teasing in his voice.

"Nay," Reid snapped. He hoisted the lass into the saddle, then swung up behind her.

He spared a moment to survey what remained of the de Reymont men's camp. A few men lay wounded on the ground. Others had been killed. The coward who was so quick to give up his mistress was nowhere in sight.

It didn't matter if he alerted someone to the attack. By the time the English could muster a response, he and his men would already be in Scotland with the lass. Besides, Reid rode with the strength of the entire Scottish army behind him. The Bruce protected those who served him, which was more than could be said for the English King.

One by one, the torches were snuffed as the men prepared to depart. He looped one arm around the lass, ensuring she couldn't throw herself from his horse. Taking the reins up with his other hand, he spurred his horse into motion. His men fell in behind him, and soon they were swallowed by the night-blackened forest.

Chapter Four

✦❧✦

Corinne tried with all her might to stay strong, to resist the giant Scotsman in the saddle behind her in any small way she could.

His thick forearm around her middle kept her pinned in place, his hand curling into the material of her dress at her side. She would never manage to dismount and make a break for it with him holding her so. She tried to lean forward so that her back didn't brush his chest, but the position put her off-balance.

If her cursed hands weren't so badly abused beneath her gloves, she could have used the saddle's pommel to leverage an inch of space between her and her captor, but as it was, her hands were all but useless.

For many dark hours, she could not order her thoughts into coherency. The attack, then her attempted flight and capture, tumbled over and over in her mind. What could the King of Scotland possibly want with her? And could she trust the man behind her to keep his word and leave her unharmed?

His visage was burned into her brain. In the torchlight, his face had been like chiseled stone, all hard lines and angles. Black, unbound hair fell in waves around his shoulders, and he had nearly enough scruff of the same dark color on his face to be called a beard. A scar bisected his left eyebrow, making his scowl even fiercer than it already was. His eyes had been a strange slate gray that revealed only hardness and cold determination.

Yet there had been no malice in his gaze, nor lecherous invasion in his touch. Would he and his band of barbarian warriors truly not harm her?

As a gray dawn began to break, the man behind her whistled softly to the others. They drew together—there were mayhap a dozen of them, their green and blue kilts draping over their large warhorses—then reined to a halt as they reached a stream.

Unease rose like a tide inside her. When they'd been riding, her mind had walked in circles, thinking over and over upon what had happened back at the camp. But now Corinne realized she should have been focused on what lay ahead.

As the man dismounted behind her, her gaze darted over the warriors and the quiet forest surrounding them.

"Where are we? Why are we stopping? What are you about?"

The dark Scotsman exhaled, then reached for her and pulled her from the saddle.

"We are mayhap a day's ride from the Scottish border," he said evenly. "We are stopping to give the horses—and the men—a rest. And as to what I am about…" He lifted an eyebrow, the one sliced in two by a white scar. "…I told ye already. I'm delivering ye to the Bruce."

Seeming to think that was a sufficient explanation, he pivoted on his heels, but kept a hand wrapped around her arm. He pulled her away from the stream and the others until he halted a stone's throw deeper into the woods.

"Ye have a choice," he said, turning back to her. "The hard way, or my way."

So numbed with shock was she that all she could do was stare up at him, unable to comprehend what awaited her next.

"Ye can continue to fight and struggle against me," he went on, "in which case I'll have to tie ye to a tree so that we can all get some shuteye. Or ye can accept that ye will never escape me and that ye are going to Scotland as the King sees fit."

Corinne's jaw went slack. *Those* were her two choices? Despite her fear and exhaustion, a spark of rage kindled inside her. It seemed that powerful men would never cease trying to use her as a pawn for their own ends. First her father and Halbert de Perroy, and now this giant of a Scot and King Robert the Bruce himself!

By some miracle, she managed to hold her tongue. At last, the wheels of her mind began turning once more. She would have to escape, there was no doubting that. The closer they drew toward Scotland, the harder it would be to navigate by herself across the landscape.

Yet she was weak with fatigue, hunger, and thirst. Her flight from the Scots had left her battered and bruised. And the mountain of a man glowering down at her was far too suspicious at the moment to let her out of his sights.

She must make it appear that she was acquiescing to her fate, that she was submitting to him.

She let her lower lip begin to tremble, which was all too easy, since her composure was only a few threads from snapping as it was. Lowering her gaze, she nodded. "I…I understand."

He was silent for a long moment, and she could feel his eyes on her, but at last he grunted.

"See to yer needs. I willnae be far, so dinnae consider doing something foolish."

She hurried to a thick shrub nearby. When she emerged a moment later, the Scots were unsaddling and hobbling their horses. The dark-haired Scotsman—clearly the leader of the group—guided her by the elbow to a small clearing between the trees a few feet from the stream.

"Sit."

Though his command chafed, she lowered herself to a rock amongst the ferns and loamy soil and waited while the man and the other Scots moved about their little camp.

Once he'd seen to his dun-colored horse, her captor

approached and offered a waterskin. Gritting her teeth, she closed her hand around the skin and took a long drink. Then he passed her some dried biscuits, all the while watching her closely.

When the edge was gone from her hunger and thirst, he took back the waterskin and crouched on his haunches so that they were at eye level with one another.

"What is yer given name?" he asked, his low voice surprisingly gentle.

"Corinne," she replied, meeting his gaze. In the overcast light, his eyes matched the clouds overhead— gray, shifting, and impenetrable.

"I am Laird Reid Mackenzie," he said.

"Why are you doing this?" she blurted. She silently cursed herself for the desperation in her voice, but his sudden kindness was making her want to crumble to pieces in the face of all that was happening.

He lifted one shoulder. "Because my King asked me to."

Her distress ratcheted into aggravation. "Then why is *he* doing this?"

The Mackenzie Laird stared at her evenly. "Does it matter? Ye cannae do aught to alter the King's plans."

Hot, helpless frustration surged in her veins. Aye, she was a pawn, her wishes meaningless, her ambition pointless in the face of men's schemes.

"It matters to me," she replied in a thin, tight voice.

He appraised her for a moment, then spoke again. "The King wished to thwart the union between Lord de Reymont and Lord de Perroy. He decided that the easiest way to accomplish that was to...eliminate the possibility of a marriage alliance."

Corinne sucked in a breath. "Does your King mean to...to kill me, then?"

The Laird blinked. "Nay, of course no'." The confusion cleared from his eyes. "Ye dinnae ken his character, but he is a man of honor. He doesnae murder women and children."

"A man of honor?" she muttered. "He had you kidnap me. How is there honor in that?"

An amused look crossed the man's hard features. "It isnae my place to question my King." He hesitated before going on. "In truth, I dinnae ken what he has planned for ye once I deliver ye to him, but I assure ye he willnae harm ye."

The Mackenzie Laird stood suddenly. "Get some rest while ye can," he commanded. "We'll push hard until we reach the border."

"And then?" she murmured, looking up at him.

"Then it will take another day to reach the King's camp in Lochmaben. And after that, I dinnae ken, for ye willnae be my concern anymore."

With that, he strode to one of his men and murmured some instructions. The others began bedding down on the ground, wrapping extra lengths of blue and green checked plaid around themselves. The Laird accepted a folded swath of wool from the man he was speaking to, then returned to Corinne's side and stretched out beside her.

"Remember, lass, dinnae think to cause trouble," he muttered as he hunkered down into the ferns.

Weariness suddenly pulled fiercely at her, and she let herself slide from the rock onto the mossy forest floor. Pulling her cloak tight against the chilly autumn air, she gave over to an exhausted sleep.

Chapter Five

R eid didn't buy the de Reymont lass's demure act for a second. He saw the fire in her sea-green eyes even as she pretended to acquiesce to him.

Strange, then, that the lass would still be sleeping beside him, nigh unmoved after several hours on the forest floor.

Reid was a light sleeper—it was a necessary skill as a warrior. He'd had every confidence that even without tying Corinne to a nearby tree, he would wake immediately if she stirred or tried to slip away. Yet she must have been even more exhausted than he'd thought. In addition to her fatigue, he hadn't missed the fact that her hands pained her. Mayhap she'd hurt them when she'd tried to flee the Englishmen's camp.

A dozen questions tugged at him, but he pushed them aside. He didn't need to get to know the lass in order to deliver her to the Bruce. The sooner he got this over with, the sooner he could return to the Highlands.

With that thought, he rose, folding the extra length of Mackenzie plaid. At the soft noises of his rising, his men awoke, just as practiced in light sleeping as he was. As they began saddling their horses, he crouched beside Corinne.

"Wake up, lass. It's time to go."

When she didn't stir, he shook her shoulder. She murmured something, her creamy brow creasing but her eyes remaining closed.

A hank of her chin-length, bright red hair slid across her cheek and over her closed eyes. What in God's name had led to the shearing of that wild, riotous hair, he wondered idly.

Pinching a lock between forefinger and thumb, he gave her hair a gentle tug. "Wake up, Corinne," he repeated, giving her hair another wee pull for good measure.

She sat up suddenly, her tresses askew and her eyes wide. In annoyance, she huffed, blowing the offending locks out of her face. Then her eyes met his and she stilled. Comprehension filled their depths, with first distress and then that same determined glint he'd seen before flashing in them.

Repressing his curiosity, he rose and helped her to her feet by her elbow.

"We've a long way to go before nightfall," he said curtly. "See to yer needs and return quickly."

He watched her face closely, but he needn't have. Her thoughts were written clearly on her delicate features. Her gaze drew distant as she considered, and her lips parted slightly on a breath.

She thought this was her chance to escape, no doubt. She was rested, had at least a few oatcakes in her belly, and was still on English soil.

He could practically see the calculations she made in her head as she nodded slowly and turned away from him, presumably to tend to her needs and return, as he'd ordered.

Of course, he could have stopped her there. He could have gripped her arm and spun her around, thrown her over his shoulder and onto his horse's back once more. But he'd learned after twelve years as the leader of his clan that oftentimes a lesson experienced was far more effective than a lesson merely told.

"I may be a few minutes," she said over her shoulder, blushing fiercely.

Reid nodded and watched her disappear into the dense woods. He turned and strode to his men, who had already mounted and were awaiting his orders.

"This will take but a moment," he said.

"Are ye sure, Laird?" old Hamond said, pointing at something over Reid's shoulder. "The wee lassie already has a head start on ye."

With a sigh, Reid turned to find a thatch of wild orange hair darting away through the trees. He mounted his horse with a grunt, then called "Wait here," over his shoulder as he urged the animal after the fleeing lass.

In mere moments, he was only a few strides behind her. She dared a glance over her shoulder, her eyes round. Abruptly, she changed course, making a hard right turn around a large pine tree.

Reid tried to rein his horse after her, but the turn was too tight, and he overshot the tree, his horse neighing his objection as he came to a halt. The lass was clever, Reid would give her that. Yanking the horse to the right, he spurred the animal after her once more.

Even in the thick forest, he gained ground on her, for his steed was sure-footed and trained to maneuver in tight quarters. The lass darted left, but this time Reid gave her enough of a lead to cut the corner off her turn, gaining yet more ground.

She turned again, and up ahead Reid saw that she meant to cross the rushing, rocky creek they'd camped beside, but higher upstream. He muttered a curse. He wouldn't drive his horse across an uneven creek bed, but that didn't mean he couldn't pursue her on foot. He'd be damned if he let a wee English chit best him.

Without hesitation, she launched herself into the creek, the surging water instantly snatching the hem of her skirts and cloak, tugging them downstream. Reid reined in his horse and leapt down, charging after her. He reached the water just as she got to the halfway point. She was only a few arm's lengths away now.

Seeing how close he was, she sprang toward the opposite bank, but her foot must have slipped on a rock underwater. She lurched sideways with a shriek, then crumpled into the stream, her skirts and cloak billowing as she went.

Some rational part of Reid's mind knew that the water was shallow, and that there was no danger of the lass drowning or being swept away. But logic vanished in that moment. Instinct—and fear—took over.

He dove forward, snatching her up before she toppled completely underwater. Scooping her into his arms, he carried her back toward the water's edge. With the stream swirling ferociously around his knees, he picked his footing carefully until he reached solid ground.

He set her down unceremoniously on the hard-packed ground, crouching in front of her. Before she had time to regain her wits and attempt to flee once more, he imprisoned her wrists in his hands.

Breathing hard, she lifted her gaze and stared at him defiantly, her eyes burning.

"Yield," he commanded, returning her hard stare.

"Nay!" she shot back. She tossed her head so that her short-cropped tresses were flung out of her eyes.

Reid ground his teeth for a moment, willing forth some of the calm, rational demeanor he'd had to master as Laird. "Lass," he said, forcing his voice to be even. "Ye willnae defeat me in this. I am stronger than ye. I am bigger than ye. And I willnae fail in my mission to deliver ye to my King. Yield, and save yerself further embarrassment and pain."

Corinne's blue-green eyes grew bright. It took Reid a moment to realize that it was from the shimmer of angry tears.

"You are...you are a monster," she choked out. "Just like all the rest."

Shite. Reid was an arse. In less than a day, the lass had proven herself brave and determined. Aye, it was his job to deliver her to the Bruce, but that didn't mean he had to break her spirit while doing so.

He let a long breath go. He didn't like playing the role of barbarian. He was a hard man, aye, and expected his orders to be followed. Yet Laird Murdoch Mackenzie and Reid's mother hadn't raised him to be a bully, to force others into submission just because he physically could.

"Ye are truly determined to return to yer fiancé, arenae ye?" he muttered.

"Nay," she blurted.

Caught off-guard, Reid sharpened his gaze on her. Color seeped into her cheeks, but she met his eyes unflinchingly.

Reid chewed on that for a moment. The lass fought against him tooth and nail, yet she wasn't fighting to reach her fiancé?

"Ye wish to return home, then, is that it? To yer family?"

"Nay," she repeated, her eyes turning hard. "I was already plotting my own escape when your men attacked."

Reid thought back to the night before. He'd assumed that the lass had merely fled when they'd attacked, wisely deducing that it would be safer to hide in the woods than wait for his men to find her. But had she actually been caught in the middle of executing her own getaway? Reid's attack must have thwarted her plans—and mayhap if he'd struck an hour later, he never would have found her at all.

He barely managed to suppress a rueful snort. Leave it to this bold, fiery-haired Englishwoman to take matters into her own hands.

But where was she so desperate to go? And why did her eyes light with hateful fire at the mention of both her family and her fiancé?

Reid grudgingly set the questions aside. He could indulge his curiosity some other time. Right now, his men—and the King himself—were waiting on Reid to get this lass to Lochmaben.

Slowly, he released her wrists, eyeing her to ensure she didn't attempt to break away once more. When she remained seated on her soggy skirts, he said, "I was telling ye the truth when I said that I dinnae ken what the Bruce intends to do with ye. All I ken is that he wishes to stop this marriage alliance from going forward. It seems as though ye want the same thing."

Her fierce gaze faltered. "What are you getting at?"

Reid lifted one shoulder in a casual shrug. "Once the Bruce is satisfied that de Reymont and de Perroy cannae ally against him, he'll have no more need of ye. I imagine he'll let ye go to wherever it was ye were planning on escaping to."

It wasn't a lie, exactly, for Reid had no notion of what the Bruce intended to do with the lass once she was at his camp. The logic of Reid's assessment was sound, though in truth, Reid couldn't claim to understand all of the Bruce's moves and countermoves. No doubt the King was already scheming several steps ahead, and the lass was just one small cog in his plans.

She pulled her lower lip between her teeth, working it as she considered. Unbidden, Reid's eyes dropped to her lush mouth. He tore his gaze away, pretending to scan their surroundings. All was calm and quiet except for the stream's merry gurgle behind them. In fact, the only thing amiss was the sudden knot in Reid's stomach at the sight of Corinne's moistened, plump lip.

Damn it all, he needed to concentrate. Sensing she was close to capitulating, he spoke gently. "As I said before, ye can fight me every step of the way, but ye willnae win. Or ye can come with me to the King, and mayhap get what ye want in the end."

At last she seemed to make a decision. She lifted her chin, meeting his eyes. "I *will* have what I am after," she said.

Reid almost asked what could inspire such fierce determination in her, but he clamped his teeth down on the question before it slipped out.

"Verra well," he said, rising. "No more of these mad flights, then." He extended a hand to help her stand.

Without taking his hand, she dragged herself to her feet. She was only wet up to her waist, but her water-logged cloak and skirts had to be heavy. Her gloved hands were wet as well. She kept them hanging awkwardly by her sides like wooden blocks. "Then don't give me reason to flee."

The boldness of the wee chit nearly made Reid chuckle. "I willnae," he said instead.

Taking her elbow, he guided her back to his patiently waiting horse. He took up the reins, but instead of mounting, he walked with Corinne back to his men.

As they reached the others, he turned to her. "Take off yer cloak so that it can dry."

To his surprise, she did as he said, though her hands fumbled with the tie at her neck. He passed the sodden cloak to one of his men, who draped it behind his saddle.

Alain held up a spare length of plaid, drawing Reid to his side.

"So, have ye subdued the wee hellion, then?" Alain asked.

Reid took the plaid and gave Alain a hard look. "I believe we've reached an… understanding."

Alain chuckled. "Whatever ye say, Laird. I'll just be glad to be rid of the English chit."

As Reid approached Corinne, part of him had to agree with Alain. The lass had caused a great deal of trouble in less than a day. When he slung the plaid around her, Reid's shoulder pinched with a faint twinge of pain where she'd bitten him. He'd had to chase her down twice now. And to add insult to it all, his boots squelched with creek water.

Still, as he lifted her onto his horse and mounted behind her, he could not deny his fascination with the lass. She wasn't at all what he'd been expecting when the Bruce had told him he was to fetch an English noble-man's daughter. He'd assumed she would be pampered, delicate, and easily cowed in the face of a band of High-land warriors.

Instead, he'd been saddled with a stubborn, willful wee scrap of a lass whose hair matched her fiery spirit.

He nudged his horse into motion, pulling her close with an arm around her narrow waist. Her bottom fit snugly against his groin, and a tendril of her wild hair tickled his nose with its faint lemon scent.

Despite the crisp edge to the autumn air, warmth surged in Reid's veins.

Aye, this was not at all what he'd expected.

Chapter Six

A s the sky turned from slate gray to charcoal, the Mackenzie Laird reined in his large dun horse. Corinne sagged with relief. How could these Scotsmen ride over rough terrain and through dense woods with few rests, yet not be falling out of their saddles with fatigue?

They must all be made of stone. The Laird had certainly felt like a rock wall behind her as they rode. His chest was so broad and hard that she had bounced off it several times, yet his firm hand wrapped around her waist had kept her in the saddle before him.

It was far too intimate for an English lady to be wedged between a kilted man's thighs the way she was. Corinne tossed the thought aside. She cared not what a lady was and was not allowed to do, but considering she intended to become a nun, she shouldn't have noticed just how warm and solid Laird Reid Mackenzie was.

Nor the fact that he smelled like wood smoke and wool and sharp, sweet pine.

As he dismounted, his heat vanished, making her hunch into the green and blue plaid he'd given her. Blessedly, the rains had stayed at bay during the day, allowing her plain brown woolen skirts to dry, yet the evening was growing rapidly colder.

She let him pull her from the horse's back, his hands encircling her waist. When her feet were on the ground, he leveled her with a sharp look, his gray eyes steely.

"Can I trust ye to see to yerself for a moment, or are ye going to run again?"

Corinne didn't have the energy to bristle, yet a flicker of warm ire kindled in her belly. The barbarian had more than proved that he could force her into submission. She hated to admit it, but he'd been right—he was bigger and stronger than she was by far, but more than that, his will was wrought of iron. Never had she met a man so commanding, so determined, so wholly obeyed by his men, than the Mackenzie Laird.

"Aye," she muttered, hating the sound of defeat in her voice.

As she trudged to a copse of bushes nearby, she reminded herself that she wasn't giving up—only accepting a minor setback. She would *allow* the Laird—nay, she couldn't pretend that she had any power over him. She would *accept* that he was taking her to the King of Scotland.

If the King truly meant to destroy her forced union with Halbert de Perroy, all the better. And once the

Bruce was through with her, she would find a convent to join. It mattered not *which* convent, for she trusted her abilities with ink and quill enough to know that she would be accepted as a scribe—welcomed, even.

Who knew, she might even stay in the Scottish Lowlands. As long as she was allowed to perform her work, she cared not if she ever returned to England.

She emerged from the bushes to find the dozen Mackenzie warriors setting about arranging a makeshift camp between the trees. The horses had been hobbled, and one of the men, a gnarled old giant with gray-dusted brown hair, was making a fire.

"Bring some kindling with ye, lassie," the old warrior called as she approached.

Corinne bent and awkwardly tried to pick up a few sticks at her feet. Her stiff, sore hands protested, making her wince and suck in a breath.

"Let me." Suddenly the Laird loomed over her. "Dinnae mind Hamond," he said, taking the sticks gently from her aching hands. "Go sit by the fire and warm yerself."

She nodded, too tired to do aught but obey him. She lowered herself onto a rock as the warrior called Hamond coaxed the fire to life.

The Laird dumped an armload of wood next to Hamond, then retrieved a waterskin and pouch of food from his saddlebags. The other warriors settled themselves around the fire with food and drink as well, though Corinne noticed that they gave her a wide berth.

The Mackenzie Laird seemed to ignore the invisible

wall separating her from the others, for he approached and sat right next to her. She accepted the waterskin and more biscuits, along with dried venison from the pouch.

As she gingerly lifted the skin in both hands, the Laird's low voice made her start.

"Yer hands pain ye. What is wrong with them?"

"Naught," she said, too quickly. Heat rose from her neck to her face. "I am fine," she added in a more even voice.

He eyed her for a long moment. "Ah. My mistake."

Seeming to drop the topic, he turned to the food pouch and rummaged in it for a moment. Then he drew out a small green apple. "Try this," he said, tossing the apple in the air to her.

Without thinking, she reached for the fruit, but when it landed in her open palms, she gasped at the smarting pain. The apple rolled from her throbbing hands into the dirt.

The Laird clicked his tongue and reached for the apple, polishing it against the plaid across his thighs. But when he met her gaze, his eyes were surprisingly gentle.

"Tell me the truth," he murmured. "Ye are hurting."

A breath slipped from her lungs. "Aye."

"Mayhap I have something in my saddlebag that can help. Let me look at them."

He reached for her, but she recoiled on instinct. He stilled, his large, callused hands suspended between them. "I willnae harm ye," he said.

Something about the soft, low rumble of his voice made her extend her hands toward him.

As if he were handling a newly hatched chick, he took up one glove and pulled ever so slightly. Though they were made of soft calfskin, the rasp of the gloves against her hand made her gasp again. The feel of the cool night air on her skin was a relief. He removed her other glove with the same care, but once her hands were exposed to the flickering orange firelight, he froze.

Corinne looked down at her hands. They actually appeared better than they had a few days past when her father had taken a cane and then a switch to them. Aye, the bruises had darkened to a deep purple across her knuckles, but the welts on her palms had mostly closed, though they were still red and raw-looking.

Slowly, the Laird cupped her hands in his and turned them into the firelight. The silence stretched as he continued to stare, and Corinne felt her face grow hot once more.

Belatedly, she realized that the other men had fallen silent as well, their eyes pinned to her mangled hands.

"Who did this to ye?"

The Laird's voice was so low and deadly soft that Corinne almost didn't hear his question. He glanced up at her, his eyes tight and hard.

"Who did this to ye?" he repeated. "Was it yer fiancé? Is that why ye were trying to run away when we attacked?"

"Nay," she replied, growing increasingly embarrassed under the men's stares.

The Laird must have sensed her discomfort, for he whipped his gaze to the others. "Sleep," he ordered. "We ride at dawn tomorrow."

As they had earlier that morning, the men settled themselves on the ground, pulling plaids around their shoulders and heads. Though Corinne didn't doubt they could still hear her, for they lay only just on the other side of the fire, the heat in her cheeks cooled slightly now that so many sets of eyes no longer bore down on her.

"Who then?" the Laird prodded.

Though a lump rose in her throat, Corinne swallowed it. She lifted her head and met the Laird's gaze. "My father."

A storm brewed in the Laird's flinty eyes. "What kind of man does this to his own daughter?"

"The kind who wishes for sons," she said. "And barring that, at least his daughter's obedience."

The Laird released a breath, and some of the uncomfortable tension evaporated between them. "Let me guess. Ye arenae particularly obedient."

"Nay," she said, surprising herself with a breathy chuckle. "Haven't you noticed?"

He grunted, but there was a hint of humor to it. As soon as it had arrived, however, his mirth vanished as he held her gaze.

"And yer fiancé? Why were ye running from him?"

She tilted her head. "De Perroy and my father…they are alike. I only met the man twice. He's three times my age, of course, but that is not why I decided to run. He…he was the one who told my father to take me in hand, to teach me a lesson I'd not soon forget." She lifted her hands to demonstrate. "I knew that a life with him would be filled with such…lessons."

And Corinne knew herself. No beating, no cruelty, no torture would ever deter her from her path as a scribe. Which meant that she could either die at de Perroy's hands, broken and bloodied, or she could escape to a nunnery and live as she wished.

"And where would ye have run to, if I hadnae found ye?" the Laird murmured, seeming to sense the direction of her thoughts.

"A convent," she replied, smiling faintly. "An original plan, wouldn't you say, Laird?"

"Call me Reid," he said softly. "And it doesnae have to be original to be effective."

She smiled again before going on. "I had taken refuge at a nunnery near my father's holding many a time. I knew I could not return there, for it would be the first place he and de Perroy would look. But I imagined that there would be another abbey near enough for me to slip away from my father's guards and take sanctuary. That is why I did this." She blew on a shorn red lock of hair that had fallen across her face.

"So ye cut it yerself," Reid said, his eyes amused as they traveled over her head. "I had wondered about that."

"All novices must have their hair cut when they take the pledge to join the church," she said. "I thought to speed the process along. Besides, it tricked you into thinking I was a boy when you first saw me."

He reached up and coiled a short strand around his finger. Corinne stilled, his nearness suddenly overwhelming. As his gray gaze slid along the lock of hair he fingered, she caught his scent, of smoke and pine and warm wool. She wondered abruptly what the rough growth on his face would feel like against her own smooth skin. His broad shoulders, clad in a simple shirt and an extra length of plaid, almost completely blocked out the fire as he leaned forward slightly.

"Aye, ye had me fooled for a moment, but once ye were in my arms, I kenned ye were a woman." His soft, low voice was like a velvet caress, sending warmth into her face and rippling across her skin.

Reid sat back suddenly, releasing the strand of hair. He turned toward the fire, and she saw his Adam's apple bob as he swallowed. She, too, had to swallow hard against the erratic pounding of her heart in the back of her throat. It was fear, she told herself—fear of being in the presence of such an intimidating man. A little voice in a corner of her mind whispered that it was also fear at the tug of fascination she felt toward him.

Never had she experienced such sensations before—a coiling in the pit of her stomach, a flush all over her body, her heart thumping wildly against her ribs—and all set off by a word, a look, a glancing touch of fingers to hair.

Whatever madness this was, Corinne wanted no part of it. She would let Reid Mackenzie take her to the King of Scotland, aye, but after that, her work as a scribe awaited.

Reid cleared his throat. "I have some salve in my saddlebags that might help with the welts on yer hands."

"Nay," she said, hastily pulling on her gloves once more. "They are already healing."

In a sennight or two, she might even be able to lift a quill once more.

"Rest then," he said, glancing at her.

She did as he bade, lowering herself to the ground and pulling the plaid tight around her body. But despite the weariness in her limbs, she stared into the dying fire for a long while, listening to Reid breathe beside her.

Chapter Seven

"Lochmaben is only another hour away," Reid said, sitting rigidly in the saddle with Corinne tucked between his thighs.

She turned her head, glancing at the forest they rode through. A strand of her hair slid across Reid's lips.

"Oh?" she replied softly.

The lass had seemed lost in thought throughout the morning and afternoon. Her creamy brow had been creased, her ocean-colored eyes distant.

For his part, Reid had woken in a foul mood. It was because he longed to be home, he told himself, not because today would be his last day with the perplexing Englishwoman sharing his saddle.

Though his men hadn't said aught, he could sense a softening from them toward the lass. Alain and the others remained quiet, with nary a comment about how eager they were to reach Lochmaben and turn the lass over to the Bruce so that they could be on their way to the Highlands. It had to be because they'd seen her abused hands. English or nay, no woman deserved to be treated thus.

He could have eased their pace if he'd wanted to. The horses were tired, and so was Corinne. He could have found an excuse to draw out their ride, to camp one more night before reaching Lochmaben. But to do so would be admitting too much to himself—that he admired her spirit, and that he found her nearness...distracting.

Nay, he would not drag this out. They would reach Lochmaben by nightfall, and then she would be the Bruce's problem.

Seeming to sense the direction of his thoughts, she turned her head partially toward him. "What will you do after we arrive in Lochmaben?"

He cleared his throat. "My men and I will return to the Highlands."

"And what are the Highlands like?"

"Och, lass," Hamond said, reining his horse closer. "The Highlands are like no other place on God's green earth. Mountains like ye wouldnae believe."

"And lochs filled with the clearest waters," Alain added.

"Purple heather blanketing the hillsides," Hamond continued. "Waterfalls, fairy pools—"

"And whisky enough to stop that wagging tongue, Hamond," Cedrick, one of the best Mackenzie warriors, cut in.

The men chuckled at that.

Corinne laughed lightly, and a strange, twisting sensation stole through Reid's chest.

"That sounds lovely."

"Aye, milady, it is," Leith said, bobbing his blond head. This had been the lad's first journey away from the Highlands. He'd proven himself on the battlefield, though he still bore a youthful eagerness about him that made Reid feel old. "Ye should see it one day. No words can describe the Highlands' beauty, especially Eilean Donan."

"Eilean Donan?" Corinne said, glancing over her shoulder at Reid.

"The Mackenzie clan keep," he answered.

"It is the strongest castle in the Highlands, for the strongest clan," Leith went on proudly. "Its walls are ten feet thick, and its towers are—"

"Leith," Reid cut in, his mood darkening. "There is no need to bore the lass with details—she'll never see the place."

A somber silence fell over the group until Corinne spoke up again.

"What will you do once you return home?" she asked quietly.

"See to my people and attend to clan matters."

That sounded simple enough, but what actually awaited him was far more complicated. He'd need to meet with Laird Arthur MacDonnell to discuss their alliance, and no doubt send more men to the MacDonnell border to combat the MacVales' raids. Laird MacDonnell was itching for a clan war against the MacVales, and it would fall to Reid to defuse the situation. And now that winter was approaching, it was his responsibility to ensure his people were prepared.

And then of course he needed to marry and produce an heir.

Reid bit down on a curse. Though the Mackenzies had accepted him as their Laird, other clans would see his position as a weakness. A bastard-born Laird without an heir—he was more vulnerable than he cared to admit.

Corinne fell silent, mayhap sensing his rapidly blackening mood.

All too soon, they broke through the tree line and rode onto an open, gently rolling moor. In the fading light, Reid spotted the Bruce's army camp, a bluish-white splotch against the browning hillsides.

Reid spurred his horse into a gallop, his men following suit. As they drew closer, Reid brought his forefinger and thumb to his mouth and let out a loud, high whistle. An answering whistle sounded from the camp, cutting through the gloaming.

When they reached the outer edges of the sprawling sea of canvas tents that served as the King's headquarters, Reid slowed. Several guards came forward to take their animals' reins. Reid dismounted, then helped Corinne down.

"Tell the King that Laird Reid Mackenzie has returned," he told one of the guards. "Along with the de Reymont lass."

The guard nodded. "The King has asked that ye be taken to him immediately upon arrival, Laird. Milady, ye may rest and refresh yerself until ye are summoned."

Corinne glanced up at Reid, her eyes wide and dark in the fading light. "Very well," she said reluctantly to the guard.

"This way, milady."

Two guards flanked her and guided her into the camp. Reid had to resist the strange urge to go after her. Would this be the last time he saw her?

"Follow me, Laird," another man said. Reid snapped his gaze from Corinne's back and let the soldier take the lead, leaving his men to see to themselves for the time being.

As they began winding through the maze of canvas tents, Reid noticed that the camp was abuzz with activity. Men were gathering weapons, drawing down tent poles, and loading wagons with supplies.

By the time they reached the Bruce's tent near the heart of the sea of canvas, Reid was beginning to suspect that the camp, which had served as the Bruce's base of operations for nigh on five years, would not be here much longer.

The guard motioned Reid into the tent and held the canvas flap back for him. When he ducked inside, he found the Bruce and a handful of others dismantling the King's quarters. Sheets of parchment were being shuffled from the large oak desk into chests, the desk itself had been swept bare, and all but a few askew pieces of furniture remained.

"Ah, Reid!" the Bruce said, setting aside a large map that he'd been folding. "I'm glad to see ye back, man. And I assume that since ye are here, ye have done as I've asked and brought me the de Reymont lass."

"Aye, Sire," he said, eyeing the others in the room. "She is refreshing herself, but yer guards told me I was to come to ye straightaway."

"Indeed. Leave us," the Bruce said to the others.

They quietly filed from the tent. Without them, the space looked even starker and more chaotic.

"I take it ye are moving yer camp," Reid commented, glancing at the sparse remains of the King's headquarters.

"No' moving," the Bruce replied. "Dismantling."

Surprise rippled through him. Surely the Bruce couldn't be retreating from the Lowlands. He'd already reclaimed the Borderlands for Scotland and had just proven that he could strike as far south as York. Why would he cede Lochmaben?

"Dinnae scowl so much, man," the Bruce said. "This is a sign of victory, no' defeat. Come, sit with me." Out of habit, the King gestured to the left of the desk, but only one chair remained there, resting on its side. The Bruce's russet brows dropped. "Or mayhap we'll stand."

Reid clasped his hands behind his back and gave the King a curt nod.

"The fact is," the Bruce began, "we dinnae need this camp anymore. The Lowlands are securely Scotland's once more. Hell, the Borderlands and most of Northern England are ours as well." The Bruce exhaled, a tired smile curling his lips. "Truth be told, we've nearly accomplished everything I set out to do when I took the throne…could it truly be nigh on fourteen years past?"

"Ye've done right by our people, Robert," Reid said. "We couldnae ask for a better King."

The Bruce smiled warmly, but then his dark eyes clouded. "There remains much to do, of course. The Pope still hasnae acknowledged me as King, nor that Scotland is a sovereign nation separate from England. But speaking of England…" The smile was back, his weathered face drawn in unadulterated joy. "I have some good news."

"Aye?"

"When Edward arrived in York to find that his city was safe but hobbled by a defeat at our hands…he sent word asking for a truce."

Reid felt his jaw slacken. Good God, it was as close to freedom as they'd ever come in this long, bloody war.

"He'll leave us be, give up the fight over the Border-lands and Berwick and all the rest, as long as we dinnae continue marching southward," the Bruce went on, emotion shining in his gaze. "It is finally happening. All our work, all the lives sacrificed over the years, all the battles lost and won—we are on the cusp now, man."

Reid scrubbed a hand over his face, a wild chuckle rumbling in his throat. "This is… By God, this is incredible!"

"Aye," the Bruce replied, shaking his head in wonder. "We are still negotiating the terms, but if all goes well, the truce will be in place before year's end."

"Our warriors will be home all winter," Reid breathed. "We might finally take a breath in peace."

"Aye, though I am no' sharing the news widely just yet, for I would ensure that this truce holds before raising our people's hopes," the Bruce said. "But assuming that it does, I'll no longer need this camp to serve as a base of operations."

"Where will ye go, then?"

"I am eager to rejoin my family. I'll return to Cardross for a time to be with my wife and children—we are building an estate there—and then I'll go to Perth. Scone Abbey has been the home of our parliament for years now, but we've been so busy making war that we've hardly had time to govern." The Bruce smoothed a hand over his trimmed russet and gray beard. "But it is time to look beyond the next battle or siege and think of our country's future."

Reid smiled wryly. "Dinnae take offense, Robert, but it is hard to imagine ye hanging up yer chainmail and leading the country from an abbey rather than a battlefield."

The Bruce snorted, but then he sobered, his gaze growing wistful. "It's time I settle down, I think—with my family, and with the task of governing the nation we fought so hard for."

He blinked the sudden mist from his eyes and fixed his gaze on Reid once more. "I'd like to see ye do the same, Reid."

"Aye," Reid replied, his brows lowering. "I have been glad to serve ye, Robert, but I've been away from my clan too much. It has been a year now since Logan and I came to our peace, and two since Euna..." He gritted his teeth. "The clan deserves an heir, a future Laird who willnae be tarnished by illegitimacy."

The reconciliation with Logan, Reid's younger half-brother and the rightful Laird of the Mackenzies by dint of blood if not birth order, had been an enormous weight lifted from Reid's shoulders. He'd thought Logan responsible for the death of Laird Murdoch Mackenzie, the previous Laird. Twelve years ago, Reid had driven Logan away, considering him dead to the clan for what he'd done. Then Reid had stepped into the role of Laird, a role that had never been meant for him given his illegitimate birth.

When Reid had learned of Logan's innocence last year, he'd realized Logan was actually the rightful heir to the Mackenzie Lairdship. Though Reid had been born two years earlier than Logan, it was a poorly kept secret that Reid's mother Brinda had arrived for her marriage to Laird Murdoch Mackenzie already three months pregnant—with Reid.

But Logan had refused the Lairdship, choosing to remain in the Borderlands with his new wife Helena as keeper of Craigmoor Castle, the powerful stronghold Reid had helped the Bruce reclaim a year past.

Even with Logan's blessing, and with his clan's acceptance, Reid had always feared the consequences of a bastard-born man as the leader of the Mackenzies. It created instability. And an opening to be challenged.

Reid became aware of the Bruce's keen eyes watching him. "Have members of yer clan been giving ye trouble?" the Bruce asked, seeming to read the direction of Reid's thoughts.

"Nay," he said quickly. "They accept me, but it isnae them I worry about. It's our neighboring clans. The MacRaes and the MacDonnells have been steadfast allies, but the MacVales continue to cause trouble. If I dinnae shore up my line of succession, the MacVales may try to make a move against us."

"Ye need a wife, then," the Bruce said.

A sudden ripple of unease coursed up Reid's spine. Suddenly he felt like a pawn, and the Bruce had no doubt plotted out several moves across the board for him.

"Aye," Reid said carefully.

"Good," the Bruce said, "because I have one in mind for ye."

Reid's gut twisted with trepidation. "Oh?"

"Aye." The Bruce met his gaze, his dark eyes piercing. "The de Reymont lass."

Chapter Eight

Corinne had been led to a small tent somewhere in the middle of the complex maze of canvas. She'd been given a basin of water so that she could wipe away the dust and dirt of travel, and a tray of steaming, thick stew. A Mackenzie warrior must have also discreetly delivered one of the gowns they'd taken during their attack, for she found a blue woolen dress folded outside her tent a few minutes after she'd arrived.

She washed, ate, and changed, feeling surprisingly fresh considering all that had happened over the last two and a half days.

The cot in the corner of the tent beckoned, but before she could lie down, someone outside cleared his throat and rapped on the wooden pole at the entrance.

"The King wishes to see ye now," the guard standing at the entrance to her tent informed her.

A sudden burst of nerves filled her stomach. Reid had portrayed the King as decent and honorable, yet he'd admitted that he had no idea what the Bruce intended to do with her other than hold her until her marriage alliance could be dissolved.

Corinne steeled her spine, nodding for the guard to lead the way. She had never met a King before, but the Bruce was not *her* King. She willed herself to be brave, to demand that in return for having her kidnapped, she be allowed to join a convent once he'd accomplished his goals.

After several twists and turns through the network of tents, the guard stopped before the largest of them all.

"Ye'll wait here until the King summons ye in," the guard said, bracing his feet before the tent's opening.

She eyed the guard for a moment. He was a few years older than she, mayhap five and twenty, with dark hair and several scars on his face, along with a crook in his nose. He wore a plain linen shirt and a red and blue checked plaid belted around his waist. That seemed to be standard attire for Scottish warriors, regardless of the sharp autumnal edge to the air.

Corinne smoothed her blue skirts, wishing she'd brought her cloak. Night was rapidly falling, and with it the temperature. She shifted from foot to foot while the guard stared straight over her head as if she wasn't there.

Muffled voices drifted through the canvas beside her.

"…but I've been away from my clan… It has been a year now… and two since Euna…"

The low, confident voice was unmistakable—Reid was already inside the King's tent.

What was he speaking on, and to whom? She shuffled closer, attempting to make it look as though she was only trying to step warmth into her feet.

"The clan deserves an heir, a future Laird who willnae be tarnished by illegitimacy."

Corinne pulled in a cold breath. Was Reid speaking of himself? How could he be illegitimate and yet also the Laird of the Mackenzies? In all his dealings with his men, she'd never once seen them question him or hesitate at one of his orders. Yet the heaviness in his voice revealed the weight of his worries.

Reid's voice dropped for a moment, and all Corinne could make out was a muffled rumble. But then his voice rose once more.

"...the MacVales may try to make a move against us."

"Ye need a wife then," another voice, sure and steady, said. Could that be...the King of Scotland himself?

"Aye," came Reid's guarded response.

"Good," the other voice said, "because I have one in mind for ye."

"Oh?"

"Aye. The de Reymont lass."

Corinne's legs crumpled beneath her. She sagged into the tent's canvas siding and would have fallen all the way through if the guard hadn't snatched her up by the shoulders.

"*What?*" came Reid's outraged bellow.

The guard blinked in comprehension at her, awkwardly placing her on her feet.

"I'm sure it will be just another moment, milady," he said. "Can ye stand?"

"A-aye." It took Corinne a moment to recognize the shaking, thin voice as her own.

She righted herself, staring at the swath of canvas separating her from Reid and the Bruce.

This was to be her future? Pawned off to yet another man to appease some scheme or other? What of her plans, her dreams? What of her work as a scribe?

"I willnae marry an Englishwoman, Robert!" Reid roared on the other side of the canvas. "Ye ken I need to marry a Scotswoman—a Laird's daughter, no less."

"Reid," came the Bruce's smooth, even voice, "calm yerself. I have thought this through. It is what's best for Scotland—and it will help ye, too."

"Help me?" Reid shouted. "How can it help me to be saddled with an English bride? I'm on shaky ground as it is, damn it!"

Even as a flood of embarrassed heat rushed to her face, Corinne withered inside. Reid didn't want to be *saddled* with her? As if she were some horrible, unwanted burden.

"My marriage needs to form an alliance with one of my neighboring clans, no' bring their wrath upon me— and give my enemies more room to question the legitimacy of my claim to the Lairdship!" Reid went on.

This was all too much. Corinne had barely escaped one terrible match. And now she would be made to give up her dreams and be thrust at a man who didn't even want her. Her throat knotted and frustrated tears burned in her eyes. She felt as though she were going to be sick.

Through the blur of tears, she met the guard's uncomfortable gaze. His face had turned as red as the slashes of dyed wool in his plaid. He straightened his stance, visibly working to wipe his face of all embarrassment, but there was simply no pretending that they couldn't both clearly hear the conversation inside the tent.

After a moment of consideration, the guard finally took pity on her. He cleared his throat noisily, cutting into Reid's next tirade. Without permission, he stuck his head through the tent's flap.

"Lady Corinne de Reymont awaits as requested, Sire," he said loudly.

The tent fell dead silent.

Someone inside coughed softly. "Show her in, please, Andrew."

The guard, Andrew, stepped back and held open the canvas flap for her. Swallowing hard, Corinne lifted her chin and entered.

Chapter Nine

W hen Reid's gaze landed on Corinne, he knew instantly that she'd heard everything.

Her face was flushed red with humiliation, and her eyes shone with tears. Yet somehow she managed to carry her head high and her back straight as she stepped into the tent.

The storm raging inside him went still for a moment as he wondered where in the world the wee lass found such fortitude.

She looked even smaller than he remembered, or mayhap it was because he could see her slender frame without her cloak or a plaid bundling her up. Though she was taller than most women, she was slimly built. Her petite breasts swelled erratically against the tight-fitted bodice of her gown as she fought to breathe. Her gloved fingers twisted in the blue wool of her skirts. That act of rage must pain her still-healing hands, but she didn't seem to notice.

Corinne's burning blue-green eyes landed on the Bruce.

"Sire," she said, giving him the faintest possible curtsy. She turned her gaze to Reid. "Laird Mackenzie."

"Lady Corinne," the Bruce said smoothly, appearing unruffled by Corinne's obvious embarrassment and fury.

The Bruce cleared his throat, clasping his hands behind his back. "It seems safe to assume ye overheard my decision that ye and Reid should wed."

"Aye," Corinne said through gritted teeth. "But I must object, Sire."

Something twisted in Reid's gut. She wanted this as little as he did. Why should that give him both relief and pricking displeasure at the same time?

"Oh?" the Bruce murmured mildly. "It seems ye and Reid both object."

Her gaze flicked to Reid for an instant, her cheeks growing redder, before she returned her attention to the Bruce.

"In the first place, I am English, as Reid has so… loudly pointed out," she began. "Which means you are not my King, and I am not your subject, Sire. You cannot simply order me to marry anyone."

"Yet here ye are on my soil, Lady Corinne," the Bruce countered. "And what's more, yer King willnae stand against me in this matter, for even if he cared— no offense meant, milady, but ye are one lass from a small corner of Edward's vast and unruly kingdom—he kens all too well he cannae best me." He lifted his brows. "Any other objections, or may we move forward?"

Corinne's mouth fell open. Taking advantage of her stunned silence, Reid jumped in.

"Ye havenae addressed my opposition, Robert," he said, his voice heated. "Ye ken verra well that I need to marry a Scotswoman—a Laird's daughter—to protect the Mackenzie Lairdship from challengers. The Mackenzies are one of the largest, most powerful clans in the Highlands, but that could be destroyed if another clan sees fit to question my line of succession."

"Ye said yerself that yer people accept ye as Laird," the Bruce said.

"Aye, but——"

"But the MacVales will cause trouble, aye." The Bruce waved his hand in dismissal. "The MacVales are a quarrelsome, lawless lot. They'll make trouble for ye no matter who ye wed."

"My allies will see it as a slight," Reid shot back. "They'll demand to ken why I passed over a chance to unite my clan with theirs in favor of wedding an Englishwoman."

He glanced at Corinne and immediately regretted the way he'd nearly spat the last word. It wasn't her fault he was in such a bind. But legitimacy meant everything to him and his people. His bastardry cast a long shadow of doubt over the clan's future. He couldn't burden them with even more trouble than he already had.

"Ye would have had to choose one lass to wed eventually," the Bruce countered. "That means at least one of yer allies would've been left slighted. And when that happened, ye would have used all yer skills as a Laird to smooth things over, to find a solution that ensured yer alliances continued." The Bruce shrugged. "That is what ye will have to do now."

Reid opened his mouth, but before he could speak, Corinne, who'd apparently recovered herself, launched another attack.

"I am meant to go to a nunnery," she blurted.

The King blinked. "Yer father wasnae sending ye to marry Lord de Perroy?"

Corinne's bluster faltered. "Nay, that is, he was, or he would have."

"Then how were ye meant go to a nunnery?"

She lifted her chin. "I was in the process of taking myself there when Reid and his men attacked."

"Ah," the Bruce said. "That explains the…" He motioned vaguely toward her sheared red locks.

"I'll find my way to a convent," she threatened. "You cannot simply force me to marry."

"Milady," the Bruce said gently, "I can, and I am."

From the sizzling fury in her eyes, Corinne would not accept that. She would no doubt fight tooth and nail, just as she had before, to gain her freedom.

Reid's stomach sank at the thought. If the Bruce had his way—and knowing him, he almost certainly would —Reid would be bound for life to a woman who would prefer a nunnery to him.

She had fire burning in her veins, of that he was certain, yet she'd made it abundantly clear that she longed to become a nun. That would mean a cold, lonely, unhappy future for both of them, all to appease the Bruce's whim.

Bloody hell, what was the Bruce getting him into?

"Why are ye doing this, Robert?" Reid demanded through clenched teeth. "Ye said that this was good for Scotland, and for me—why?"

The Bruce turned to him. "It is an elegant solution to two problems. Ye need a wife. I need the lass married off." He lifted his palms as if there was naught more to say.

"I need a *Scottish* wife," Reid ground out.

"I've already addressed that," the Bruce replied. "It doesnae matter whom ye marry. Regardless, ye will miff some of yer allies, and yer enemies will give ye trouble. Besides, yer marriage to a MacRae or a MacDonnell lass does little to aid the larger cause."

Reid clenched his fists until his knuckles popped. "Ye said there was to be a truce. How does wedding an English lord's daughter to one of yer loyal Lairds help the cause?"

"Ye think after all we've done to get here, I would cede ground to Edward now?" the Bruce demanded. "I willnae allow Edward's lords to strengthen themselves with an alliance along the border. Nor will I allow de Reymont and de Perroy to target innocent Borderlanders once their forces are united. Nay," he said, swiping a hand through his hair. "The Borderlands have been through enough. I cannae allow the English to regain power there."

"I am already here," Corinne cut in. "The alliance between my father and de Perroy will be dashed once they realize that I am lost to them both." She stepped closer to the Bruce, her eyes pleading. "I was only a pawn to be traded between them. Without me, you can consider the alliance all but dead. I could remain in Scotland if you prefer, but what difference does it make whether I marry Reid or enter a convent?"

The Bruce gazed at her with sympathy. "Ye are determined, I'll give ye that, milady. But ye wouldnae be secure, even in a convent. One of yer father's men, or de Perroy's, could have ye taken and forced into the marriage. Nay, the only way to ensure that the alliance can never go through is by marrying ye to someone else."

He turned to Reid. "Though I ken ye cannae see it now, I am honoring ye, Reid. This is a sign of my trust in ye. I believe ye are the best man to ensure that Lady Corinne is safe—as yer wife. Ye are doing a service to the cause—and yer King."

"I'm no' one of yer Bodyguard Corps," Reid growled. "If ye want the lass protected, have one of them look after her."

"Ah, but there is the problem," the Bruce said, a rueful smile lifting his lips behind his beard. "The men in the Corps have a pesky habit of falling in love and getting married. Take yer brother Logan and Lady Helena, for example. Or Colin and Sabine. Or Kirk and Lillian. Or—"

"Ye've made yer point," Reid interjected. He raked a hand through his hair, looking up at the tent's canvas ceiling.

Numb resignation began to settle over his mind. The Bruce had clearly thought this out to his liking, and once the man took hold of an idea, he was like a dog with a bone, seeing it through to the end.

"Nay," Corinne said, glancing wide-eyed between the Bruce and Reid. "You cannot—you cannot simply—"

"I am Robert the Bruce, King of Scotland," the Bruce interrupted. He leveled her with one of his most commanding stares, then turned the look on Reid. "And I am ordering ye to wed."

Reid's ears rang with the declaration. It felt as though the tent's walls were pressing in. Though some part of him still longed to resist, to argue with the Bruce until he ran out of breath, a larger part of him knew he would never triumph. More than that, he'd pledged himself to serve and obey his King. He was bound to submit.

He bent into a stiff, shallow bow. "As ye command, Sire," he ground out.

When he straightened, his gaze clashed with Corinne's. Her blue-green eyes were round and brimming with disbelief.

"Now that we have that settled," the Bruce said lightly, "I can marry ye here and now."

"Nay," Reid snapped. He held no illusions that he could find a way out of this cursed union, but marrying Corinne in the Bruce's half-disassembled camp tent would create problems—*more* problems, that was—later.

"It may be hard for my people to accept an unknown Englishwoman as the lady of the clan," Reid went on. "They might be more likely to tolerate her if they see us wed with their own eyes."

The Bruce considered this for a moment. "Verra well, but dinnae delay. I want ye wed as soon as ye reach

Eilean Donan. Can I trust that ye'll see this done, Reid?"

Teeth locked, Reid gave a curt nod. But then a thought occurred to him. "Do ye truly believe de Reymont and de Perroy are a threat? Will they come after Corinne?"

"This will cause a few ruffled feathers, no doubt, but I dinnae believe they have the will or the resources to wage war against me," the Bruce replied. "If they cause trouble, I'll deal with them. And I may even press de Reymont to give Lady Corinne's dowry to ye, Reid. Ye ken that's what I'm good at." A wry grin lifted one half of the King's mouth. "Creating a stir and then making the most of it."

Reid worked his jaw for a long moment, but there was naught left to say. He was good and trapped now.

"We'll leave for the Highlands at dawn tomorrow morning, then," he said tightly.

The Bruce nodded. "Verra well." He turned to Corinne, who still stood dumbstruck and wide-eyed, and gave her a little bow. "It was a pleasure to meet ye, Lady Corinne. I hope we meet again under more...agreeable circumstances. And Reid," he said, straightening, "I meant what I said. I trust ye as much as I trust any of the men in the Corps. In fact, I consider ye an honorary member, of sorts."

The King gave Reid a lopsided grin, then sobered once more. "I hope someday ye understand that this decision is a mark of my respect for ye, and gratitude for all ye've done for me."

Reid forced himself to bend under the King's praise.

When he rose, the King ushered them toward the tent's entrance. "No doubt ye are both weary from yer travels. My men will ensure yer comfort for the night. And I'll make sure to see ye off tomorrow at dawn."

As Corinne passed woodenly through the tent flap, the Bruce gripped Reid's arm to halt him.

"The lass has fire in her blood," the King murmured, his dark eyes dancing. "Who kens, mayhap this will prove to be a love match. I have had luck with such things before."

The Bruce released Reid's arm with a soft chuckle. As he exited the tent and followed Corinne's rod-straight back into the darkened maze of canvas, Reid had to disagree with his King.

This was going to be a disaster.

Chapter Ten

T wo days.

Corinne had wasted two whole days in a numb, disbelieving torpor.

Somehow, she'd managed to make her way back to her tent in the Bruce's camp after receiving the blow— she was to marry Reid. Despite the relative comfort of the tent's cot compared to sleeping on the ground, she'd passed a near-sleepless night staring into the darkness. Then at dawn, as promised, Reid had fetched her and they'd ridden from the camp.

North. Toward the Highlands.

Toward his home. Where she would be his wife.

Distantly, she was aware of his taut displeasure as they rode atop his horse, and of his resigned silence when they made camp in the woods the night after they'd departed Lochmaben. Yet she'd been too absorbed in her own shock to pay him much heed.

Likewise, she was vaguely aware of a shift in the

other Mackenzie warriors. They all seemed to be in varying degrees of a foul mood, and it could only partly be attributed to the fact that the weather had finally turned and a cold rain fell steadily through the trees. Though none of the men spoke to her, Corinne assumed that what had soured their temperaments was the thought of her, an Englishwoman, as the lady of their clan. They hadn't minded her so much when they'd only been delivering her to the Bruce, but now she was to be their mistress.

The mistress of a clan of Highlanders who would likely hate her for simply being English—the thought gnawed at her for two long, cold, silent days. Though she assumed Reid had meant to do her a kindness by refusing the King's offer to wed them immediately, his reasoning left her knotted with trepidation. His people would loathe her. They would not accept her as the clan's mistress, mayhap not even if they saw her wed Reid with their own eyes.

Reid didn't want this. His people didn't want this. And *she* didn't want this.

There was only one last resort, but time—and opportunity—was running out. She had to escape somehow, to find an abbey and claim sanctuary, or else she would be trapped in this nightmare forever.

As a blue-gray twilight began to fall on their second day out of Lochmaben, Corinne began to feel the stunned fog lift from her mind. She needed to think clearly, to make a plan—and then act.

Escape wouldn't be easy. Though Reid seemed as unhappy by the King's order to marry as she, he'd obviously resigned himself to his duty. He'd already proven that she was no match for him physically. She would need more than just a half-formed plan to break away and run.

As her thoughts began spinning like wheels, flickering lights emerged in the falling darkness ahead. To her surprise, Reid continued on toward the lights until they broke through the trees on the outskirts of a small town.

"What are you doing?" Corinne blurted.

Reid cleared his throat behind her. "I thought it would do us all good to get out of the rain for the night."

Neither Reid nor his men appeared in the least affected by the cold and damp conditions. They were like unmovable mountains—the rain seemed to simply run off them. It was for her benefit, then, that he thought to stop. Aye, even in her thick wool cloak, and pressed against Reid's solid warmth, she was wet and chilled to the bone.

She quickly reassessed her budding escape plan. No doubt a town this size would have an abbey or at least a chapel where she could claim sanctuary. And once she was inside, not even the King of Scotland's command that she marry could override the church's protection for a sanctuary seeker.

Corinne scanned the cluster of darkened buildings as they drew nearer, searching for a telltale spire or bell tower. *There!* At the far end of the town, a dark, narrow column rose above the rest of the structures. That had to be a church.

The horse halted, pulling her out of her thoughts. Reid had reined in before a two-storey wooden building with a lantern hanging next to a sign that read The Stag's Head.

"See to the horses," he said to the men as he swung down from the saddle. "I'll arrange for ye all to sleep in the barn."

The others began dismounting and guiding their animals around the right side of the inn. Reid reached up and pulled her from his horse's back.

"Am I to sleep in the barn as well?" she asked, her numb feet squelching when they met the muddy ground.

"Nay, I'll get us a room."

"*Us?*" she squeaked. For the first time in two days, she felt too hot as sudden panic spiked in her veins. If she could not find a way to be alone, it would be nigh impossible to slip away to the church across town.

But it was more than that. Her mind flooded with images of Reid looming in the doorway of a small chamber, then stepping inside and closing the door so that they were alone together. Would he share a bed with her? Would he—

"I dinnae intend to claim the rights of a husband," he said. "Yet."

Though the last word was spoken in a flat, emotionless voice, a ripple of warmth fluttered low in her belly. Aye, she had to reach that church, else she do something foolish like consider what it would be like to share the marriage bed with Reid.

"I'll sleep on the floor," he went on. "Ye'll forgive me if I dinnae fully trust ye no' to attempt to flee again."

This time, the heat rushing to her face had naught to do with unwanted thoughts about beds with Reid in them. Was she so transparent that he'd already guessed the direction of her thoughts? She'd never been skilled at hiding her emotions, but she would need to be more careful than ever if she was to escape the fate that awaited her in the Highlands.

"Suit yourself," she said, turning toward the inn's door.

Reid got there before she did and pulled the door open for her. A blast of warmth and light hit her, and she hurried inside with an eager shiver. She moved to the roaring fire at one end of the inn's common room while Reid spoke with the innkeeper and arranged both barn space for his men and their horses and a room for Corinne and him.

After dropping several coins into the innkeeper's hand, Reid motioned Corinne away from the fire. She reluctantly followed him up a flight of wooden stairs and down a long corridor lined with a half-dozen doors.

He stopped in front of the last one and swung the door inward.

Corinne's gaze instantly landed on the bed. It was small and narrow, but looked clean. It sat against the wall opposite the door, under a shuttered window. A table and two chairs and a brazier with an unlit fire laid in it rounded out the sparse accommodations.

"I'll see about having a warm meal sent up," Reid said gruffly.

Corinne nodded and stepped into the room, walking a slow, small circle. But the moment the door closed behind Reid, she yanked off her dripping cloak and tossed it over one of the chairs. Scrambling to the bed, she crawled onto the mattress and reached for the latch on the shutters.

The wooden peg slid easily from the latch, and the shutters opened on silent hinges. Corinne stuck her head out the window and peered into the dripping darkness. The ground looked frighteningly far away, but she had little choice. She'd have to jump.

But not yet. Later. Reid would return in a moment, and if he caught her trying to escape, he'd no doubt hunt her down and capture her in short order. If she could slip out in the middle of the night, though, he might sleep for several hours before realizing she'd disappeared.

This would be her best chance at securing her freedom. And most likely her last.

She hastily closed the shutters, but she left the latch undone—one less thing to fumble with in the dark later on. A creak on the floorboards outside the door alerted her to Reid's return. Hurriedly plunking down on the edge of the bed, she smoothed her damp blue skirts.

Just as she finished arranging herself in what she hoped was a casual slump, the door swung open. Reid entered bearing a tray with two steaming bowls of soup, a large hunk of bread, and two mugs of ale.

He set the tray on the table and cast her a sideways glance. Then he tilted his head, indicating that she should join him in eating.

Heaven above, he was a man of few words. Yet he

could accomplish more with one raised eyebrow or pointed stare than anyone Corinne had ever known.

She rose from the bed and sank into one of the chairs.

"Thank you," she murmured as she gingerly lifted a spoon in her gloved hand. "For the food, and for the inn." Let him believe that she was coming to accept her fate, she thought as she swallowed the first warm spoonful of soup.

"How are yer hands?"

She flexed her fingers around the spoon. "Better, I think." Though the still-healing skin on her palms was tender, the dull ache from the bruises had faded a great deal.

An awkward silence fell as they ate. Corinne kept her gaze carefully lowered to her food. There was no telling what Reid's sharp gray eyes would see if he looked too closely into her face.

"How much longer until we reach Eilean Donan?" she asked when the meal was nearly complete.

"Four days, mayhap five if this rain continues."

Once more, quiet fell over the small chamber. Corinne silently cursed herself. Why was her tongue as useless as a block of wood in the moment she needed to pretend that naught was amiss?

But of course, *everything* was amiss. Here she was, alone in this cramped inn room with a Highland Laird who seemed to fill the space with his broad frame and penetrating gaze. And they were to be married in less than a sennight.

Corinne stood from the table abruptly. "I am weary. I think I will retire."

"Take off yer dress."

Her mouth fell open, and she forgot not to stare straight into Reid's flinty eyes.

His eyebrows dropped and his mouth turned down behind his dark stubble. "I meant...yer dress is wet."

"A-aye?" she managed.

"Remove it and lay it next to the fire so that it will be dry by morning."

Corinne clamped her mouth shut with a click of her teeth. "You certainly aren't shy about giving orders," she muttered.

"Nay, I'm no'." He crossed his arms over his chest, and her gaze involuntarily slid over the large, hard contours of muscle pressed against his shirt.

When her eyes lifted to his once more, she found some unreadable spark in their steely depths. He rose swiftly, turning to the still-unlit brazier. "I'll light the fire if ye want a moment of privacy."

Heat rushed to her face. The blasted man wouldn't give her an inch, would he? Reid seemed to simply expect her to do as he commanded without hesitation or argument. Yet he, too, must sense how awkward this all was—the two of them alone, not yet married but ordered to be soon enough.

She should thank him for turning his back to her and kneeling before the brazier, for not demanding that they share the bed, for not touching her at all other than when they were forced into close proximity atop his horse. Yet all she could manage was to stand there blushing fiercely, feeling foolish and too warm and acutely aware of his broad, muscular back.

Think, silly girl! she chided silently. Removing her dress would make her escape in the middle of the night that much more difficult. On the other hand, arguing with Reid about the merits of remaining in a wet gown would only draw his suspicion. The choice was abysmal but clear.

Muttering a decidedly unladylike curse under her breath, she began tugging on the laces running down her back.

But by the time the fire roared merrily in the brazier and Reid had stood, dropping two flint stones into the pouch on his belt, Corinne had only managed to make a tangled mess of the laces.

Reid eyed her for a moment, one eyebrow arched at her hissed string of curses.

"Let me." He turned her by the shoulders so that her back was to him.

Corinne looked up at the ceiling, balling her still-tender hands before her in frustrated embarrassment. When he began to tug gently on the laces, her face warmed.

"These damned ribbons are too thin," he muttered, his low voice surprisingly close to her ear. She twitched, biting her lip to keep from gasping.

"At least ye are dressed for travel and no' in some silly noblewoman's frippery," he continued, seeming to be speaking more to himself than her as he worked on the laces.

His fingers moved higher up her spine. "Bloody hell,

what have ye done to these poor ties?" His warm breath fanned her skin where her shorn hair left her nape exposed.

Gooseflesh pricked down her spine and over her chest. "These blasted gloves make it hard..." she offered lamely.

"Soon enough ye willnae need them," he said, giving a firm tug on the laces, which seemed to do the trick.

Aye, she reminded herself through the blood rushing in her ears, soon her hands would be healed and she could resume her work as a scribe—but not unless she escaped marriage to the formidable Scotsman distracting her with his murmurs and warm breath and fingers grazing her back.

She began to turn around, but apparently he wasn't through with her yet. His big, warm hands settled on her shoulders and he began to peel away the damp wool. Another shiver slammed into her as her shoulders were bared. His thumb snagged on the band of her linen chemise, and for a breathless moment she thought he meant to remove it along with her dress. But then the chemise slid back into place even as he continued to pull down the gown.

Shamefully hot and prickly with awareness, Corinne tried to help, hoping to hasten the end of this embarrassingly intimate moment. She snatched the front of the dress and tugged, but her hands refused to be of much use.

Reid clucked his tongue, taking one of her elbows in hand and lifting it so that he could pull it free of the dress. He did the same with her other arm, then began working the dress down her hips.

With naught to do but stand there like a helpless idiot, Corinne glanced down at herself. To her mortification, her breasts were pressing against the thin linen of her chemise. She realized belatedly that her breaths were coming short and shallow, revealing the petite shape of her breasts—including the tightened tips.

If God had any mercy, He would have let Corinne die of embarrassment in that moment. Instead, she was left acutely aware of just how alive she was. Her heart slammed against her ribs, her blood roared in her ears, and her skin burned with sensation where it rubbed against her chemise.

Reid's hands at last freed her gown from her hips and let the material fall to her feet. Corinne hurriedly stepped from the pile of damp wool, only to stumble as her foot caught on one of the traitorous laces. She lurched forward, but suddenly Reid clamped both hands around her hips, steadying her.

They stood frozen like that for half a heartbeat before he withdrew as if she'd burned him. He snatched up the gown, clearing his throat loudly.

"I'll just…" He shook out the dress with a snap of his wrists and spread it over one of the chairs nearest the brazier. For a man so sure and capable when it came to everything else, he was taking an inordinate amount of time getting her gown to hang just right over the chair.

Corinne took the extended moment to dash to the bed, shucking her short boots as she went. With a swift pull, she yanked the covers up to her chin.

"Good night," she said, her voice sounding loud and forced in her ears.

"Good night," he rumbled, still not facing her.

She turned toward the wall, letting her gaze drift up to the unlatched shutters. Behind her, she could hear Reid shuffling around the small space for several moments. Then he moved toward the bed.

Her breath froze in her lungs, yet Reid's weight never dipped the mattress beside her. Instead, the floorboards creaked as he lowered himself to the ground.

She forced herself to breathe evenly. She would have to at least feign sleep for a few hours until she was sure Reid was unconscious and she could slip out the window.

But when she at last ripped her gaze away from the shutters and closed her eyes, her head spun with the memory of his hands branding her hips through her thin chemise.

As time stretched and the fire burned low, Corinne cursed the Bruce for having her kidnapped. She cursed Reid for his stubborn commitment to duty.

But most of all, she cursed herself for the longing burning like a fanned ember in the pit of her stomach.

Chapter Eleven

R eid stared at the ceiling until the fire had burned to naught but coals. He resisted the urge to shift against the hard wooden planks beneath him. He'd endured far worse physical discomfort than sleeping on the floor—but never had he experienced a pain quite like the acute ache underneath his kilt at the moment.

Damn Corinne for making this so difficult. Reid didn't know if he meant the journey to Eilean Donan, their impending marriage, or the unwanted need burning through his veins. Regardless, things were not going as planned.

A taunting voice in the back of his head whispered that he had naught to complain about. He found his future wife courageous, intriguing—and damned alluring.

Lust spiked in his gut as he remembered the brushing contact his thumb had made along the creamy skin of her slim shoulder. That skin had rippled with gooseflesh—had it been from the cold, or was she affected by his touch?

The firelight had teased against her chemise, giving him a maddeningly fleeting glimpse of her delicate curves underneath. Her hips, though on the trim side, had felt made for his hands when he'd steadied her. And damn it all if he hadn't had the insane desire to pull her roughly against him, bury his nose in the riot of red hair brushing her neck, and let his hands drink their fill of her body.

Aye, what could be so wrong about desiring one's soon-to-be wife? Reid ground his teeth in the darkness. Unfortunately, everything.

Desiring the lass was quickly turning an already tangled situation into an all-out disaster. His allies—the MacDonnell Laird especially—would be outraged when they learned of his marriage to an Englishwoman.

Assuming that the breakdown of a possible marriage alliance didn't start a clan war with his allies, Reid would still have to deal with the likes of the MacVales, who plagued the MacDonnells' eastern border and refused to form alliances of any kind. Serlon MacVale, Laird of the clan, seemed to relish remaining in isolation—and creating chaos amongst his neighbors as well. If a wedge of discontent formed between the MacDonnells and the Mackenzies, MacVale would no doubt take the opportunity to exploit it for his own gain.

And all that presumed he could wrangle his slippery wee English bride to the Highlands without further incident. She'd made it abundantly clear that she wanted naught to do with the Bruce's arranged marriage.

Desiring the chit was simply masochistic. How could Reid lust for a woman who would prefer the cold, drudging life of a nun?

As if prompted by his thoughts, he heard the bed creak softly. Reid kept his breathing slow and steady, but his ears pricked. Was the lass just rolling over? Nay, for he could hear Corinne's breaths coming soft and short somewhere over him.

She was trying to look at him in the dark, he realized. He remained motionless, feigning sleep. What was the lass about?

From the soft rustling, he gathered that she'd pushed the covers aside. Then to his vexation, he heard her fumbling with the shutters over the bed.

Would she truly jump from a second-storey window in the middle of a dark, rainy night just to be away from him? The frustrating thought burned away the lingering lust warming Reid's body. He was as displeased as she about the Bruce's order—bloody hell, he had an entire clan legacy depending on a marriage alliance—but he would see his duty done.

She must have swung the shutters open, for the patter of rain outside grew louder in the blackened chamber. The clouds completely obscured the moon, leaving Corinne to move in the dark. A faint, light-colored smudge rose up from the bed—Corinne's linen chemise.

He heard her take a deep breath and knew she was about to jump.

Surging up from the floor, he flung an arm out and snatched the first thing he came in contact with—

Corinne's ankle, judging from the delicate bones under smooth skin.

Corinne shrieked in surprise and fright. He yanked her ankle hard enough to send her thumping down onto the mattress. With one hand, he slammed the shutters against the blustering rain. Then he threw himself on top of her so that she couldn't wriggle away.

"Let me go!" she cried frantically. She squirmed beneath him, but he caught her wrists and pressed them into the mattress. The weight of his torso and legs on top of hers was enough to render her nearly completely motionless.

"Must I tie ye to the bed, woman?" he barked, letting his anger—at the Bruce, at Corinne, at this whole damned situation—boil over. "How many times must ye be shown—there is no escaping this."

She cried out wordlessly, struggling even though they both knew it was futile. Beneath him, he felt her begin to shake. Realization dawned—she was sobbing.

"Dinnae make me into a monster, Corinne," he said roughly. He dragged in a breath, willing his anger in check. "Dinnae make it this way, when ye ken I am in the same bind ye are."

"Then let me go!" she cried. "Release me. Let me take sanctuary in a church."

"And tell the Bruce what?"

"That I got away. That you cannot violate the sanctuary of a religious house. The Bruce will have to accept—"

"Nay." The word was as hard and flat as a lead anvil.

"Why not?" she demanded, her voice thick with emotion. "Are you so proud that you cannot let it appear that I bested you?"

"It is no' a matter of pride," Reid ground out, "but of duty. I pledged to serve Robert the Bruce as his loyal subject. I cannae disobey his order."

She released a shaking breath. "Duty is a poor excuse."

Reid stiffened. He thought of all the times he'd answered the Bruce's request for aid, for warriors, for supplies during these harrowing years of war. He thought of all the Mackenzies who'd died for duty—to him as their Laird, and to their King and country. "Men have given their lives for it," he growled.

"And now you would take *my* life to satisfy your duty," she whispered.

"Ye think marrying me and dying are one and the same?" he snapped.

"I will be forced to live a shadow life, just like my father and de Perroy intended, and that is as good as being dead."

"What the bloody hell does that mean?"

Something seemed to break in her, for she went limp beneath him. A sob rose from her throat. "You don't understand. You don't know me at all."

Reid stared down at her in the darkness. The sound of her tears was like a nail being driven into his chest. Damn it all, she was right. He didn't understand what drove her with such unwavering determination to escape —not only him, but her father and her fiancé.

He eased off her slowly. As he shifted his weight to

the side, she curled into a ball, muffling her sobs in her hands.

"I ken ye dinnae wish to wed me," he said carefully, "but I am no' like yer father and de Perroy. I'll never raise a hand against ye."

She continued to cry as if she hadn't heard him. Mayhap now wasn't the time for words. The lass was scared, alone, and cornered as surely as he was in this cursed union.

Gently, he looped an arm around her and drew her against him. She stiffened for a moment, but then she buried her face in his shoulder and let the tears come.

She felt so fragile in his arms, her body shaking as sobs wracked her. Like a bolt of lightning, it struck him —he was to marry this woman in a matter of days. She would be his to protect, to look after. To raise an heir with.

The weight of that responsibility hit him for the first time. He'd been so focused on alliances and enemies, on his legitimacy and lineage, that he'd hardly considered what it would mean to share a life with Corinne.

If her tears were any indication, she *had* considered what that would mean—and found him lacking. He couldn't blame her—he'd kidnapped her, held her captive, dragged her to the Lowlands and now the Highlands, and next he would bind her to him for eternity. And all without her getting a sliver of choice in any of it.

Of course, he hadn't had much choice either, but that didn't make things any easier for her.

Once again, Reid felt like a complete arse.

"There now," he said, awkwardly patting her back.

What else could he say? That they would find their way? What if they didn't? What if she hated him for giving her naught but a shadow life, as she'd put it, whatever that meant?

Reid cursed himself. He'd never been one for flowery words or eloquent turns of phrase. He led his clan with strength and decisiveness, not tenderness and charisma. Damn it all, he was only good at taking action.

He dragged in a breath, catching a faint whiff of lemons in Corinne's hair. He knew the action he wanted to take at the moment, but he had no idea if it would help or make him more of a monster in her eyes.

"Bloody hell," he muttered. Without thinking, he laced his fingers through her cropped hair and lifted her head away from his shoulder.

Just as another sob rose in her throat, he dipped his mouth to hers and kissed her.

She stilled, the sob catching on an inhale. Her lips tasted of salt from her tears, but they were lush as ripe fruit beneath his.

He waited for her to pull back, to shove against his chest, but to his surprise, she remained motionless. Experimentally, he angled his lips to capture her mouth more fully. She softened ever so slightly in his arms.

That small loosening of her coiled body was enough to send a surge of desire through him. His fingers tightened in her hair, and he was rewarded with a little gasp. At the parting of her lips, his tongue sought entrance.

Another wave of need hit him as he delved into the damp heat of her mouth. Unbidden, his manhood stirred, the ache from when he'd undressed her returning to his bollocks.

Hesitantly, she curled her hands in his shirt, opening to him. He took all she gave, caressing her velvety tongue with his.

The sudden urge to tighten his fist in her hair, to rip her thin chemise in two, to spread her legs and drive into her, nearly stole his breath. Never had he felt such an abrupt and fierce desire to possess a woman before—not even with Euna.

Corinne made a low noise in her throat, dragging him from his thoughts. She was meeting the strokes of his tongue now, following his lead. The urgency in her kiss matched his own. The realization—that need consumed her just as it did him—sent his cock straining rigidly under his kilt.

He yanked his mouth from hers, reveling in the desperate moan of dissatisfaction she gave at his departure. But just as quickly, his lips fell on her throat, and she sucked in a breath of surprise. He pushed her hair out of his way with his nose as he forged a path to her earlobe. When he took the lobe between his teeth, he was rewarded with yet another inhale.

By God, she was so responsive to his touch, like kindling primed for a spark. In that moment, he nearly lost his white-knuckled grasp on control. He nearly rolled her onto her back and shoved their clothing out of the way to claim her there and then.

But some last shred of sanity stopped him. Nay, this wasn't the way to do this. As a man born in bastardry, he knew the costs of a rash act of passion all too well.

The Mackenzie Lairdship needed a legitimate heir. He couldn't put his people through more questions of legitimacy. Nor would he put Corinne—or any child borne of their union—through those same questions.

With every drop of willpower he possessed, Reid lifted his mouth from Corinne's blazing skin. Panting, he rested his forehead against hers.

"Rest now," he managed at last.

He could feel her questioning gaze on him, but she didn't speak. Was she as astounded by what they'd just shared as he was? He longed to read her ocean eyes, but in the dark, her thoughts were shielded from him.

After a moment, she lowered her head to his shoulder once more, letting a long breath go. It fanned across his neck, sending a pulse of need through him.

She must have been exhausted, for after only a few minutes, she went soft against him, her breathing slow and deep.

Reid remained motionless, but he knew he would not be joining her in sleep. Not with her snuggled up against him, wearing naught but a chemise, her lemon-scented hair tickling his chin and her kiss branded on his lips.

Nay, several parts of him would remain very much awake this night.

Chapter Twelve

✵

Corinne woke reluctantly. As she began drifting back to consciousness, she clung to the warm comfort surrounding her.

Warm, *hard* comfort. She felt her brows furrow in confusion. Where was she?

A light tug on one of her tresses brought her fully awake with a gasp.

"Ye slept deeply."

Reid's voice rumbled through her. By God, she was practically lying on top of him! She attempted to scramble away, but promptly bumped into the wall. She was good and wedged into the narrow bed between the wall and Reid's large frame.

Her cheeks blazed in embarrassment at all that had happened last night—her attempted escape, Reid besting her yet again, and then her weak dissolution into tears, followed by a kiss that had left her...confused was a vast understatement. Yet Reid had been...kind.

"Easy, lass," he said, gently pulling on the strand of hair again. "Dinnae jerk so, else I might come away with a clump of this stuff."

Corinne hesitated. An inch of air now separated her body from Reid's. She still wore only her chemise, but he must have pulled the blankets over them some time in the night, for she was cozily tucked to her chin. He had not hurt her or overpowered her, as they both knew he could.

Her eyes felt puffy, her throat raw. Even as a knot of grief rose in her throat yet again at the thought of her fate, his gentle teasing this morn took the sting out of her shame and frustration.

She let a breath go. "You can have it," she muttered, glancing up where his finger was wrapped around one of her unruly orange locks.

"Ye dinnae like it?" he asked, sliding his thumb along the coiled strand.

"Nay, of course not."

She darted a look at his face. He was so close. His slate-gray eyes were fixed on her hair, his dark brows drawing low. The scowl, combined with the white scar bisecting his eyebrow, made him look fierce, yet strangely she wasn't afraid of him.

"Why no'?" he demanded.

Corinne blinked. "It is ugly."

"Says who?"

"My father." A tangle of anger and shame pulled tight in her stomach. "I should have been fair-haired. And demure. And not so gangly."

"*Should* have?"

Her lips quirked. "I am my mother and father's only child. They needed a son. Instead they got me. The only consolation to having just one daughter would be if she was a great beauty, someone who could command a powerful alliance with her charms alone."

Reid's frown deepened. "Yer father sounds like an arse."

At the blunt words, she gave a decidedly unladylike snort. "He is."

"And yer mother? Why did she allow yer father to treat ye so?"

Corinne sighed. "I think my mother prefers to remain as invisible as possible, so as not to draw my father's attention to her own failings."

Reid grunted. "No wonder ye are so prickly. I imagine it was either that, or be swallowed whole by the likes of them."

An unexpected burn rose behind her eyes at his unexpected understanding. "Aye," she murmured.

Reid pinned her with his gaze, suddenly intent. He let his finger unravel from her hair and propped himself on one elbow.

"I am coming to accept our fate, Corinne," he began, his voice a low caress. "And I hope that someday ye can, too. But regardless of how we feel, we *will* be married. I thought…" An uncharacteristic hesitancy flickered across his eyes. "I thought that mayhap we should learn a wee bit more about each other."

A shaky breath slipped past her lips. She'd been so focused on escaping that she'd hardly considered what sort of man Reid was. Yet she couldn't deny her curiosity about the large, ruggedly handsome man lying opposite her in the bed.

"Very well," she said at last. "Tell me something of yourself."

One of his dark brows rose. "That is rather broad."

She pulled her lower lip between her teeth and gnawed on it for a moment, thinking. "What did you mean in the Bruce's tent when you said that you were illegitimate?"

He huffed a breath. "Ye arenae one to tiptoe around it, are ye, lass?"

When she opened her mouth to retort, he held up a staying hand. "Nay, I dinnae mind telling ye, for ye ought to ken before we are wed. Though I am recognized as the Laird of the Mackenzies, I am no' a blood heir to the Lairdship."

Corinne lifted herself onto one elbow, mirroring Reid. "Is that…unusual in the Highlands?"

One half of his mouth lifted ruefully. "Oh aye, unusual. And problematic."

"How did you become the Laird, then?"

"That came to pass under…difficult circumstances twelve years past, but I'll have to go back farther than that to explain."

She nodded, eager to know.

"Murdoch Mackenzie was the previous Laird. To bind an alliance with a neighboring clan, the MacDonnells, he agreed to wed Brinda MacDonnell—my mother. But when she arrived at Eilean Donan to marry Murdoch, it soon became clear that she was already pregnant."

"With you?" Corinne asked.

"Aye. I was born less than six months after their marriage, big and strong, no' wee from being early." He smiled faintly. "My mother chose the name Reid before I was even born. It means red, ye ken. Murdoch had bright red hair, and I think some part of her hoped I would too. It would have made it easier to at least pretend I was Murdoch's son."

He tilted his dark head and cocked an eyebrow. "As ye can see, though, her wish didnae come true."

Though he still bore a trace of a smile, Corinne could see that some part of the old wound of his illegitimate birth hadn't healed.

A sudden wave of guilt washed over her. Here she'd been complaining about her red hair not a moment before, and Reid's mother had likely prayed desperately for such a color. Reid, too, must have felt marked by his dark hair, a bastard-born black sheep.

Her guilt must have been written on her face, for he reached out and playfully tugged on a strand of hair again. "Yer parents must be blind fools, for I think the color very becoming on ye."

Warmth rushed over her face at the compliment. She opened her mouth to deflect the praise, but all she managed was a little flustered breath.

Reid released her hair, growing sober once more.

"The fact that my mother had come to him carrying another man's bairn was grounds enough for Murdoch no' only to send her away and annul the marriage, but also to break the alliance with the MacDonnells. But Murdoch was a good man."

"Your mother was allowed to stay and the alliance remained in place, then?" Corinne asked.

He nodded. "Though nigh everyone in the clan kenned that I couldnae be Murdoch's bairn, he treated me like his own son. He was a proud man, and I cannae imagine it was easy, but he protected both my mother and me from the worst of the stain of bastardry."

"What of your blood father? Do you know who he is?"

"I ken naught of him, for my mother wouldnae speak a word about him, no' even his name." Reid's eyes grew stormy. "I'd like to believe that she loved the man, that mayhap she hadnae wished to be sent to Murdoch, a stranger to her then, to be wed. I dinnae ken if she was protecting Murdoch or my blood sire, but whatever the case, she took her secret to the grave several years ago."

Corinne hesitated before her next words, but he'd said they should get to know each other better, and she longed to understand the clouds of unreadable emotion crossing his eyes.

"Mayhap she was protecting *you*," she said softly. "Mayhap she didn't want you to know your blood father."

"I have considered that," he replied. "I dinnae ken the man's nature or character, yet I cannae deny that I have longed to. Dinnae misunderstand, I loved Murdoch. I consider him my true father. Yet another man's blood runs through my veins. Someday I hope to learn just what he shared with my mother—and what I might share with him as his son."

Corinne nodded. "I understand. Even though I have as much in common with my parents as fish and fowl, they have made me who I am in many ways."

Reid chuckled softly, and the rumbling seemed to travel through the mattress and into Corinne's bones. Her skin suddenly felt tight and warm.

"You said you became Laird under difficult circumstances," she said, hastily redirecting her attention. "What happened?"

Reid's eyes went hard, a muscle twitching in his jaw behind his dark stubble.

"Though Murdoch accepted me as a son, it was no secret that I was in fact a bastard. The clan elders grew concerned that the line of succession for the Lairdship would be in jeopardy—until my mother bore another son, Logan, two years after my arrival. There was no doubt that Logan was Murdoch's bairn, nor that he would become the next Laird of the Mackenzies."

His gaze drifted to the now-cold brazier, his voice low and soft.

"Murdoch raised us side by side, trained us in the ways of fighting, negotiating, leadership—how to be a Laird. Still, it was assumed that Logan would succeed Murdoch. The Lairdship was his by right of blood and birth. But then, when I was two and twenty, Murdoch pulled me aside and told me that he wished to name me as his heir. It was a great honor—a sign that he truly thought of me as his firstborn son."

Surprise fluttered through Corinne. "How did the rest of the clan react to that?"

"Before he told anyone, Murdoch wished to inform

Logan of his decision. He took Logan and our younger sister, Mairin, away from the castle, hoping to explain his wishes in private. While they were gone, a storm broke. We at the castle began to grow worried. We formed a search party, but just as we were going to depart, Mairin emerged from the woods, crying hysterically. When she could form words, she said that Murdoch was dead."

Corinne sucked in a breath. "What had happened?"

Reid's jaw worked for a moment. "That was our question as well. Just then, Logan stumbled out of a nearby alehouse, drunk and ranting about how our father had passed him over. I knew Murdoch had intended to tell him of his decision to make me heir, and I…"

He swallowed hard.

"I assumed the worst of my brother. Since Murdoch hadn't publicly named me his successor, I thought Logan had killed him so that he would remain the heir. I accused him of killing Murdoch before our clanspeople and drew a blade on him. We fought, and I cut his face." He lifted a thumb and drew it down his left cheek from eye to jawline. "Here. And he cut me here." Reid ran a finger over his scarred eyebrow.

The chamber fell dead silent for a long moment.

"Did…did you kill him?" Corinne whispered.

"Nay," Reid replied, his voice hard as stone. "He fled. I thought to hunt him down, but the clan needed me. We'd lost our Laird and his heir in one fell swoop. So I assumed the duty of the Lairdship, a role I'd been trained for, but that I was never meant to have."

"And now?" Corinne asked. "Did you ever learn what happened to Murdoch? Or Logan?"

Reid let a long breath go, some of the tension easing from his jaw. "Aye, there lies one of the only bright spots in our family. A year past, I encountered Logan fighting for the Bruce's cause at a siege on a Borderlands castle. I confronted him and accused him of murder yet again, demanding that he answer to the charges. But he had our sister, Mairin, with him. She'd been kidnapped years before and had endured a long captivity at the hands of the English."

"What?" Corinne blurted. Good heavens, how much could one family go through?

"She is well now," he said hurriedly. "She is in the Highlands with others dedicated to the Bruce's cause. But when she was still a wee bairn, she was kidnapped outside Eilean Donan. No ransom request ever arrived, so we never kenned why she'd been kidnapped—until Logan rescued her. Apparently she was being used against him to force his service in a bounty hunter organization." He waved a hand as if that explained everything. "It was a messy business, but it's through."

Corinne sat bolt upright, belatedly remember that she only wore her chemise. Snatching the blankets over her chest, she stared at him, wide-eyed. "'It's through?' That is all? You forgave Logan for killing your father because he saved your sister?"

"Well, nay," he replied. "But the fact that he had Mairin, and that she begged me to hear him out, prevented me from killing him on the spot and gave him a chance to explain himself."

"And?"

"And apparently Murdoch never had the chance to tell Logan of his decision, because before he could speak, Logan asked to be allowed to lead a contingent of Mackenzies in the Bruce's army. Murdoch said nay, for it was a volatile and violent time, and he didnae think Logan ready at only twenty. Logan felt slighted, passed over, and stormed away to get pissed in the alehouse."

"And Murdoch's death?"

Reid's features hardened with grief. "An accident. Mairin was only a bairn of five at the time. She grew frightened when she heard Logan and Murdoch arguing. She ran away and climbed a tree, but a storm broke and Murdoch feared for her safety. He tried to climb up after her, but he slipped and fell."

He closed his eyes for a moment before going on. "Mairin carried the guilt of that accident for years, blaming herself for our father's death while never being able to speak of it. Only a year past did I learn all this—that I had torn our family apart with my accusations, that I had frightened Mairin into silence, and then lost her too, just as I'd lost Logan."

"But you have regained them," Corinne pointed out gently. "You have a brother and a sister again."

"Aye," he said. "And a clan. They are counting on me to lead them—to set things to rights for the future."

Realization settled over her. "Which is why you didn't wish to marry me. You believe they will not accept an English bride on top of everything else."

"I've caused a great deal of trouble for my clan," he said. "From the moment I was born, my existence raised uncertainty about the clan's future. With Murdoch's death and Logan's exile, I took on a role that wasnae meant for me. I opened the clan to questions, both from our allies and our enemies, if I was the rightful leader, and if an heir of mine could be trusted to succeed me in the Lairdship."

"And you thought to quell those challenges with a strong marriage alliance." A heavy stone sank in Corinne's stomach. Reid had been kind to suggest that they get to know each other, but the more she learned, the more she understood just how insurmountable the forces against them were.

He nodded. "A Highland bride would have done that. But the King's wishes cannae be denied."

Corinne felt her chest crumple and stinging heat rise to her eyes. It was happening again. She was not good enough. "I'm sorry I am not the bride you wanted," she muttered.

Though she knew it was impossible, she wished she could jump from the shuttered window and sprint all the way to the village's church. The only place she'd ever felt that she was good enough was at the nunnery near her father's keep. Her work there had meant something —and she was more than skilled at it. Sister Agatha had said she had a gift. If she could only—

Reid pinched a lock of her hair and tugged it, as he had earlier. She met his gaze reluctantly, but found his steely eyes surprisingly soft.

"Ye arenae the bride I *thought* I wanted," he murmured. "But God kens I've been wrong about much in my life."

Corinne stilled, captivated by his stare. His gaze dropped to her mouth, and suddenly the chamber seemed to fall away. Her heartbeat filled her ears.

Slowly, he pulled her down to him by the hank of red hair he held. His warm breath fanned her lips, then suddenly they were kissing again.

Something hot and sharp spiked in the pit of her stomach at the first brushing contact of his lips. They were firm and soft at the same time, coaxing yet demanding.

He released the lock of hair, his hand slipping around the nape of her neck. Her skin prickled at the faint scrape of his calluses, sending waves of gooseflesh rippling down her arms. Her nipples drew tight, rasping against the linen of her chemise.

Under the increasing pressure of his kiss, she parted her lips. His hot tongue invaded her mouth, pulling an involuntary moan from her throat. In answer, he growled in pleasure, sending vibrations through her lips.

She reached for him, needing more of his big, solid presence to anchor her. Her hands landed on his shoulders, and she cursed the gloves protecting her still-raw skin for separating her from the dark waves of hair resting there.

Still, she could feel the rippling strength of his muscles through the gloves. She clung to him as best she could as their tongues entwined.

His other hand slipped from around her waist and drifted up over her chemise until it was poised just under her breast. Without thinking, she arched up in silent invitation.

When he closed his palm over the sensitive flesh, she sucked in a breath. Sensation shot from her nipple straight between her legs.

He groaned, taking the weight of her breast in his cupped hand and letting his thumb slide across the aching peak.

Corinne nearly jumped out of her skin at that. Lightning coursed through her veins, making her feel weak and tense at the same time. Her breath caught on a gasp, her fingers sinking into his shoulders. What was he doing to her? Never had her body felt so awake, so needy, so—

A fist pounded against the chamber's wooden door in three sharp raps.

Corinne shrieked, bumping into the wall behind her.

"Laird, the horses are ready whenever ye are."

Over her wildly pounding heart, she thought she recognized the voice of the Mackenzie warrior called Alain.

"Thank ye," Reid snapped in the direction of the door.

The floorboards creaked as Alain retreated, and Corinne let out a trembling breath.

"We'd best get moving," Reid said to her. "I let ye sleep well past dawn."

Corinne nodded, not trusting her voice. Heaven above, what was happening to her? Reid had stirred something to life inside her that she'd lived all her twenty years without realizing existed—desire.

Her face burned as she scurried from the bed to where her now-dry gown lay draped over the chair.

Though he was already dressed, Reid busied himself with his boots and his sword belt while she quickly donned the gown.

As she secured her cloak around her shoulders, he opened the chamber door and motioned her forward.

"Ready?"

Was she? Ready to head deeper into Scotland? Ready to abandon her last hope of escape? Ready to accept that her fate was now inextricably entwined with the rugged, gruff man before her?

She drew in a shaky breath. "As ready as I'll ever be."

Chapter Thirteen

R eid helped Corinne onto the back of his horse, but before mounting behind her, he strode to Alain, who already sat in the saddle a few paces away with the others.

"I'll thank ye to await my orders rather than seeking me out to tell me that ye are ready to depart," he snapped through clenched teeth.

Alain's sandy brows rose and his lips quirked. "Forgive me, Laird. I merely thought that ye'd wish to use what little daylight we have to reach Eilean Donan."

"I do," Reid replied. "But dinnae interrupt me when I am alone with the lass."

Now Alain was clearly fighting a grin. "Ah. I see, Laird. I must have…misunderstood the purpose of ye sharing a room with the lass."

Some distant, rational part of Reid's brain knew Alain was only ribbing him. Normally, Alain's easy, teasing good humor was a boon. It had lightened the mood on many a battlefield camp or miserable journey over the years.

Yet a sudden surge of frustration burned away all reason, and Reid had to fight the urge to drag Alain from his horse and pound the smile from his face.

"She is to be my wife," he growled. "No' some lass to have a tumble with in an inn. Dinnae dishonor her with such jests."

Alain blinked, and several of the others sat up straighter in their saddles.

"Aye, Laird," Alain said earnestly. "I meant no disrespect."

Reid grunted, spinning on his heels and stomping back to where Corinne waited atop his horse.

Bloody hell, what was wrong with him? He knew Alain meant no harm, that he was likely only trying to make a difficult situation a wee bit cheerier, but damn it all if Reid wasn't feeling on edge.

Alain wasn't the source of his frustration, though— nay, that distinction lay with the flame-haired, ocean-eyed temptress sitting in his saddle. He needed a moment to think without her lemon-scented tresses tickling his nose—and he needed a dunk in an ice-cold loch to cool his cock and bollocks.

Corinne blinked at him, and he realized he'd been scowling fiercely at her. He swung into the saddle, barely biting down a groan as his legs bracketed hers, her bottom fitting snugly against his groin.

Bloody hell, it was going to be a long four days to Eilean Donan.

But of course, he reminded himself, when they

reached the castle, they would be wed, and then he could finish what he'd started at the inn.

He nudged his horse into motion, a tangle of conflicting thoughts knotting in his head. Aye, as she'd said, she wasn't the bride he'd wanted. Their marriage would only create more problems in an already fraught situation.

But accepting that he couldn't change his fate now, lusting for one's wife wasn't exactly a hardship.

As they rode out of the wee town, he noticed that Corinne's gaze was locked on something. She turned her head slowly as they continued north, her eyes following some fixed point in the distance.

He traced the path of her gaze to a kirk spire rising above the other squat buildings. Glancing down at her, he found her eyes sheened with tears.

He frowned. Desiring the lass was easy. Her wild spirit and her delicate, unusual beauty were an intoxicating combination. But *knowing* her, *understanding* her, was proving to be far more complicated.

And if Reid ever hoped to give her a decent life, one she did not long to flee from at the slightest opportunity, he needed to work harder at learning what lived in her heart and mind.

"Is that where ye meant to run to?" he murmured softly in her ear. "Last night?"

She started slightly, blinking away the tears. "Aye."

"Because ye want to be a nun so desperately?"

"Aye," she replied, but then paused. "Well, nay, not exactly."

Surprise flickered through him. "Nay?"

She glanced at him over her shoulder, her lower lip caught between her teeth. Damn it all, a fresh surge of desire hit him at the sight of her lush lip pinned in her mouth, her tongue running over its surface behind her teeth.

"I…I have a different reason for wishing to join a convent."

"Oh?" he murmured, at last managing to tear his gaze away from her mouth. He found her eyes clouded with uncertainty. "I wish to ken ye better, lass," he prodded gently. "I willnae judge ye."

She hesitated for another long moment, and Reid began to wonder if she would ever open up to him, but then she spoke at last. "I…I have been training to be a scribe."

Reid should have known better than to be surprised by aught the lass said or did. She was the most unusual woman he'd ever met, and he'd only known her for a sennight. Yet her declaration still managed to catch him off-guard.

"A scribe?" He wracked his brain for what little he knew of monastic work. "Ye mean ye are learning to write?"

Corinne cast him a withering look over her shoulder, and he nearly snorted in amusement.

"I already know how to write," she replied dryly. "I am the daughter of an English lord. I had a fine education in letters, numbers, and more."

She sighed, and they swayed together with the rhythm of the horse's steps for a moment before she continued.

"Of course, the purpose of that education was to mold me into a suitable wife, the lady of a household. It was all in the service of making me competent at running a keep."

"But let me guess," Reid said. "Ye decided no' to obey that directive."

Her lips curved. "Something about learning letters captivated me. First there was copying the alphabet, but soon I was copying passages of the Bible and poetry, whatever my tutor would lend me. I began neglecting my other lessons and spent all my time with a quill in my hand. I can still barely mend a stocking, let alone embroider or weave, but Sister Agatha said she'd never seen scribal work like mine."

"And Sister Agatha is…?"

"One of the nuns at Saint Mary's, the convent near my father's keep," she replied. "When the tutor refused to take the blame for my lack of advancement in other areas besides letters, he quit, and I began slipping away to the convent. That was when my real education began."

A soft rain started to fall, and Corinne pulled the hood of her cloak up. But so that her voice wasn't muffled, she leaned closer to him, turning her head so that he could see her profile.

"Sister Agatha recognized my gift and passion for writing, so she began teaching me the skills of a scribe. For her, it was God's work. In transcribing the Bible or a prayer book, she was disseminating God's words, helping them spread."

"And for ye?" he asked. "Why are ye so compelled by the work?"

She hesitated for a moment. "I am a faithful Christian, but I am not called to the church the way Sister Agatha and the others were. For me it is…" She looked up at him, her blue-green eyes searching. "Have you ever yearned to give the world something that will live long after you are gone?"

Her words were like an arrow aimed straight at his heart. Reid dragged in a breath. "Aye," he said, holding her gaze. "I long for that every day. As a Laird, I ken I am only a temporary keeper of my people. The clan will go on when I am gone—I can only hope to make it stronger in my time as leader."

Do right by our people, son.

Those had been Murdoch Mackenzie's words when he'd told Reid that he'd chosen him as his successor. It was an awe-inspiring responsibility—one Reid bore with fierce pride every day.

Reid remained quiet for another heartbeat before going on. "That is why I have been so focused on giving the clan an heir. It will mean strength and stability for the next generation, and those to follow."

Corinne lowered her gaze, pretending to fiddle with her gloves. "Aye, that is similar. The texts I transcribe will survive long after I am dust. I don't have any stories of my own—not yet, anyway—but the stories I write down can be passed on and shared with dozens, mayhap hundreds of others."

She huffed a little laugh. "It is foolish, I know, and mayhap arrogant, but it is something I'm passionate about—and good at. The letters flow from my quill, and I lose myself in them."

"No' foolish," he said, placing a hand over her entwined fingers. "And no' arrogant to use yer gift."

A sudden realization struck him. Her father had beaten her hands not merely to teach her a lesson, but to prevent her from being able to write. The cruelty and callousness of such an act sent hot rage into his veins.

"That is why yer father hurt ye," he said, enfolding his large hand over her smaller ones more completely. "To force ye to stop writing."

Corinne's gaze fixed on their hands, but her eyes were distant with memory. "At first, he could find no objection to my frequent trips to the convent. He thought it would do me good to learn humility and humbleness in a house of God. But when he discovered what I was truly about, he forbade me from continuing with my lessons."

"But ye arenae obedient," he said, something in his chest swelling with pride at the lass's fortitude.

"Nay," she said with a soft chuckle. "I continued learning under Sister Agatha in secret. By the time he discovered what I was up to, he'd already contracted my marriage to Halbert de Perroy. I think he was relieved that I would no longer be his problem—but also embarrassed that my unruliness would reflect badly on him to de Perroy."

She lifted her hands under his to indicate the beating she'd endured. "He told me that de Perroy had been the one to suggest such a punishment, and that the man promised far worse once I belonged to him."

Reid kept his touch on her relaxed, but his other hand clenched the reins so hard that his horse twitched and nickered in annoyance.

"The bastard willnae harm ye now—neither of them. I vow I'll never raise a hand against ye."

She glanced up at him, her eyes unguarded. "Though this was not the path I wanted for myself, I…I am grateful for your words."

Reid swallowed, forcing some of his anger down. "Yer hands seem to be healing well. Yer father didnae manage to cripple ye, if that was his intent."

"Aye, soon enough I'll be able to use a quill agai—" The words stuck in her throat, her shoulders stiffening. "That is…I will be able…"

In a stab of realization, he understood the trail of her thoughts. Aye, she would be physically able to write again, but as the wife of a Laird, she would never join a convent and work as a scribe.

Another, far more troubling thought came to him. Though he knew it would ruin the single thread of trust between them, he needed the answer if they were to be wed.

"Corinne," he began cautiously. She gazed up at him, her eyes wide and depthless as the ocean. He was an arse, but he had to know. "Yer study as a scribe and yer impending marriage to de Perroy explain why ye tried to flee to a nunnery," he said, choosing his words carefully. "But sometimes there are…other reasons a woman retreats to a convent."

She blinked at him in confusion. "What are you saying?"

"I'm asking," he said, "if ye have ever been…indiscreet with a man."

Clarity, followed by offense, filled her eyes. "You think I am not innocent?"

Reid ground his teeth until his jaw ached. "I mean no insult. But…" *Damn it all!* He dragged a hand through his hair, scanning the landscape for a moment. "I told ye of my mother marrying Murdoch while carrying another man's bairn. I cannae have any doubt hanging over an heir we produce."

Corinne's gaze burned with hurt. "I am a virgin," she breathed. "You were the first man—the *only* man—I've ever even kissed."

Surprise hit him in the gut. "Corinne, I—"

"But thank you for reminding me what this arrangement is about," she went on, angry tears brimming in her eyes. "I had nearly forgotten that I am unwanted except as a means for you to bring forth an heir."

Bloody hell, he'd made a mess of things again.

Gently, he lifted his hand from hers and cupped her chin, turning her face until their gazes locked.

"I willnae lie to ye," he murmured, his voice low and tight. "The path ye sought, the life ye wanted, willnae come to pass. But I can promise ye this—ye will be safe and well looked after as my wife."

The flicker of emotion he saw in the depths of her eyes was unmistakable—hurt. And sadness.

What he offered was fair. She could rest assured in his protection of her, and in a life free from fear and pain.

But was that enough? From the way she dropped her

gaze and hunched her shoulders away from him, it wasn't. She wouldn't try to run again, of that he felt fairly certain. Aye, she was coming to accept her lot, just as he was. Yet Reid had the sinking suspicion that the Bruce's command that they marry would consign them both to a life of misery.

He urged his horse into a faster walk, even though every step sped them closer to Eilean Donan—and their fate.

Chapter Fourteen

W hen they crested a rocky ridge a sennight after
departing from Lochmaben, the Mackenzie
warriors let out whoops and whistles of enthusiasm.

Corinne jumped in the saddle. It had been a glum,
quiet five days since they'd left the inn. The sudden
noise and excitement sent trepidation into the pit of her
stomach. They must be close to Eilean Donan.

The landscape had changed much over the last
several days. Gone were the soft hills and dense forests
of the Lowlands. For a while, they'd traveled through
desolate moors of rock and scrubby, hardy plants, only
broken by huddled clumps of pine trees, wind-rippled
lochs, and small, humble farmsteads and villages.

Now they'd entered terrain even more rugged.
Having grown up in Cumbria, Corinne had thought
she'd seen mountains, but naught compared to the
craggy, barren peaks surrounding them. She felt small,
dwarfed by such majesty.

"The men have spotted the Five Sisters," Reid said behind her, making her start again.

They'd said little to each other after she'd told him of her dashed dreams. It was for the best, for Corinne didn't trust her voice whenever she thought of his words.

The life ye wanted willnae come to pass.

Aye, it seemed that one way or another, fate was conspiring against her work as a scribe. Even as she struggled to accept that, it didn't take the sting from her eyes or the lump from her throat. The pain was made more acute with each passing day, for they drew nearer to Reid's home—and her new life.

Reid pointed, his muscular arm making an angled line over her shoulder and past her eyes.

"Those are the Five Sisters there. Ye see?"

Her gaze followed his arm toward a row of steep mountains rising in front of them. A faint dusting of snow highlighted every sharp angle and unforgiving slope along the range. Beneath its awe-inspiring façade sat a smooth lake trimmed with flame-colored oaks and dark green pines. Red deer dotted the hillsides above the lake, their breaths puffing in the chilly air.

"Each peak has a different name," Reid said, shifting his finger to the highest points jutting above the rest. "It is said that they were the daughters of a Highland chief long ago. He once had seven beautiful daughters, but two brothers from a faraway land sailed into the loch and stole two of the chief's daughters away."

Despite herself, curiosity pricked at Corinne. "What happened to the other five, then?"

"To appease the angry chief, the brothers vowed that

they had five eligible brothers to marry the other sisters. But after they sailed away, they never returned to the loch, and the lasses eventually turned to stone."

Warmth rose to her cheeks. "That is a sad tale. Mayhap the brothers shouldn't have stolen those women away."

She felt him shift in the saddle and imagined that he was frowning at her pointed comment.

"Be that as it may," he said, his voice low, "the Five Sisters are much beloved by the Mackenzies, for whenever we see them, we ken we are close to home."

He trailed his finger to the left, pointing at a valley that ran along the lake and around the base of the mountain range. "Eilean Donan lies just beyond there."

She nodded, her stomach pinching with nervousness.

Reid spurred his horse into a gallop, and they tore down the rise and into the valley. The others streamed after them, clearly eager to be home.

They rounded the lake and skirted along its northern shoreline. As the sharp, briny scent of the sea hit her, Corinne realized that the lake must actually be fed in part by the ocean, though the waters were sheltered and still.

Ahead, a dark speck of an island sat in the water just off the shore. Across from it on the north side was a clump of buildings.

"Is that..."

"Aye," he shouted over the thundering of hooves. "Eilean Donan."

To her shock, he pointed not at the little village on

the shoreline, but at the stark, rocky island. She squinted. What she'd mistaken for a towering pile of rocks was actually a massive stone castle.

As they reached the outskirts of the village, Reid and the other warriors reined in their horses. Someone shouted and pointed at them, and soon people were streaming from thatch-roofed huts and wooden buildings, calling out and waving to the returning party.

Soon the gathering villagers broke out into song, the children running merrily after the horses. Corinne fought the urge to shrink back into Reid's chest. As joyous as the homecoming was, she didn't miss the curious stares and whispers as she passed atop Reid's horse.

Reid guided them to the edge of the village, where a large system of stables sat along the shoreline. He dismounted and reached for her. When she looked down at him, his normally hard-set features were surprisingly relaxed. Of course, he was among his people. Unlike her.

He called out orders to the stable master to tend to the men's horses, then took Corinne by the elbow and led her toward a wooden dock just opposite the stables. Now that they were no longer on horseback, villagers swarmed around them.

"Welcome back, Laird!" someone called.

"Did ye slay many Englishmen, Laird?"

"What news from the King?"

As Reid and the others reached the wooden dock, he turned to face the exuberant villagers.

"All is well," he called out in a booming voice. "In

fact, to celebrate our many victories, there will be a great feast at the castle on the morrow."

The villagers erupted into cheers and merriment. Taking advantage of their uproarious joy, he turned to an armored man on the dock and shouted "To the castle, Timothy."

The man nodded and motioned Reid onto a waiting boat. Reid pulled Corinne through the crowd after him and handed her down into the boat. A few of the Mackenzie warriors climbed in as well, though it looked as though some of them wished to remain in the village to celebrate their homecoming.

Just as Timothy shoved away from the dock and began rowing them toward the castle on the island, someone called from the shoreline. "Who is the lass, Laird?"

Reid ignored the question, but when Corinne caught his eye, he frowned slightly. "They'll learn soon enough. The feast tomorrow will be in honor of our wedding."

Cold apprehension rippled over Corinne's skin. "So soon?"

"There is no point in waiting."

The words sounded frosty to her ears. She swallowed, pulling her gaze away to examine the castle.

Though it only sat a long stone's throw from the shoreline, it was clearly built with impenetrability and inaccessibility in mind. A thick stone curtain wall surrounded nearly the entire island, with three rectangular guard towers positioned along the wall so that every angle could be watched.

Inside the wall, an even larger square tower, which

she assumed was the castle's keep, rose imposingly above the others. Both the watchtowers and the keep were slitted with arrow loops and topped with crenelated battlements for defense.

As they drew nearer, Corinne began to wonder how they would enter the imposing fortress, for the curtain wall rose directly from the island's steep rocky sides. She had her answer when Timothy began to row them around to the back side of the island.

Corinne craned her neck as they glided past one of the towers, where guards wearing the same green and blue checked plaid as Reid gazed down at them. Between the largest of the watchtowers and the keep tower, a small, shallow beach appeared against the wall. Timothy rowed them onto the beach, which was hardly big enough even for the small boat.

Just as Reid lifted her from the boat to the sand, a squat, narrow gate in the wall opened with a loud squeal.

"Come." Reid took her elbow once more and ducked through the gate. They emerged from the narrow path cut in the thick stone wall into a large open courtyard—filled with smiling people.

A cheer went up as those in the castle greeted their Laird. He held up a hand for silence, and as the crowd began to quiet, Corinne felt the distinct shift of eyes toward her.

"We have returned victorious, having served King Robert the Bruce loyally," Reid boomed.

The crowd cheered once more, but now a ripple of

murmurs moved through them. A few pointed at Corinne, whispering questions behind their hands.

"And as a loyal servant," Reid went on, his voice loud and emotionless, "it is my duty to obey the King's wishes. He has deigned to give me a bride and ordered that I wed her with all haste."

Corinne stared up at Reid, stunned by his words. Whether he meant to or not, he'd just shamed her in front of his people. Aye, it was true that he'd been commanded to wed her, but need he make her sound like such a burden?

Now rumbles of confusion rose from those gathered.

Reid spoke over them. "This is Lady Corinne de Reymont of Cumbria."

"She's *English*?" someone whispered loudly.

"Look at her," another muttered.

Corinne looked down at herself, imagining what the crowd saw. She wore the same much-abused blue gown that she'd donned in the Bruce's camp. It was rumpled and stained from a sennight of hard travel. Besides their night at the inn, they'd slept out of doors on the ground and ridden through the rain and mud during the day.

She lifted a gloved hand to her hair, her face burning with humiliation. Reid had thought her a boy when he'd first laid eyes on her.

"Silence," Reid snapped, his gaze hard on his people. "We will be wed tomorrow, as the King wishes. Now see to yer duties."

If she could have, Corinne would have let the stones beneath her feet swallow her whole in that moment.

Was this how it would be between them, then, and between her and his people?

Aye, what else did she expect from the Mackenzie clan—or from Reid? He was only doing his duty, as she was. His distaste for the task was palpable. It was no wonder, then, that his people would feel free to express their displeasure as well.

Still murmuring, the crowd began to disperse, casting wary stares in her direction.

"Gellis!" Reid barked, making Corinne jump.

A short, brown-haired woman approaching middle years hurried forward from the departing mass of people. She dipped into a curtsy before Reid, sliding a look at Corinne as she did.

"I ken this may be awkward for ye, Gellis, but I'd like ye to attend to Lady Corinne. See that she is made comfortable for the night in one of the spare rooms, and help her prepare for the wedding tomorrow," Reid instructed.

Gellis blinked wide brown eyes at Reid, but then quickly dropped into another curtsy. "As ye wish, Laird. This way, milady."

Gellis tilted her head at Corinne, then set off toward the large, looming keep.

Shame and trepidation burning in her face and pricking behind her eyes, Corinne turned without looking at Reid and fell in behind Gellis.

She was in the belly of the beast now.

Chapter Fifteen

Corinne tried to quell her rising fear as she followed Gellis into the great hall. The hall was aflurry with activity, due no doubt to their Laird's arrival and impending marriage. The rushes on the ground were being hastily cleared away for new ones, and the trestle tables and benches were being arranged for the evening meal.

"The kitchens are just there," Gellis said, pointing toward the back of the great hall. "We have room enough within the castle walls for an herb and flower garden, plus a few fruit trees, but many supplies come from the village."

Realizing this might be her only guided orientation to the castle, Corinne hastened her steps until she was nearly on Gellis's heels, else she might miss a word.

"There are four storeys above this one," Gellis said as they crossed the great hall, "though the top floor is the garrison for the guards' weapons."

"And the others?" Corinne asked.

Gellis mounted a flight of spiraling stairs, lifting her skirts efficiently. "The first floor holds the Laird's chambers—his sleeping chamber and his solar." As they passed a landing, Gellis gestured to first one door and then another. "The second floor houses servants and supplies."

Several doors sat closed on the next landing, indicating that the chambers must have been divided into much smaller portions than Reid's quarters.

"And the third floor is much the same as the second," Gellis said, halting on another landing. "It is mainly a few guest chambers in addition to more servants' quarters and storage rooms."

Gellis opened the first door on the far left of the landing, motioning Corinne inside.

Corinne glanced around. The room was dark and cold, likely because it was infrequently used. A hearth sat empty along one wall. Opposite it, a narrow slit in the stone served as a window. A medium-sized bed rested with the curtains drawn back from its posters. Besides a trunk at the foot of the bed and a dressing table and chair, the room was empty.

"I hope ye'll find this adequate for the night, milady," Gellis said.

"Of course," Corinne said hastily, realizing that her silence might be mistaken for snobbish disdain.

Gellis turned to her and looked at her fully for the first time. Her gaze traced down over Corinne's soiled dress to her muddy boots, then back up to her face. But when their eyes met, Corinne didn't find disgust or animosity there, only curiosity.

"I imagine ye'll be wanting a bath before the evening meal, milady."

"Yes, please," Corinne breathed.

Gellis poked her head out the door and called for a bath.

As a wooden tub was rolled into the chamber and servants began bringing water in buckets, Gellis worked on the laces down Corinne's back.

"I have other clean dresses," Corinne said, embarrassment warming her face. "And soap. They are with the men who…escorted me here."

Gellis nodded matter-of-factly and turned to one of the chamber maids who'd just emptied her bucket into the tub. "Find Alain and see that Lady Corinne's things are gathered and brought here."

The chamber maid ducked into a swift curtsy and hurried to do Gellis's bidding.

"Leave it to a MacRae to forget that a woman would want her personal effects and a clean gown after a long journey," Gellis murmured as she helped Corinne peel away her soiled dress.

Corinne's hands halted for a moment. "Alain isn't a Mackenzie?"

Gellis looked up, her brown eyes inquisitive. "Nay. Didnae he tell ye?"

"We didn't…exchange many pleasantries on the journey," Corinne replied. The men had been largely uninterested in her when they'd been en route to the Bruce, and afterward, they'd seemed so absorbed in their sour silence that Corinne still didn't know some of their names.

"And the Laird didnae explain?" Gellis asked, her brows lowering. At Corinne's mute shake of the head, Gellis frowned. "I suppose ye dinnae ken much about the Mackenzie clan—or clans in general—do ye?"

"I know Reid is the Laird, the leader. I know his heir will be the next Laird…"

Corinne faltered. She was edging into dangerous territory. Firstly, the thought of Reid's successor reminded her that *she* would be the one to produce an heir, which tangled her insides into a ball of nervousness, trepidation, and some unidentified warmth she didn't wish to dwell on.

What was more, though, she was approaching mentioning Reid's family and birth. Though Reid had said it was no great secret among the clan that he was bastard-born, Corinne had only been here a few minutes. As an English outsider who was being forced on the Mackenzies as their lady, she doubted they'd appreciate her first few words among them being in reference to their Laird's illegitimacy.

She cleared her throat. "I admit I have much to learn." And she had to start somewhere, for unless a miracle happened, this would be her new home. "I had assumed that everyone here was a Mackenzie, but Alain is from the MacRae clan?"

"Oh, aye," Gellis responded, busying herself with folding Corinne's discarded dress. "There are quite a few MacRaes here at Eilean Donan. They are the Mackenzies' neighbors to the south, ye ken. Many of the castle guards are MacRaes—in fact, they have come to be called the Mackenzies' shirt of mail for the protection they provide."

So the Mackenzies controlled not only Eilean Donan, which boasted the thickest stone walls and most elaborate defensive planning of any keep Corinne had ever seen, but they also had the loyalty of warriors from a neighboring clan? It spoke to the Mackenzies' strength —and Reid's determination to protect his people.

"Are there people from other clans here as well?" Corinne asked, eager to understand more about this seemingly impenetrable place—and her equally impermeable future husband.

"I myself am a MacDonnell," Gellis commented, testing the water in the now-full tub with a finger. Nodding, she motioned Corinne forward.

Though the last of the chamber maids had departed, closing the door behind them, Corinne still blushed at disrobing completely. "I can see to myself," she said, hesitating at the tub's edge.

"The Laird asked me to look after ye," Gellis said evenly.

Swallowing her pride, Corinne slipped off her gloves, then pulled her chemise over her head and hurriedly eased into the water.

"Ye're a skinny thing, arenae ye," Gellis said as she approached. Then the older woman seemed to remember herself. "Forgive me, milady."

A soft rap on the door saved Corinne from responding. One of the chamber maids slipped in with her arms full of Corinne's other dresses and the few possessions that had been salvaged from the wagon. As the chamber maid ducked back out, Gellis took up the lemon-scented soap Corinne loved so dearly and began working a lather into her hands.

Corinne dunked her head underwater quickly. Though the warm temperature coaxed her to linger, she got the sense from Gellis that she should not dally. The lady's maid had been polite enough—except for commenting on Corinne's figure, about which she was already self-conscious—but Corinne got the impression that Gellis was watching her, waiting for her to slip up and prove that she shouldn't be here.

As Gellis began working the soap into Corinne's scalp, the older woman tsked softly. "What happened to yer hair?"

Corinne wished she could sink all the way underwater and not come out again. "I cut it."

"Oh? And why would ye do that, milady?"

It was time for Corinne to make a decision. She was either going to cower, blush, and wither away with discomfort here at this Highland castle, or she was going to find her spine. She glanced down at her hands, which rested on top of her knees where they poked out of the water. The marks were almost completely healed. She hadn't let her father cow her, and she wasn't going to let the Mackenzies—or the MacRaes or the MacDonnells, or anyone else—do so either.

"I was planning on entering a convent," Corinne said, willing her voice to be strong and steady. "I was meant to marry a detestable man, but I wished to become a scribe at a nunnery instead. So I plotted an escape. That was just before your Laird kidnapped me, and your King saw fit to order us to wed."

Gellis's hands froze in Corinne's hair. Corinne held her breath, her fingers sinking into her knees.

After a long moment, Gellis made a noise that was half-cough, half-snort. "I havenae heard aught as... bold as that in quite a while, milady."

Corinne released her breath slowly at the sound of surprise and grudging amusement in Gellis's voice.

They completed the bath in silence, and when the last of the lemon suds had been washed away, Gellis extended a length of drying linen to her. Once she'd dried herself, Gellis slipped a clean chemise over her head.

As Gellis shuffled through the small stack of clean gowns, Corinne remembered something that Reid had said earlier.

"The Laird mentioned that you would find serving me as a lady's maid difficult," she began, chewing on her lower lip. "Is that...is it because I am English?"

Gellis looked up, a wool gown dyed crimson in her hands. She blinked, her big brown eyes considering. "I willnae lie to ye, there will be many in the clan who willnae take easily to the idea of an English mistress."

Just when she felt that she was making progress, gaining Gellis's respect and finding her spine, a stone of discouragement sank in Corinne's stomach.

"I havenae met many English," Gellis went on, "but of course we have all suffered in this long war. We've lost good men, and struggled to keep ourselves warm and fed when the war effort requires so much." The woman shook out the crimson dress and appraised it. "I dinnae think that was what the Laird meant when he assigned me to ye, though, milady."

Corinne hesitated. "Oh?"

"Nay. I think he was more referring to the fact that I was the last mistress's lady's maid."

That was strange. Though Gellis was at least a dozen years older than Corinne, her brown hair wasn't laced with gray. Surely she couldn't be old enough to have served Reid's mother, for Reid had said Brinda had died several years ago.

"You attended Lady Brinda, Reid's mother?" she asked cautiously.

"Nay, milady," Gellis said, staring at her evenly. "I served Lady Euna, Reid's first wife."

It was as if Gellis had dumped a bucket of cold water over Corinne's head.

Reid had a wife? A first wife?

What had happened to the woman? When had they been wed?

And why in God's name hadn't he mentioned her to Corinne?

Euna. She'd overheard him mention that name when she'd been listening outside the Bruce's tent. Corinne wracked her brain for any sliver of information she could recall other than the name, but she came up empty.

A sudden, hot wave of anger crashed through her. Reid had told her all about his childhood, the struggles his family had endured, and his ascension to the Lairdship, yet he'd failed to mention—to his future wife—that he'd been married before.

Why was it left to her to listen outside tents and overhear from servants that he'd had another wife? Was this to be what their marriage would be like? Him withholding and silent, and her bitter and isolated?

A stinging memory suddenly hit her—of her father, casually informing his captain of the guard that the marriage arrangement between Corinne and Halbert de Perroy had been finalized. He hadn't even told her. Instead, he'd merely allowed her to overhear him make arrangements with the captain to transport her.

That had been right before he'd taken the switch to her hands.

She could not live like that again. Even if Reid was telling the truth that he wasn't the sort of man to raise a hand against a woman, she was still at his mercy. Did he expect her to happily play the part of a pawn, silently sipping up what trickle of information he deemed her worthy of knowing?

"Where is the Laird?" she demanded through clenched teeth.

Gellis's brows lifted. "He's likely refreshing himself in his chambers before the evening meal, milady, but—"

Without thinking, Corinne stormed toward the door.

"Milady, yer gown!"

Corinne didn't slow as she wound her way down the spiral stairs. Bare feet, chemise, and dripping hair be damned. She needed answers from Reid—now.

Chapter Sixteen

R eid sank into the heated water with a groan. Aye, he could push his body just as hard as ever in battle and on long journeys, but damn it all if he didn't feel it more than he used to.

Truth be told, the knots in his shoulders and the ache between his legs weren't just from hard riding and sleeping on the ground for the last sennight. Corinne was doing strange things to him—especially when she looked at him with hurt simmering in her sea-green eyes.

He roughly shoved aside his guilt. He'd been blunt in introducing her to his people, but there was no room for sentimentality when it came to being the Laird of a large and powerful clan. His people needed to see that he could set aside personal feelings and do his duty for the good of clan and country.

Still, his thoughts tugged upward as he began lathering a cake of soap and washing away the grueling journey. Corinne would be on the third floor in one of the guest chambers if Gellis had done as he bid. What might she be doing up there at this moment?

He'd seen the servants carrying a tub and water up the stairs earlier. It had given him the idea to bathe as well. Eilean Donan boasted two wooden tubs and enough enormous hearths to quickly heat several buckets of water at a time. Was she still bathing, as he was?

An image of Corinne naked, dripping wet and lathered in that maddeningly enticing lemon-scented soap, slammed into him like a punch to the gut. Unbidden, his cock leapt to life below the water. Gritting his teeth, Reid groaned as more erotic visions came to him.

Corinne on her back, her wild red hair splayed out beneath her. The feel of her soft breasts filling his hands. Her creamy thighs falling open in invitation.

With another groan, Reid's hand dipped below the waterline, the frustrating need to find relief nigh overpowering.

A fist suddenly slammed twice against the chamber door—hard. Reid jerked upright in the tub, but before he could bellow at whoever was interrupting his bath to leave him the hell alone, the door flew open.

Corinne stood in the doorway.

In only a chemise.

A wet chemise.

Her cropped hair was dripping onto the thin linen, making it plaster to her skin along her collarbone.

At the sight of her pale skin showing through the material, his mind ground to a halt.

"What in the bloody he—"

"You were married before."

Reid yanked his gaze from the neckline of her chemise and fully looked at her. Belatedly, he realized that she was fuming mad. Her wet hair was a disorderly red tangle on her head, her blue-green eyes blazing with fury. Her hands, which were uncovered and only faintly discolored now, were balled at her sides.

He remained motionless in the tub. "Aye," he said carefully.

Though it was the truth, it seemed to be the wrong response. Corinne's eyes widened and her brows shot up.

"When were you going to tell me? On our wedding night? Or mayhap never, if it didn't suit you?"

"Close the door," he ordered evenly.

She let out an exasperated huff, but then she blinked, seeming to truly see him for the first time since barging in. Where the chemise clung wetly to her collarbone, her creamy skin turned pink. The color traveled up her neck and into her face. Reid watched, mesmerized for a long moment, until he at last found her eyes.

Clearly, she was embarrassed and fascinated all at once. Her gaze darted over his lathered chest to his arms, which rested along the sides of the tub, to the waterline around his abdomen, and back up again.

"At yer leisure," he commented, gesturing toward the door. Aye, he was wicked for taunting her, and for enjoying her spellbound gaze on him as well, yet in that moment he couldn't muster a single shred of guilt.

Face aflame, Corinne dropped her eyes and hurried

to close the door. The act must have given her a chance to calm her nerves and gather her anger once more, for when she turned back to him, she planted her fists on her hips and stared him down.

"Well?" she demanded. "Why didn't you tell me?"

Reid's amusement faded—but not, unfortunately, his throbbing erection. He let a long breath go, attempting to focus.

"I didnae think it mattered," he said at last.

Corinne's bonny lips parted in disbelief. "What didn't matter—telling me? Or the entire marriage?"

Damn it all, this wasn't going well. He'd just been envisioning Corinne before him, but it hadn't been like this. His marriage with Euna was the last thing he wished to discuss at the moment. Still, from the pain smoldering behind the anger in Corinne's eyes, it was time he addressed the matter.

"I didnae think it…relevant to our current situation," he tried again.

"It seemed relevant enough for Gellis to mention it. How could you drag me all the way here—"

Now his own annoyance flared to life. "I didnae drag ye. Dinnae make me seem like some great barbarian."

"—bring me here, then," she continued, "and not mention that you were wed before?"

"There wasnae a good time to bring it up," he replied. "Ye seemed upset enough as it was about being forced to marry me. I didnae wish to add more to the list for ye to hate."

Corinne's hands dropped from her sides, her eyes flickering with hurt. "I am not upset that you were previously married. Caught off-guard, mayhap, but not angry. Nay, I am angry because you didn't *tell* me. You left it for the servants to mention it, and made me look a fool in front of them."

Reid muttered a curse at himself. Aye, he should have thought of that. "Gellis willnae think ye a fool."

She jolted several steps toward the tub. "It's not just Gellis. The way you spoke of me before them—the way you spoke of marrying me as naught but a duty—"

Her voice broke and her chin wavered.

Shite. Reid had the sudden urge to rise from the tub and go to her, folding her into his arms. Yet he could not come undone so easily.

"Isnae that what this is for *both* of us—a duty? An order we must obey?" he asked, though he attempted to soften his voice.

She closed her eyes for a moment. "Aye. But you are in your home, surrounded by people who love and respect you. I don't know a soul, and as an English-woman, I am your people's enemy. I know next to naught about your clan or life in the Highlands—and apparently I know even less about *you*, whom I am to wed tomorrow."

Reid let his arms slip into the rapidly cooling water. Damn it all, she was right. He'd been an arse yet again. He hadn't wanted to lower himself before his people by showing weakness or coddling Corinne in front of them, yet surely he could have done better to ease both their reception of her and her first welcome into her new home.

"I apologize," he said, the words tasting strange in

his mouth. "As Laird, it is my duty to be a strong leader for my people. I may seem...harsh to ye, but it is only because the clan needs me to be their rock."

The tension began seeping from her shoulders. She dropped her gaze. "I understand."

But clearly Corinne's discomfort would not be so easily soothed. Reid cursed himself again for putting her in such an impossible position.

"I married Euna three years past," he offered.

She froze, glancing up at him.

"She was a MacDonnell," he went on. "The eldest daughter of Laird Arthur MacDonnell. I'd been in talks with the man for years before he finally agreed to a marriage alliance."

"Oh?" she asked hesitantly.

"Aye, he is a stubborn old badger. I cannae blame him, though. No man wishes to give his daughter over to a bastard, even a bastard Laird. He feared that the shadow of illegitimacy hanging over me would stain no' only Euna, but the entire MacDonnell clan as well."

Corinne's brows drew together. "Then how did you forge the marriage alliance?"

Reid felt one corner of his mouth lift. "The Mackenzies are a far larger clan than the MacDonnells. The Laird realized at last that it would be in his interest to align himself with us."

"You threatened him?"

"The opposite," Reid replied. "I offered to help him. The MacDonnells share a border with the MacVales, a troublesome clan that does little more than raid and stir up discord. The MacVales refused to join the Bruce's efforts at freedom. Because they havenae lost men and supplies to the cause, they've grown more powerful—and bolder. They've been pestering the MacDonnells for decades, but lately they've done more than reive a few cows and sheep. They began burning crops, and even a few crofts."

"And how did you help?"

"I sent the MacDonnells several of our warriors to help them patrol their borders." Reid lifted a shoulder, making the water ripple around him. "It didnae hurt that many of the men I selected had been eyeing MacDonnell lasses as well. The marriages and bairns that resulted, plus the added protection, showed Laird MacDonnell that I was serious about our alliance. He finally agreed to the marriage."

Corinne pulled her lower lip between her teeth, and an involuntary spike of heat stabbed him.

"What happened?" she asked.

"A few months after our wedding, Euna was carrying a bairn. But several months before the bairn was to arrive, she began to bleed. Both Euna and the bairn died shortly after. That was two years past."

Corinne lifted her fingertips to her mouth, her eyes going wide. "I...I'm sorry," she murmured. "That is a terrible loss."

Reid cupped a palmful of tepid water and splashed it over his face. He took his time washing away the remnants of soap lather on his chest and arms, buying himself a few moments to carefully phrase his next words.

"Euna was a good woman, and her death was a

deep wound to her father and the rest of her family. To lose an heir was also a blow to the clan."

Corinne took another step forward. Now she stood right at the edge of the tub, her gaze searching his face. "And a blow to you as well?"

"Euna and I were both doing our duty to our people, naught more," he murmured. "Though I respected her, we didnae share feelings beyond that."

Reid let his eyes skim over the candlelight reflecting on the surface of the water. "Our marriage was meant to no' only unite our clans, but to end the uncertainties surrounding the Mackenzies' future in light of my birth. A legitimate union with another Highland Laird's daughter would have strengthened my position, and an heir of that union would have been unquestionable."

Out of the corner of his eye, he saw Corinne shrink into her shoulders, and he realized that yet again, he'd hurt her.

Before she could withdraw, his hand darted out and closed around her wrist, holding her in place.

"That is all in the past now," he said.

"Your first marriage may be in the past," she said. "But your concerns for your clan and your alliances remain the same. Just as before, you must wed out of duty, only this time, your bride creates naught but problems for you."

"That is true," he replied. Her eyes rounded in indignation at his blunt admission and she tried to pull her wrist free, but he held fast.

"Ye have bitten me," he went on, tilting his head toward his bare shoulder, where faint red tooth marks were still visible from the first night they'd met. "Ye have run from me. Ye've made me feel like an arse for…well, for being an arse."

He turned her wrist over and ran his thumb along the sensitive inner skin. To his satisfaction, a ripple of gooseflesh traveled up her arm.

"Ye've kept me awake at night," he murmured, his voice a low rumble. "Ye've made me painfully hard with wanting ye. And worst of all, ye've made me respect ye —*ye*, an Englishwoman—for that hellfire spirit of yers."

He slowly released her wrist, but she remained frozen, rooted in place. His hand skimmed up her bare arm, savoring her velvety skin.

"Aye, ye've been naught but trouble," he breathed, his gaze hungrily sweeping over her. Her hair still dripped onto the neckline of her chemise. The wet spots had spread to the tops of her breasts, making the linen cling mouthwateringly to the gentle curves.

Closing his hand around her elbow, he slowly pulled her down until she sat perched on the edge of the tub. The water had gone cold now, but it did little to alleviate the heat pounding through his veins—and into his cock.

Surely he'd gone mad. Corinne was right—his union with Euna had made sense. It benefited not only him, but also his people.

A marriage to Corinne, however, brought him naught but problems. Yet he couldn't deny the growing desire he felt for her.

It was easier to tell himself that he was only wedding her out of duty, a grudging acquiescence to the King's command. The truth was far more unsettling. He

EMMA PRINCE

wanted her—wanted her spread beneath him, aye, but also wanted her as his wife, his partner. Such wanting was dangerous, for it meant he was willing to set aside the needs of his people for his own desire.

A warning bell sounded in some distant corner of his mind, but thoughts of duty and responsibility slipped through his fingers like sand with Corinne so close, her warm, bright scent, of lemons and woman, driving him wild.

Reid reached up, lacing his fingers in her damp hair. Her wide ocean eyes dropped to his mouth, and he knew her thoughts had fled as well.

He pulled her down, letting his breath tease her lips for a long moment. He needed her to know exactly what was about to happen, to make her burn for wanting it as badly as he did.

But the wee hellion would not be made to wait. With a sound of frustration, she strained against his hold in her hair and joined their lips.

A bolt of white-hot need tore through Reid. He drank in the taste of her lips like a drunkard with whisky. Tilting her head, he deepened the kiss, his tongue invading her mouth.

She yielded to him then, letting him take control. He rumbled his pleasure. Though he liked her spirit, he found it incredibly erotic that such a strong-willed woman would surrender to him—in this area, if naught else.

His other arm looped around her waist, drawing her farther over the tub's rim. His damp arm made her chemise cling between them, taunting him with its thin barrier.

All thoughts of the cursed scrap of linen vanished when her hands tentatively came to rest on his chest. It was the first time she'd touched him, skin to skin. Heat blazed over his chest as if she'd branded him. It traveled below the waterline straight to his needy cock.

His fingers sank into her hair and his arm tightened around her waist. But she must have been more precariously perched on the tub's edge than he'd realized, for she suddenly tumbled toward him, shrieking against his lips.

Corinne landed with a splash in his lap. Like a cat, she scrambled wildly up, sloshing water over the sides as she fought her way free of the tub.

A bark of laugher rose in Reid's throat even as he helped her up. The fates seemed determined to drive him nigh mad with lust, then yank Corinne from his arms just when he had her where he wanted her.

The laugh died when his gaze landed on her, though.

She might as well have been standing naked before him. Her soaked chemise was like a second skin—a *transparent* second skin.

The delicate curves of her breasts were tipped with beaded nipples the same lush pink as her lips. Her narrow waist flared gently into her hips, where a dark wedge of auburn curls protected her womanhood.

Reid's cock strained with need. Belatedly he realized that while she was *nearly* naked, he had risen upright in the tub in naught but his skin, the last of his bathwater lapping around his calves.

Corinne's eyes rounded, her gaze darting down over the length of him before jerking away. She made a strangled noise that Reid guessed was an attempt to clear her throat.

He reached for the stack of drying linens beside the tub. A few had gotten wet when Corinne had fallen in, but he quickly looped one around his waist, then straightened and extended one to her.

She snatched it up, hastily wrapping it around herself.

Reid couldn't help but hate the piece of cloth now blocking his view.

"Will I see ye in the great hall for the evening meal?" he asked, willing his voice to be even.

"I-I am tired from our journey," Corinne replied, her cheeks glowing red. "I think I will retire to my chamber."

She turned to go, but just as she reached for the door, she hesitated.

"Reid?"

His damned cock surged hopefully as she glanced over her shoulder at him.

"Aye?"

"Thank you. For your apology, and for telling me the truth. And for..." She waved at the tub, her blush growing impossibly deeper.

Though he gave her a curt nod, something warm expanded in his chest.

"Get some rest," he said, his voice coming out

gruffer than he'd intended. "Tomorrow is an important day."

She slipped out the door, closing it softly behind her. Reid was left to stare at the remains of his bath, wondering how Corinne had left him in a tangled knot of need yet again.

Chapter Seventeen

Corinne woke with a start when Gellis entered her chamber.

"Time to rise, milady," Gellis said brusquely. "Today is an important day."

Corinne's heart leapt to her throat. Both Reid and Gellis seemed to feel the need to remind her, but they needn't have. It was Corinne's wedding day. For better or worse, she would never forget it.

Gellis helped her through her morning ablutions, then lifted the blue-green silk gown from the trunk at the foot of her bed. The gown had been meant for her wedding to Halbert de Perroy, but now, thanks to one of the men who'd raided her wagon, she'd wear it today.

Gellis clucked her tongue in muted approval as she slid the gown over Corinne's head and began lacing the bodice tight. It fit Corinne perfectly, of course, because it had been made for her, yet Corinne was awed into silence when she glanced at the polished silver plate Gellis had brought to serve as a looking glass.

The material matched her eyes perfectly. The wide scoop neck revealed her delicate collarbone and the upper swell of her breasts, which were on display thanks to Gellis's tight cinching. Gellis fitted a belt of braided silver silk around the fitted waist, just above where Corinne's hips flared and the material fell in rich, loose waves to the floor.

"There isnae much we can do with yer hair," Gellis commented, eyeing Corinne's head, "but I think I can manage something."

By the time Gellis was done combing and twisting and fitting a garland of green herbs and leaves into her hair, Corinne gazed in amazement at her reflection. Tears stung her eyes as she stared at herself.

Part of her had always known she would be wed to some powerful man or other. She'd been trained practically from birth that her purpose in life was to marry, bear children, and serve her household. Yet for so many years, she'd believed that she could change her course, rewrite her fate, and become a scribe.

Now here she was, a bride with the hair of a nun, her future husband not an English lord but a Highland Laird. It seemed that all her plans had tangled together to become something known and new, something foretold and never anticipated all at once.

Gellis slipped out of the room to ensure that the rest of the wedding preparations were progressing, leaving Corinne to sit on the edge of the bed, fear and uncertainty and anticipation churning together in her empty stomach.

A long while later, Gellis returned and instructed Corinne to go to the castle's sea gate. The great hall was empty, though noises of frantic cooking drifted from the kitchens at the back. When she entered the yard, it was also deserted except for the few guards posted at the watchtowers. They looked down at her in silence as she crossed the yard to the sea gate.

Timothy and his small rowboat awaited her there, though neither Reid nor any of the other castle inhabitants were anywhere in sight.

In silence, Timothy rowed her to the village and helped her onto the dock. He motioned her into the heart of the town, where Corinne noticed a crowd gathering. Their backs were turned to her, but someone must have noticed her approaching, for a murmur went through those gathered, and they began to part.

As they made way for her, she realized they'd congregated before the village's small church. Two figures stood on the stone steps before the chapel—a man in black robes, and—

Involuntarily, her breath caught in her throat. Reid stood beside the priest, his dark hair pulled back into a queue at the base of his neck and his face freshly shaven. Even from this distance, she felt the moment when his stormy gray eyes locked on her.

His shoulders stiffened beneath his clean linen shirt. He wore the green and blue Mackenzie plaid belted around his waist, as he always did. Though his clothes were simple, he looked every inch the commanding

Laird, his dark head towering over everyone else's from the steps, his feet planted wide, and his hands clasped behind his back.

Corinne's legs faltered for a moment, but before the silent, watchful eyes of all the clan, and held captive by Reid's gaze, there was no going back now.

Mustering all the poise and confidence she possessed, Corinne strode forward—toward Reid and her future. No matter what came next, no one could call her a coward on her wedding day.

She met him on the steps, blushing under his intent gaze. He opened his mouth to say something, but the priest cut in and began the ceremony.

Time seemed to blur and stretch as the priest moved through the rituals. Corinne could have heard a pin drop when he asked if anyone had cause to object to the union, yet it was a tense, uneasy silence. Numbly, she repeated her vows and stared at Reid's moving lips as he did the same.

The day was overcast and sharply cold, and by the time the priest pronounced them man and wife before God, a chill had settled into her bones. Reid's swift, light kiss brought a staid cheer from those gathered, but the crowd quickly fell silent once more.

Reid took her hand and guided her through the crowd toward the dock. Timothy waited, mutely rowing them back to the castle. Other boats, carefully super-vised by Mackenzie and MacRae guards, were allowed to launch as well so that the villagers could join the wedding feast at the castle.

When they scraped against the small sandy inlet on

the back side of the island, Reid lifted her from the boat and carried her through the sea gate to the great hall. The kitchen staff must have been hard at work throughout the ceremony, for the tables were now laden with roasted meats, steaming vegetables, fresh bread, and an assortment of puddings and late-season fruits for the feast.

Reid carried her to the table on the raised dais at the back of the hall, setting her down into an ornately carved wooden chair. He took up the even larger chair beside her, gazing out at the villagers as they began to filter in for the celebration.

"I didnae have time to arrange for musicians or entertainers," he murmured, watching his people slowly take their places at the long trestle tables below the raised dais.

"That is all right," Corinne said, exhaustion and tension tightening her throat. "No one seems in the mood to celebrate."

His brows lowering, he opened his mouth, but she held up a hand to stay him. "I do not mean to criticize them—or you. I understand why they are not pleased by this union."

Reid's face darkened further, and Corinne realized belatedly that she'd said the wrong thing. But the deadening weight of first her own nervousness, and then the stonily somber ceremony, had left her too wrung of energy to amend her words.

She hadn't known what to expect today, but some part of her had hoped for a pleasant, happy wedding.

Though no one had been outright rude, the clan's displeasure was like a thick fog hanging in the air.

Reid's apology last night—and the scorching kiss they'd shared—had buoyed her, giving her hope that mayhap things wouldn't be so bad. But if today was any indication, her new life would be aught but smooth.

Those in the hall ate mostly in silence, with the occasional restrained toast to the Laird's health and the clan's strength breaking the uncomfortable hush.

For her part, Corinne ate little and said even less. Under the stares of those gathered, she hunched into herself. Where was her bravery from earlier at the church? It had melted, dripping away like armor made of ice.

At last, Reid cleared his throat and stood. The hall stilled, all eyes locking on their Laird.

"For the sake of my bride's modesty, I have already had Father Ewan bless our marriage bed," he said. "There will be no bedding ceremony. Enjoy the rest of the wedding feast."

With those curt words, he scooped Corinne up from her chair and strode across the hall toward the spiral stairs.

Again, staid cheers rose, but they fell away as soon as Reid's foot landed on the first step.

Corinne held herself tense in his arms as he made his way to his chamber. Once he was inside, he set her on her feet and closed the door behind them.

Though she had been here last night, she'd been so focused on her anger—and then the sight of Reid bathing—that she hadn't paid much attention to the chamber itself.

Like her room, it was simply furnished. An enormous bed took up nearly half the space. There was a trunk and an armoire, a dressing table and chair, a hearth with a fire flickering in it, and fresh rushes on the ground. A few colorful tapestries depicting battles hung on the walls, softening the otherwise stark stone.

"I hope ye dinnae mind leaving the feast," Reid said.

"Nay," she murmured. She was suddenly struck by what was about to happen. They'd spoken their vows before God and the clan. They'd made a public showing at the feast. The only thing left to do was—

Blood roared in her ears as she stared up at Reid. Though she was taller than most women, he towered over her. He seemed to fill the large chamber with his commanding, assured presence.

His steely eyes were inscrutable beneath dark brows. He must have sensed her rising panic, for he didn't mince his words.

"Are ye ready, lass?"

"Aye," she breathed. As ready as she'd ever be.

Chapter Eighteen

R eid watched Corinne carefully. She was like a cornered cat, eyes round, shoulders tensed, and gaze darting around the room.

He had to do this right, else whatever sliver of trust she had in him would be destroyed for good.

"Ye are beautiful," he murmured, taking a slow step forward.

Corinne glanced down at herself. "Aye, the dress is very fine. The belt complements it well. And Gellis managed to make my hair—"

"Nay," he cut in. "*Ye* are beautiful."

She looked up, catching her lower lip between her teeth.

Reid took another step forward, reaching out to gently grasp her chin. "I ken ye are nervous," he said, sliding her lip free. It glistened faintly in the light from the fire in the hearth. "But it will be good between us."

"H-how do you know?" she asked.

"What did it feel like when I kissed ye at the inn?"

Her copper brows drew together. "It felt…good. Warm." At his expectant look, she went on. "You… tasted good. And my skin tingled and heat shot through me."

At her words, a fire of longing began to kindle in the pit of his stomach. "And when we kissed last night?" he asked, his throat suddenly tight.

"The same," she replied, her face flushing. "Though I wanted something…more. It ached."

"It can be even better. When we join—" he had to clear his throat before going on, "—ye'll ken what ye ache for, and what will relieve it."

She swallowed, nodding.

He reached for the leafy garland atop her head and carefully removed it. A few locks of wavy red hair fell around her face, framing her delicate features. Setting the garland aside, he laced his fingers through her hair, letting the soft strands slide across his palms.

With one last step, he closed the distance between them and tilted her head up. Bending, he kissed her lips softly. Some barely leashed animal inside him longed to tighten his hand in her hair, plunder her mouth, and draw a desperate moan from her throat, but he willed himself to go slow, to be gentle.

Her hands tentatively found his shoulders, and even through his linen shirt, heat like a brand sank into his skin. As he deepened the kiss, her lemon scent enveloped him, sweet and bright and just a little sharp.

"I love the smell of ye," he murmured against her lips. His hands found her waist and unfastened the silver belt there. Then they traveled up until they rested just under the swell of her breasts.

He'd meant to move slowly, to give her time to learn his touch, just as he needed time to learn her body, but then her fingers threaded into his hair, loosening it from its tie. He groaned, both hands lifting to cup her breasts.

She stilled, but then when his thumbs swished over the peaks, she sucked in a hard breath and arched into his palms.

God help him, she was so responsive to his every touch. Aye, it would be good between them, just as he'd promised—assuming he could hold himself at bay long enough to please her.

He gritted his teeth as his cock surged in response to the feel of her pert, hard-tipped breasts in his hands. Damn it all, he *would* please her, even if he went blind from withholding his own release.

His lips found hers, and although he'd promised himself he'd be gentle, he took her mouth in a rough kiss. She met his intensity, though, opening to him and twining her tongue with his.

He hadn't realized he'd begun to back her toward the bed, but suddenly she bumped into one of the corner posters. He took the opportunity to grind his hips into hers.

"This is how ye ken I want ye," he rasped. "This is what ye do to me."

He let his head drop to her collarbone as his hands began fumbling with her gown's ties. He dragged his lips along her throat and down to the swells of her breasts peeking over the neckline of the dress.

She moaned, her head falling back against the poster and her fingers sinking into his back.

He needed her naked—*now*.

With a grunt of frustration, he clawed the rest of her laces free. The gown loosened from her shoulders even as he began to tug it off.

But when he'd peeled away the fine silk and she stood before him only in a chemise, she stilled. Her eyes were dark pools in the low light from the fire, her skin pale with nervousness.

Despite all the blazing passion between them, she was still a virgin, frightened on her wedding night for what was to come.

"I ken it hasnae been a smooth road for us thus far," he murmured, trailing the backs of his fingers along her jawline. "The circumstances that brought us here have been…fraught."

"Aye." She watched him, her features guarded a she waited for him to go on.

"Ye were right earlier—the wedding wasnae a happy event for my people. They are displeased, and I certainly havenae helped matters by going on about our union as an obligation."

She swallowed, her throat bobbing faintly.

"Yet standing before ye, a brave, beautiful, determined woman, thoughts of duty, of the King's orders or of my clan's disapproval, scatter from my mind," he said. "All I can think of is how ye drive me half-mad with wanting. Ye are unlike any woman I've ever kenned."

Aye, he wanted her. But after so many years as Laird, it was strange for him to consider his own wants.

Under the burden of bastardry, he'd been raised with the knowledge that his very existence was a problem. Aye, his family had been loving, but as the eldest son, he'd been acutely aware of his responsibilities to his clan—and of the failing of his birth.

Because of that, he'd worked harder at serving his people, fulfilling his every responsibility to them, to compensate for his bastardry. He'd stepped in as Laird when Murdoch had died and Logan had fled. He'd married Euna for the alliance it would bring. And he served the Bruce for the betterment of not only his country, but also his clan, so that they could be proud of their role in the fight for freedom.

But now gazing down at Corinne, his own burning desire engulfed all thoughts of responsibility.

"At first, I only saw the bad in the Bruce's order for us to wed," he said, watching the firelight dance across her features. "But now I realize that even if we hadnae been forced to marry, I would still long to claim ye as my own."

And from the need pulsing in his veins and squeezing his chest, he would have defied King, clan, and duty to have her. The thought frightened him, yet that was how strong his desire for her was.

"Thank God for the Bruce's order, else I would have destroyed everything for ye, Corinne."

She sucked in a breath, her eyes as wide and depthless as the sea. Suddenly she was reaching for him, dragging him down to her until they were kissing once more.

The trust in her kiss and the welcome of her arms as they looped around his neck snapped something deep inside him. With a growl, he fisted the material of her chemise, pulling it up and over her head.

Forced to break their kiss, he stepped back, panting.

Her lithe body was gilded in soft light from the fire. Every slim angle and delicate curve made her look like a golden angel. Reid's hungry gaze stole over her breasts, her narrow waist, and the crux where her long legs met.

"Lie on the bed," he managed, his voice like gravel.

She sat on the edge, then scooted to the middle, pulling back the covers as she went.

Without taking his eyes off her, Reid yanked his shirt over his head and unfastened his belt. As his plaid began to unravel around his hips, he snatched it up and tossed it aside.

At her gasp, he slowed, letting her look her fill as he stepped out of his boots. Her gaze was like a caress, sliding over his shoulders and chest, down his abdomen, and fixing on his jutting, rigid manhood.

Before she could become nervous once more, he lowered himself to the bed beside her.

"I've dreamt of tasting yer skin," he murmured. "Of being inside ye."

He cupped her hips and drew her closer until they were flush against one another. He let out a groan at the feel of her velvety skin touching his, of his cock pressing into her belly.

Slowly, so as not to frighten her, he rolled on top of her. She went stiff for a moment, but then he lowered his mouth to her breast, his lips brushing her nipple.

She gasped and arched off the bed—giving him all the better access to each perfect breast.

He kissed and laved her until she writhed with need, her breath stuttering. Instinctively, her legs spread and lifted, cradling his hips between them. Ever attentive to her breasts, he let one hand slip between them. His fingers brushed the curls protecting her womanhood. They were already damp. Another pained groan rose in his throat to know that she was nearly ready for him.

He dragged a finger along the seam of her sex until he brushed that spot of a woman's pleasure. Corinne hissed out a breath, her head twisting against the sheets in a wild tangle of shorn red tresses.

Reid stroked and kissed her until her fingers turned to talons on his back and her hips began undulating against his hand.

Rising up on one elbow, he gripped his aching manhood and guided it to her entrance.

Though Corinne's breath came ragged, she stilled, looking up at him through the dim light. He met her gaze steadily, holding a lungful of air until she gave him a little nod.

He eased forward, entering her one torturous, exquisite inch at a time. With each passing moment, he could feel her coil with increasing tension until she made a little sound of pain.

"Breathe, sweeting," he ground out through clenched teeth. A bead of sweat slid down his forehead as he fought for control. Damn, she was so wet, but so tight that he knew he was hurting her.

She relaxed a hair's breadth, and he knew he had to

put them both out of their suffering. He torqued his hips forward, burying himself to the hilt. His groan of restrained lust mingled with her whimper of pain.

Damn it all, he'd promised himself to make this good for her. Muttering a curse, he lowered his head and flicked his tongue over her ear. Her inhale encouraged him, so he dragged his teeth over her lobe, holding himself deep inside her to give her time to adjust to his size.

He felt her body ease ever so slightly. He trailed kisses down to her breasts once more, and her legs unclenched around his hips. Though he shook with the effort of restraining the desire to pump into her, he slid a hand between them again and found that pearl of pleasure.

At last, she released a breath, but then quickly pulled another one in as he teased and caressed her. When she was panting once more, he began to move, drawing himself out and thrusting back in slowly.

As he built a rhythm, her legs began to tremble and her back arched off the bed.

"Aye, that's it," he breathed, already feeling his control slipping at the sight of her pleasure. "Come for me."

With a shudder and a cry, she came undone. A bonny flush traveled from her pert breasts up her neck and to her cheeks as she rode the wave of pleasure.

That was his undoing—seeing her unbound, swept away by ecstasy as he drove into her.

Pleasure coiled and then exploded within him. He thrust hard—harder than he should have, some distant voice chided, for she was a virgin. Yet he could not hold the sudden urge to possess her completely at bay.

At last, he sagged over her, panting. God, it had never been like that for him before. Never had he needed to fight so hard to maintain control, to temper the wild, animalistic part of him that wanted to claim a woman as his own. Corinne had done that.

"Are ye well?" he breathed, gazing down at her.

Her eyes latched onto his. Beneath the gloss of pleasure, he saw something else in their depths—vulnerability.

"Aye," she murmured. "Very well."

He eased himself onto the bed, pulling her into his arms as he went.

"Sleep now…wife."

The word felt strange in his mouth. He'd never gotten used to using it with Euna. Yet as he brushed a few unruly locks of flame-colored hair from Corinne's forehead, he let it sink in.

No matter the circumstances that had brought them together, they were bound now for the rest of their lives. It was his duty—nay, his *privilege*—to protect and care for her.

Though it was a weighty thought, it made his heart swell against his ribs as he surrendered to sleep.

Chapter Nineteen

As she had at the inn, Corinne woke in the steely warmth of Reid's arms. And as before, he was playing with a lock of her hair, coiling it around his finger like a ribbon.

"Morning," he said, the word rumbling through his chest where her head lay nestled.

"Morning," she mumbled, too shy all of a sudden to raise her head and meet his eyes.

Heaven above, what they'd shared last night...her face grew hot with the memories.

His big, callused hands skimming her skin. His firm lips and velvety tongue on her breasts. And the hard length of him—so big she'd feared they could never join —buried deep inside her, filling her until pain and pleasure had blended into one, and she'd shattered into a thousand pieces of light beneath him.

"Are ye well?"

He'd asked her the same last night. Then, she'd been

in a daze, still drifting down from the euphoric heights he'd taken her to.

Now, in the gray light of day that slipped in around the coverings over the arrow slits, she found the question harder to answer.

"I am well," she replied, hesitating. "Last night was…not what I thought it would be."

Reid abruptly sat up, dislodging her from his chest. He loomed over her, his dark brows drawn together. But instead of offense or anger, she found concern clouding his flinty eyes.

"Are ye hurt?"

"Nay," she said quickly. Well, that wasn't quite true. She was sore between her legs, but the ache was only to be expected.

"What, then?" he prodded. "Did ye…did ye no' find it…enjoyable?"

Now she was sure her face had caught fire. "Very enjoyable," she squeaked. She cleared her throat, trying again. "I only meant…I didn't know it could be like that. So…intimate."

Reid's features eased and he lowered himself to one elbow. If she wasn't mistaken, mirth tugged at his lips. "Aye, these things do tend to be intimate."

Corinne buried her face in the bed linens. She knew she sounded like an utter fool, but she couldn't seem to find the right words.

Before last night, she'd been resigned to her fate, yet she'd never imagined there could be such pleasure in their joining—or from what it represented. She'd thought she could keep herself separate from Reid somehow, that she could do her duty to him as his wife, yet hold some part of herself away.

The truth was, she'd been struggling to restrain her feelings for some time now. At first it had been easy. He was wickedly handsome, aye, and a man dedicated honor and responsibility. Yet she'd wanted naught to do with him, for he stood in the way of her freedom, her dreams.

As she'd come to terms with the inevitability of their marriage, she'd grudgingly accepted that he was better than Halbert de Perroy, but hadn't allowed herself to consider her fascination with him.

But now, after entwining themselves body and soul in marriage, there was no hiding from it—she was coming to care for him. How could she not? He was loyal and protective of his people, sure and steady, dedicated and determined in all that he did. She could only hope to be a recipient of such devotion.

And it was all so real now. She was married to the rugged warrior-Laird lying next to her, and she the lady of a powerful Highland clan. To her surprise, a seed of pride and happiness budded in her chest at the thought.

She lifted her head, meeting his inquisitive gaze. "I...I liked it," she said bashfully.

A slow, roguishly proud grin broke over his face. "I liked it, too."

But then his smile faded, and he pinned her with a serious look. "There is one last thing I must do to put an end to these marriage rituals."

She stilled, uncertain. "Oh?"

"Aye. Ye may no' like it, but it isnae negotiable."

"What is it?" she asked, trepidation coiling in her stomach.

"I must fly our bedsheet."

She felt her eyes go round, but before she could speak, he continued.

"I thought to save ye the embarrassment of a bedding ceremony last eve, but the clan must ken—ye were innocent when ye entered this chamber, and now ye are my wife in every sense."

Corinne scooted back, lifting the covers to peer at the sheet beneath them. Sure enough, a spot of blood marked the white linens. A hot blush rose to her face at the evidence of her lost innocence. Aye, she was well and truly wed now.

"It is crude, I ken," Reid said gently. "But I willnae permit any doubt in this area. And I believe it will help the clan accept ye as their lady."

Though the thought of her virgin's blood on display made her want to shrink into the floorboards, she forced herself to speak. "I understand," she managed.

And to her surprise, she did. It was *her* clan now, too. Just as they needed to accept her as their Laird's wife, so too did she need to accept their concerns for the future of the Lairdship. If proving the legitimacy of any heir that might come of Reid and her union did that, then she could relinquish her pride for the greater benefit.

Reid's slate eyes simmered with pride as he gazed at her. "Ye are a strong one, arenae ye, wife?"

"Aye," she replied, her chest swelling.

Reid drew her to him for a slow, smoldering kiss.

When at last he released her, Corinne's breath came short and her blood hammered hotly in her veins.

"I have been away from the clan for more than a month," he said, his gaze lingering on her as he reluctantly rose from the bed. "There is much I must see to. Will ye be all right on yer own?"

Corinne clutched the covers to her chest as she watched him dress, mesmerized by every hard line and chiseled, muscular angle of him. It wasn't until he'd pulled on a shirt and pleated his plaid around his waist that she could think straight.

"I have much to do as well," she replied at last. To gain the trust and respect of the clan, she would need to be the true mistress of this large keep. The thought was daunting, yet she had to start somewhere.

And no time was better than today.

CORINNE SLIPPED out of the chamber a short time after Reid and scurried up the stairs to her old room. She dressed quickly, making a mental note to ask Gellis to move her few belongings into Reid's chamber. Then she headed for the great hall.

She found a few servants wiping down the long trestle tables that had been used for the feast, though the hall was nearly empty now. It seemed that people in the keep had risen before the autumn sun to break their fast.

Lifting her skirts, she hurried to the kitchens. Inside, several women bustled about, apparently cleaning up from the morning meal.

Corinne cleared her throat discreetly, and all eyes shifted to her. The scullery maids stilled in their pot-scrubbing, the servants turning to her as they wiped their hands on their aprons.

"Good morn," Corinne began. "Thank you for the wedding feast last night. I appreciate your hard work."

A few of the servants dipped into curtsies, but the lot remained silent.

"I thought to acquaint myself with the running of the kitchens," she tried again. "In case there is an area where I might help, or…"

A rotund, short woman stepped forward from the others, planting her hands on her hips. "I'm Bitty, milady, the cook. Thank ye for visiting, but I dinnae think ye'll find much to help with here. I'm sure ye'll be busy seeing to other matters."

Corinne blinked. She'd been taught that it was the lady of the keep's responsibility to plan meals with the cook, monitor supplies, and ensure that the kitchens ran smoothly. Truth be told, Corinne wasn't sure how to do any of that, for she'd shirked her lessons many a time in favor of practicing her quillwork. Still, oughtn't she try to be a proper mistress of Eilean Donan?

Yet it seemed as though Bitty was dismissing her before the others. Slinking away now would seal in the servants' minds that Corinne was weak and incompetent.

"Pleased to meet you, Bitty," she said, straightening her spine. "Thank you for thinking of my other respon-sibilities, but naught could be more important than keeping the castle well fed."

Bitty eyed her. "That is indeed what we've been doing all the years before ye arrived, milady."

Corinne faltered. "Everything is running…smoothly then?"

"Aye, milady," Bitty replied. "The winter stocks are strong, the meals planned, and we dinnae hear complaints from anyone. I keep a tight, clean space here, as ye can see."

Corinne glanced around. The double hearths roared cheerily, the working surfaces were clean and orderly, and the servants had seemed well-occupied—that was, until Corinne had interrupted them.

"Do ye have experience running a kitchen, milady?" Bitty asked. "Or a special request? Or mayhap some expertise that could be applied here?"

The only experience or expertise Corinne had was in transcriptions. And she had never paid much heed to food before. Her palate was neither sophisticated nor picky; she merely ate what she was served and tended to enjoy it.

Corinne silently cursed herself. Why had she thought she could simple swoop in and smoothly take over the running of such a large and well-established kitchen? She'd only managed to make a fool of herself before the cook and the other servants.

She began to back her way toward the door leading to the great hall. "It seems that all is in order here," she said in a lame attempt to save face. "My compliments to you Bitty, and the rest of you."

Just as she reached the door, her elbow hit a large pot of porridge perched on one of the counters. The pot wobbled, then crashed to the floor, splattering porridge everywhere.

"I'm so sorry!" Corinne fell to her knees and righted the pot, but the damage had already been done to Bitty's clean floors.

"It's all right, milady," Bitty grumbled, motioning two scullery maids forward. "Leave it for the lasses."

Reluctantly, Corinne stood and watched as the girls began mopping up porridge with rags.

"I'm sure ye have elsewhere to be, milady," Bitty said pointedly after a moment.

Cheeks burning, Corinne nodded and hurried from the kitchens.

She nearly ran into a tall, slimly built man with gray at his temples who was walking past the kitchen door.

"Forgive me," she sputtered.

"Beg pardon, milady," the man replied, giving her a stiff bow. He must have noticed her red face, for he pursed his lips. "Is all well?"

Corinne sank her teeth into her lower lip. "Mmhm," she mumbled, trying to shove aside the flustered tears that pricked in the back of her eyes.

"The Laird sent me to find ye," the man continued, gazing placidly down his nose at her. "I am Wallace, the castle seneschal—or steward, as ye English would call it."

He bowed again, somehow making the gesture even more rigid than the first time.

"Ah," Corinne said, grasping for her confidence once more. "I had hoped to meet you today."

Wallace tilted his head stoically. "The Laird asked

that I show ye the castle grounds. I take it ye've already familiarized yerself with the keep?"

Though she wouldn't call herself familiar with the massive tower, she nodded, eager to learn more.

Wallace motioned her toward the doors that led from the great hall to the yard. When she stepped outside, she was surprised to find a faint dusting of snow covering the ground and clinging to the castle stones. Though she wished she'd brought a cloak, she didn't want to delay Wallace, who seemed a man of an exacting nature.

Wallace led her on a brisk walk around the perimeter of the wall. They passed the southernmost and eastern guard towers before the yard widened on the northern end of the island. An orchard of nearly leafless trees lined the back of the open space, skirting what appeared to be a training area for warriors. Though the grounds were mostly empty now, there were several archery targets, a rack of wooden practice weapons, and a wide expanse of hard-packed dirt, lightly covered in snow, where Corinne imagined the men sparred.

Several buildings sat against the stone curtain wall, though Wallace said she needn't bother seeing them, for they were mostly for storage. Instead, he guided her to the largest tower besides the keep, then motioned her in.

"The castle has its own smithy," he commented as they stepped inside. The blast of heat from the smithy's forge was welcome after touring the castle out of doors. The blacksmith paused his hammering of a horseshoe and gave Corinne a nodding bow.

"This way," Wallace instructed, pointing her toward the flight of stairs in the corner.

As she wound her way up, she passed several more chambers, some of which contained weapons, others appearing to be sleeping quarters for the guards. At the top, she stepped through the door leading to the battlements along the wall.

From this height—four storeys up—Corinne could see the entire village spread along the shoreline nearest the island castle. Beyond it, thick green forests touched with white snow stretched to the base of the jagged, imposing mountains she'd seen on their way here. She could also see the mouth of the sea-lake in which the castle sat, its blue-gray waters blending with the clouds overhead in the distance.

"It is an impressive stronghold," she said as Wallace came to her side.

"Indeed, milady."

"Is there…aught I can do to help? Areas where we should discuss improvements, mayhap?"

Wallace cleared his throat, his lips pursing once more as he remained silent for a moment. "The Laird has brought honor to the clan in his service to the King," he began.

"Aye," Corinne said, feeling her brows draw together.

"He has been called away quite a bit in the last several years. As such, the running of the keep has fallen to me—and Bitty, and Seanad."

"Who is Seanad?"

"The head of servants, milady." Wallace coughed

lightly again. "We have been charged with the smooth operation of this castle, both when the Laird is here and when he is away. So ye see, there isnae much that requires yer oversight."

Or her meddling, he seemed to be silently saying.

Corinne swallowed against the lump rising in her throat. "And where is the Laird just now?"

"He is in the village, and will likely remain there until nightfall."

"I see," she murmured. "And Seanad?"

Wallace waved his hand toward the main tower. "Seeing to something or other in the keep, I'm sure."

Calling forth the last of her pride, Corinne nodded. "I'll see myself down and not take up any more of your time, Wallace. Thank you for showing me the castle."

He tilted his head in acknowledgement even as she began hurrying down the stairs. Feeling the eyes of the guards on the battlements and in the watchtowers, Corinne crossed the yard and stepped into the great hall. She rubbed her hands against her arms, but the chill seeping into her bones wasn't entirely from the frosty air outside.

It was so much worse than she'd thought it would be. She was neither needed nor wanted here. Even if she gained the respect of the clan, they had no room for her in the daily work of maintaining the keep. She'd given up her hopes of becoming a scribe, only to find that her role of mistress at Eilean Donan had already been filled. She was useless.

Ducking her head against the curious stares of the servants lingering in the great hall, she crossed to the spiral stairs and began ascending, unsure of where she was headed.

As she reached the first landing, a woman was just stepping into Reid's chamber, her arms full of folded bed linens.

"Och! Excuse me, milady!" the woman said when she turned and nearly ran into Corinne.

"It's all right," Corinne murmured. "I was just…" She let the words die, for the only thing she'd been about to do was find a quiet chamber somewhere and give in to the tears clogging her throat.

"I am Seanad," the woman said, peering over the stack of cloth in her arms.

Despite her despondency, Corinne felt a stirring of surprise. The woman was only a handful of years older than she was, her dark blonde hair pulled back into an efficient bun and her blue eyes earnest. She must be very accomplished to have earned the role of head of servants so young.

"Pleased to meet you," Corinne replied. "I was hoping to speak with you."

"Oh?" Seanad shifted the load of bed linens slightly. "What about, milady?"

A few hours earlier, Corinne would have happily offered to assist Seanad, to help her manage the servants or devise a schedule of tasks. But she faltered, not eager to be brushed aside yet again.

"I…I simply wanted to meet you," she said, twining her hands in the folds of her skirt. "I have met Bitty and Wallace this morn, and have come to discover that you are the third leg holding the castle up so well."

"Thank ye for the kind words, milady," Seanad said, but then she glanced up and down the stairs. "Were ye going into the Laird's chamber—or rather, yer chamber?" Seanad tilted her head encouragingly toward the door.

"I...yes," Corinne said, puzzled.

Seanad nudged the door open with her hip, then stepped inside. Corinne followed, shifting to the side so that Seanad could close the door behind them.

Once they were alone, Seanad set the stack of linens on the dressing table and swiped a lock of hair out of her face. "I hope ye dinnae think me loose-tongued, milady," she said, facing Corinne, "for I dinnae permit gossip amongst the servants, but I must just say—ye are a brave one for facing those two."

Surprise hit Corinne so hard that she stepped back and sank into the wooden door. Unbidden, a wild laugh rose in her throat. "Not brave enough, I'm afraid."

"Dinnae tell me—Wallace looked down that long nose of his at ye, and Bitty practically whacked ye with a wooden spoon to shoo ye out of her kitchens."

"Just about. I made a terrible mess—literally—in the kitchens, and I seem to have offended Wallace somehow."

"Nay, he is just like that," Seanad replied matter-of-factly. "And Bitty will be fine. She merely likes to imagine herself the queen of her domain, ye ken."

Hot tears—for the difficult day, and for Seanad's unexpected kindness—suddenly pricked in Corinne's eyes. She quickly blinked them away, not wishing to blubber on her first day as lady of the keep.

"Was it like this before…with Lady Euna?"

Seanad gave her a kind smile. "As a matter of fact, aye. Lady Euna mainly busied herself with needlework and weaving."

Two more things Corinne had next to no skill at.

"I…" she began, having to swallow the tightness in her throat before going on. "I wish to help, but I seem only to be in the way."

Seanad stilled, her eyes warm. "I saw ye yesterday, milady—at the wedding. I was in the back, but I could see yer fine gown and the green garland in yer hair. Ye were beautiful. But I also saw something else."

"Oh?" Corinne murmured.

"I have a little habit at weddings. When all eyes are on the bride, I like to look at the groom, to see his face as he watches his lass approach."

A flutter like butterfly wings took flight in Corinne's stomach. "And what did you see?"

Seanad smiled. "He looked like a man dying of thirst laying eyes on a clear, sparkling loch. I've never seen the Laird look…well, no' in control of himself."

Heat rose from Corinne's neck to her face. "Thank you."

"I ken it must be hard, coming here an outsider and being thrust into a clan that is used to doing things on our own. But ye'll find yer way, milady."

Corinne gave a sad chuckle. "In truth, I should be grateful that you and the others have things so well managed, for I cannot boast many skills other than with a quill."

Seanad crossed her arms, drumming her fingers

against her elbows as she considered. "The Laird keeps the castle ledgers in his solar."

She nodded toward a narrow door next to one of the tapestries. Corinne hadn't noticed it before. It must connect Reid's sleeping chamber to his solar so that he wouldn't have to exit to the landing and enter through the solar's main door.

"As the lady of the keep, ye are more that welcome to try yer hand at them," Seanad said.

Relief and gratitude flooded Corinne. Keeping ledgers was something she was certain she could do, and it would mean getting to hold a quill once more.

"That is an excellent idea. Thank you."

Seanad nodded, then patted the pile of linens next to her. "I'd best return to my duties, milady. The Laird asked that I change yer bed linens so that the matrimonial sheet could be flown."

Feeling her face heat, Corinne's gaze darted to the rumpled bed. The covers were thrown back, and even from across the room, she could see the small red stain in the middle of the linens.

"No need to be embarrassed, milady. The clan will appreciate the assurance, is all—as does the Laird." Seanad lifted the fresh linens and turned to the bed. "Oh, and I've instructed Gellis to bring yer things down. Ye are in good hands with her. She keeps to herself a wee bit, being a MacDonnell, ye ken, but she'll look after ye properly."

"Thank you again," Corinne breathed, once more feeling overwhelmed by Seanad's kindness.

As Seanad set about her task, Corinne slipped through the narrow door leading to the solar.

On the other side, she found a quiet, dim room that she instantly knew she liked. Though the only source of light came from the narrow arrow slits that protected the castle, there were more than a dozen of them in this chamber, providing a soft gray glow.

A massive wooden desk dominated the space, its top mainly clear other than several writing supplies laid ready for use. More thick, colorful tapestries warmed the walls, interrupted by a few shelves with various bound ledgers stacked upon them. A fire was laid waiting to be lit in the hearth.

To her, it was perfect—quiet, simple, and meant for work. Work she knew how to do.

She made her way to the desk and lowered herself into the cushioned chair before it. Reverently, she lifted the quill, already trimmed and tipped, into her hand.

Aye, she could do this. For Reid. For the clan. For herself.

Chapter Twenty

"Ye only paid me two sheep instead of four!"

"Two was what I owed ye, and two is all ye deserve!"

Reid pinched the bridge of his nose, barely managing to bite back a curse.

Rabbie MacRae and Dillon Mackenzie continued their squabbling, seemingly unaware of the stares they were drawing in the great hall, or of their Laird's increasing annoyance.

"Ye lie, Dillon!" Rabbie spat. "We agreed on four, but ye're too much of a bloody arse—"

"Silence!" Reid barked. Both men's heads snapped to him, at last remembering their place.

It had already been a long day, and it was only just past noontide. Reid had spent all day yesterday in the village, meeting with shopkeepers and farmers who'd come into town to settle disputes now that he'd returned. For those cases that were not easily settled, he'd invited the disputants to Eilean Donan so that they could air their grievances and he could rule on them.

Of course, that meant several long days like this one stretching ahead of him, days spent listening to farmers quarrel about sheep and shopkeepers argue over transactions that happened months ago.

Reid shifted in his large, carved wooden chair, eyeing the two men from the dais.

"Rabbie, ye lent yer three lads to Dillon to help with the harvest season," Reid began.

"Aye," Rabbie replied.

"And ye claim that the agreed-upon payment in exchange for their labor was four sheep."

"Ye said so yerself, Laird."

"Nay, Laird," Dillon cut in, "ye said two. I distinctly recall—"

"Quiet, the both of ye," Reid snapped. He ground his teeth, dragging a hand through his hair.

Damn it all. He vaguely remembered helping the two quarrelsome neighbors reach an agreement earlier that spring. Dillon had only daughters and needed help in his fields during the harvest season. Rabbie had strapping lads, yet that meant many mouths to feed and the constant need for either grain or sheep's wool to trade for it.

The problem was, Reid couldn't recall exactly what ruling he'd made so many months past. So focused had Reid been on fighting the Bruce's battles and maintaining peace along his own borders that these smaller disputes often fell through the cracks. But this was the work of a Laird—if he overlooked his people's troubles, they would soon lose trust in him.

"Did Rabbie's lads work hard and get yer harvest in?" he asked Dillon.

"Aye," Dillon said grudgingly, looking sideways.

"Ye dinnae have any complaints about them, then?"

"Nay, Laird, but—"

"And ye, Rabbie," Reid cut in. "How many sheep now fill yer flock?"

Rabbie scowled. "Nigh on one hundred, Laird."

"I have come to a decision. Ye'll split the difference. Dillon will pay three sheep to Rabbie. Three sheep for three lads' labors, nay more, nay less."

"But Laird!"

"It isnae fair, Laird!"

Reid held up a hand for silence, and the two men reluctantly bowed in acknowledgement of the decision, though he heard both of them muttering under their breaths.

As he watched them slink from the great hall, Reid drummed his fingers in annoyance on his chair's arm. He'd either shorted one man a sheep he'd been promised, or made another man pay one sheep more than they'd agreed back in spring. Either way, he'd been unfair. But he couldn't very well admit that he'd been too preoccupied to remember their original bargain.

As one of the village's blacksmiths and the stable master approached, preparing to air out their disagreement over a faulty horseshoe, Reid rose.

"That is all for today," he said. "We'll continue tomorrow."

As the hall emptied, Reid let a long breath go. He needed to hit something. Though he knew it was a foolish, juvenile thought, he wished that more of these disputes could be settled with fists rather than words. It was no way to lead, of course, but Reid had always been a man of action.

He stepped down from the dais and crossed the hall. What he needed was to train with his men. It would release some of his pent-up energy—and mayhap distract him from thoughts of Corinne.

Yesterday in the village, his mind had kept conjuring forth images of her pale skin, her parted lips, her moans of pleasure. And today, he felt like a damned green lad, achy between the legs and daydreaming about her when he was supposed to be focusing on settling disputes.

He'd returned so late from the village last night that she'd already retired. He found her sleeping in his wide bed, her face covered by a mass of unruly red locks and her breathing slow and deep. She must have been exhausted. Though he longed to pull her into his arms and taste her mouth, he couldn't bring himself to disturb her.

That morn, he'd risen well before dawn and slipped out before she'd awoken, intent on busying himself else he find a reason to linger with her all day in their bed. Instead, all he'd managed to do was fumble his way through several disputes, his mind on her lips, her breasts, her sweet, wet—

Cold blasted him as he yanked open the hall's doors and stomped into the yard. Aye, this was what he needed—to run himself ragged before he did something foolish like hunt her down and take her against the nearest hard surface like a brute.

As he approached the training grounds, he found a clump of his men standing on the hard-packed dirt, but instead of sparring, they were talking.

"...see that hair? It can only mean one of two things," one of them was saying, his back turned.

"She was making her way to a nunnery," Leith, the fresh-faced lad who'd been along for the Bruce's mission, said firmly.

"So I heard," the first man, Galen, murmured conspiratorially. "As I said, one of two things."

"Go on, Galen," another urged.

"She's either a cold English fish meant to be a nun," Galen said. "Or no' a virgin at all."

White-hot anger blinded Reid for a moment. He quickened his pace, closing in on the group like a charging bull.

"Dinnae ye disrespect our lady, Galen," Leith retorted.

"Shut yer flap, Leith," Galen retorted. "Everyone kens a virgin is supposed to have long, flowing hair. That English chit is naught more than a——"

Before he could finish, Reid rammed into him, shoving him so hard that he was thrown into the others gathered around him. Before Galen could right himself, Reid grabbed a fistful of his tunic and spun him around. With all his might, he drove his fist into Galen's dumb-founded face.

The crack of Galen's nose breaking cast a stunned silence over the group of men.

"How *dare* ye speak ill of my wife—yer lady!" Reid roared, shaking Galen so hard that blood from his nose spattered onto the sleeves of his shirt.

"Do ye see that?" he demanded, yanking Galen up and pointing to the top of the keep, where the white sheet from their matrimonial bed hung from the battlements. Though it was four storeys up, the tiny red spot could be made out from the yard. "That is *my wife's* innocence. The lady of the Mackenzies. Yer mistress."

"Forgive me, Laird," Galen mumbled through the stream of blood running down his face. "I didnae see ye. I never would have—"

"It doesnae matter if ye *saw* me or no'!" Reid bellowed. "Ye disrespected her all the same." He cast his gaze around the lot of them. "Ye all did. I only heard Leith speak in her defense."

The men lowered their heads in shame, all except Leith, who glared at the others.

"Laird," one of the men said tentatively. "We were wrong, and we beg yer forgiveness. It is only…"

"Out with it," Reid barked.

"We thought ye were as unhappy as we to have an Englishwoman as yer bride," he mumbled. "We thought ye shared our sentiments, seeing as how the only reason ye married the lass was out of duty to the King."

Reid's blazing rage was doused so quickly by surprise that his mouth fell open and he involuntarily loosed his hold on Galen. Galen stumbled back, holding his broken nose gingerly.

Bloody, stinking hell. Was this what his clan thought

—that he detested his union with Corinne so much that they had leave to disrespect her?

He knew he'd hurt her before, speaking more of duty and obligation than aught else when he'd introduced her and told his people of their impending marriage. He'd been an arse, aye, but now he saw that it was far worse than that.

He'd thought by presenting a stony façade to the clan, he'd shown his strength as their leader—he would do whatever it took to protect them and serve their King, including marrying an Englishwoman. Yet now he saw that by acting so cold, *cruel* even to Corinne before them, he'd done naught to stop their frosty reception of her. Worse, he'd led by example.

She was already in an impossible situation as an outsider, an Englishwoman among Scots. Through his own selfishness and inattention, he'd failed to lead his people as a Laird ought, letting their displeasure fester.

It wasn't too late, though. Only a day and a half had elapsed since their wedding, and two since they'd arrived at Eilean Donan. Reid could show them with his own actions how Corinne deserved to be treated, and how fortunate they were to have such a strong, smart, spirited woman as the lady of the clan.

Reid leveled a hard stare at the waiting men. "I should have ye lashed—all of ye. And ye," he pointed at Galen, "could have yer tongue cut out for what ye said about yer lady."

Galen blanched, his face appearing all the whiter in contrast to the blood running from his nose.

"Instead," Reid went on, "ye'll all go to the village

and muck out the stables for a fortnight. Except Leith." The young lad straightened under Reid's assessing gaze. "Ye'll help me train the *real* warriors for a fortnight."

"Ye are merciful, Laird," Galen said, dropping his head. "I am sorry I shamed ye."

"Ye shamed yerself," Reid growled. "Dinnae do so again, for if ye—*any* of ye—disrespect my lady wife again—if ye even *think* ill of her—I'll rip ye limb from limb and banish what's left of ye from ever setting foot, or arm, or head, on Mackenzie land again. Am I understood?"

"Yes, Laird," they replied in crisp, decisive unison.

Turning his back on them, Reid strode toward the keep, his legs moving faster and faster.

He needed to make this right, to show his people just how lucky they were—how lucky *he* was—to have her.

Which meant he needed to find Corinne—now.

Chapter Twenty-One

R eid threw the doors to the great hall back so hard
that they banged against the stone walls. Several
servants jumped, halting what they were doing to stare
at him.

His gaze landed on Seanad, who was just stepping
into the great hall from the stairs.

"Where is Corinne?" he barked, barging forward.

Seanad blinked, but his capable, even-keeled head
of servants regained herself quickly.

"She is in yer solar, I believe, Laird. Would ye like
me to fetch her for—"

Before she could finish, he swept past her and up the
stairs, taking them two at a time. When he reached the
first landing, he went straight for the door to the solar.

"Corinne," he said as he threw open the door.

She squeaked and leapt nigh out of her skin—and
definitely out of his desk chair. She'd been hunched over

something, quill in hand. She glanced down at the open ledger on the desk and gasped.

"Oh, drat!" She pinched the sleeve of the butter-yellow dress she wore and dabbed at a blot of ink on the parchment with it. Giving the ledger one last swipe with her sleeve, she sighed in relief. "That saved it." But then her eyes fell on her sleeve and the blotch of dark ink marring the yellow-dyed wool. "Drat again."

He couldn't help himself. Reid roared with laughter. Corinne jumped once more at his loud mirth, her cheeks flaming red.

"Forgive me," she said, raising her voice over his merriment. "I hope you do not mind that I have been using your solar to work on the ledgers."

"It is I who should ask forgiveness," he replied, his chuckles fading. "I shouldnae have startled ye." He stepped into the solar, closing the door behind him. "And of course ye can use the solar. It is yers as much as it is mine now."

As he approached, he glanced at the fire that had burned low in the hearth. "Have ye been in here all day?"

Her face flared even brighter, and her gaze slipped to the floor. "Aye. I seem to be in the way everywhere else."

Reid froze, his anger from earlier spiking once more. "What happened? Have ye been mistreated?"

"Nay," she said hurriedly. But then she dug her teeth into her lip, a telltale sign Reid was beginning to recognize.

He let a breath go. "Out with it," he urged gently.

"Truly, naught happened," she insisted. "I simply… thought to take over the management of the keep, but I learned that everything is in good hands already."

"Bitty and Wallace?" he asked.

She cracked a shy smile. "My offer to help was unnecessary, it seems."

"Surely Seanad wasnae rude to ye."

"Nay!" she replied. "Seanad has been naught but kind and helpful."

Reid nodded. Seanad was respected by all in the clan for her hard work and even temperament, but Bitty and Wallace both could be thorny when they felt they were being questioned. Bitty had even shooed Reid himself out of the kitchens a time or two when he got in her way around mealtime.

It wasn't as bad as he'd feared, then. Corinne hadn't been subjected to the open derision he'd witnessed in the yard. Still, he didn't like the idea of her hiding up here in the solar.

"What had ye so occupied?" he asked, stepping alongside the desk.

When his gaze landed on the ledger, his jaw slackened at what he saw.

The page was filled with the normal markings—he could make out Wallace's small, angular hand, Bitty's hurried scrawls, and Seanad's looping notes. The three of them had managed the ledgers for years now, keeping track of the coffer balances, supplies, crop yields, and more.

But alongside the familiar marks was a fourth hand —Corinne's. It was flowing yet precise, each letter a miniature work of art. She'd carefully nixed errors and added corrections, incorporated notes in the margins, and even added a few artful flourishes to delineate the different types of records kept in the ledger.

"I've been looking over these," she said, gesturing toward the figures on the parchment. "At first I merely wanted to familiarize myself with the clan's accounts. Then I noticed a few little miscalculations that were easy enough to fix. I think I've devised a simpler way to record things as well."

He looked up at her in stunned silence. She spoke so matter-of-factly about what she'd done, yet to Reid it might as well have been magic. He'd never had the patience to pore over the ledgers, which was why he'd pawned off the work to Bitty, Wallace, and Seanad. Yet he finally understood what Corinne had said about Sister Agatha calling her gifted.

"This is…" He shook his head in astonishment. "This is amazing, Corinne."

Her gaze darted to his face, her eyes guarded.

"I mean it," he went on. "The patience to do this kind of work, the attention to detail. And the artistry…" This wasn't a mere utilitarian use of a quill to record facts, but how a painter would wield a brush, or a sculptor a chisel.

She lifted one eyebrow, a slow, teasing smile lifting one side of her mouth. "I told you before that I was skilled. Didn't you believe me?"

He huffed a laugh, this time at himself, for she was right. "I suppose I didnae understand before."

"This is naught," she said, waving at the ledger. "I wish I could show you what a *true* transcription could look like."

When the words were out, she stilled, her gaze dropping to her ink-stained fingers and the quill caught in one hand.

He grew sober at that, for they both knew that path was no longer hers to follow.

His heart twisted in his chest. Though she could not be a scribe in a convent, he wanted to do something for her, show her that he valued her for her skills and passion.

A seed of an idea drifted to him like thistle fluff on the wind. He snatched at it, letting it take root and bud.

"I have a problem," he began, his thoughts racing ahead.

Her brows drew together. "Oh?"

"Aye. Ye see, as Laird, it is my responsibility to settle disputes within the clan. Sometimes the issues are large, such as marriages, deaths, family alliances, and the like. And other times, they are small—just today I doled out three sheep from one farmer to another, though mayhap it was meant to be two, and mayhap four."

"Mayhap?" she echoed.

"Aye, for the agreement was made several months ago, and I must admit that the details of the original bargain slipped from my mind."

Understanding suddenly flashed in her blue-green

eyes, but she quickly guarded it with a wary look. "What are you saying?"

"How would ye like to be the clan's record-keeper?" he asked. "To transcribe all agreements, negotiations, punishments, rulings—whatever ought to be marked down so that it cannae be disputed or questioned later."

Holding his gaze, she slowly lowered the quill to the desk and dropped it beside the open ledger. She blinked, but he didn't miss the sheen of emotion dampening her eyes.

For one long, terrible moment, Reid feared he'd hurt her worse than ever before. Mayhap he should have thought the idea through before presenting it to her. Mayhap he'd offended her in some way he hadn't had time to consider, or—

Suddenly, she launched herself at him, slamming into his chest and wrapping her arms around his neck.

"Thank you," she mumbled in a thick voice against his shoulder.

His arms looped around her, holding her close. His heart did an odd little flip inside his ribcage—strange but surprisingly pleasurable. God, it was good to have her pressed against him. But more than that, it felt right to make her happy, to be the one to bring tears of joy to her eyes.

He buried his nose in her hair, inhaling deeply. "I've been thinking of ye all day," he murmured against her ear.

To his supreme satisfaction, she shivered and pulled him tighter. "Oh?"

"Aye. Of how beautiful ye are. And of what we shared the night before last."

"Oh?" she repeated. Though she teased him with her coy act, he could feel the rapid swell of her breasts where they molded against his chest. The mere reminder of their wedding night made her breath catch.

With a growl of anticipation, he dipped his head and claimed her mouth in a hungry kiss.

Chapter Twenty-Two

Corinne's heart hammered wildly as Reid descended on her, kissing her with such fierce urgency that her breath whooshed from her lungs.

Could this be real? Reid had come up with a way for her to be helpful to the clan *and* make use of her skills? She kissed him back hard, using her lips to wordlessly tell him how much his idea meant to her.

In response to her own boldness, he rumbled his approval low in his throat. He tilted his head to deepen the kiss, and their tongues tangled in a sensual embrace.

Heated memories flooded back to her—of their bodies joining, of Reid's driving strength over her, around her, inside her.

Reid abruptly broke their kiss and swept his arm across the desk beside them, shoving everything—quill, ledgers, inkwell, and all—to the far end of the vast wooden expanse. Just as swiftly, he lifted her behind the knees, wrapping her legs around his waist, and carried her to the desk's edge.

Corinne gasped in shock, but when her bottom came to rest on the desk's surface, her legs still hooked around Reid's hips and the hard ridge of his manhood wedged between them, she understood what he intended.

And oh, what a wickedly erotic intention it was.

His lips fell on hers once more, but then he trailed kisses down her neck and over her collarbone. In anticipation, her breasts grew tight and needy, the tips pearling beneath the bodice of her gown.

As he clawed frantically at the laces down her back, his mouth dropped to one aching breast. Even through her woolen dress and chemise, a bolt of sensation shot through her. She moaned, her head lolling back as he shifted to her other breast.

When he had her laces loosened enough, he simply yanked down on both dress and chemise. Cool air hit her exposed skin even as she heard a faint ripping noise.

Ah, well, she thought distantly. The gown would need attending anyway, since she'd gotten ink on the sleeve. What would the staid, serious Gellis say when Corinne handed her not only a stained gown but a torn one?

All thoughts of her lady's maid fled when Reid's lips closed around one of her beaded nipples.

Corinne arched, moaning with abandon as he laved first one and then the other breast. His hands clamped on her hips and he ground his rock-hard manhood against the crux of her legs through her skirts. She was already damp there, she realized, the heat building layer upon layer as he continued with his attentions on her breasts.

"Bloody hell," he hissed, his warm breath drawing her nipples even harder still. Before she could ask what was the matter, he pulled away, stepping out of the circle of her legs.

"Reid—" she began, her voice raw with need.

"I have to taste ye," he rasped, gripping her skirts. "Tell me ye'll let me."

"A-aye," she replied, though in truth she wasn't sure what he meant.

In one swift motion, he threw her skirts up, exposing her lower half. Before she could contemplate what he was about, he lowered himself between her legs and skimmed a finger along her sex.

She felt completely exposed with her skirts around her hips, her feet dangling from the desk and Reid positioned between her knees. Yet his teasing touch made all her shyness and inhibitions flee. She shuddered as his finger found that sensitive spot between her folds. But what he did next stole the breath from her lungs.

His hot tongue slid where his finger had been, licking her, taunting her, making her hips tilt in wanton invitation for more. He rumbled his pleasure against her sex, sending vibrations straight to her core.

She could not seem to get enough air. Her fingers clawed at the smooth wood beneath her, looking for purchase, but the only thing anchoring her in the storm of sensation was Reid's big, strong hands on her hips.

"Oh, God," she panted as the pleasure began to ascend toward the breaking point.

Reid abruptly stood, his gaze like molten metal as he stared down at her. "No' yet, love," he grated. "No' until I'm filling ye with my cock."

The wicked words should have made her blush, but instead of warming her face, they sent spikes of hot desire between her legs. She suddenly felt empty in a way she'd never experienced before—aye, she needed him inside her.

He yanked his kilt up, exposing the long, hard length of his manhood to her brazen gaze. The tip touched her wet entrance, pushing, filling, just as Reid had promised.

He drove himself to the hilt, his pants of exertion and barely held control mingling with her moans at the overwhelming sensations. He paused, giving her a moment to adjust to his size. She was still tender, even two days after their wedding night, and she felt drawn tight, barely able to take him.

But then one of his big hands brushed her exposed breast, and the wave of pleasure she'd been riding a moment before began to rise once more. She let herself fall back completely onto the desk, surrendering to the building ecstasy.

Now Reid began to move, pulling out of her and driving back in—hard. His thrusts shook the heavy wooden desk beneath her with their force. She, too, was jolted with each powerful plunge. She locked her legs around him tighter. All she could do was hold on as he pushed her closer and closer to a shattering release.

Through the mounting pleasure, Corinne realized just how much restraint he'd shown on their wedding night—for her. To make it good for her, and to avoid hurting her as best he could.

But he wasn't being gentle now—and it was so much better this way.

He loomed over her, one hand clamped onto her hip and the other cupping her breast as he drove into her again and again with enough force to steal her breath and make her legs tremble around his hips. Reid was every bit the fierce, wild Highland warrior now. She loved this untamed side of him.

Her pleasure suddenly spiraled upward, the sensations cresting and breaking in a surge of ecstasy. She arched off the table, crying out as wave after wave of pleasure swept her. Just as she began to drift back to earth, Reid shouted his own release, holding himself deep within her. At last, the tautness in his body began to drain and he slumped over the desk.

"Bloody hell," he breathed, easing out of her after a long moment. She let her quivering legs fall from his hips with a ragged exhale.

Tenderly, he smoothed her skirts down and eased her chemise and gown back over her chest.

She stared at him, her heart still thrumming swiftly. "That was…"

"Forgive me," he rasped. "I dinnae ken what came over me. I hope I didnae—"

"Nay," she blurted, pushing herself up. "Don't apologize. That was incredible."

He met her eyes then, and his gaze smoldered with stormy passion once more. "*Ye* are incredible."

As she stood, he pressed a slow kiss to her lips.

Drawing back, he looked down at her, brushing a wayward lock of hair from her face.

"This is just the beginning for us, Corinne," he murmured. "I promise ye, it will only get better from here."

She wasn't sure if he was speaking of their lovemaking, or the emotion she felt budding in her heart and saw reflected in Reid's gray eyes, or mayhap simply her new role as the clan's scribe. Whichever he meant, she could not deny the burst of warmth spreading through her. It was something like happiness.

Chapter Twenty-Three

"**A**re ye ready?"

Reid watched as Corinne made one final tiny slice into the quill's tip, making it perfectly pointed.

"Aye," she replied, setting aside the paring knife and gathering her supplies—quill, ink well, ledgers, and blotting sand.

Reid's chest swelled as she straightened from the desk, her writing materials in hand and her teeth digging into her lip.

He'd never be able to look at that desk the same after what they'd shared on it yesterday. Just as he'd feared, nigh moments after laying eyes on her, he'd taken her roughly against the nearest flat surface. Yet the fact that her desire had matched his had been even more arousing than the sight of her splayed beneath him.

Feeling the stirrings of lust once more, he quickly leashed his thoughts. Though taking a wildly erotic tumble with Corinne had been amazing, he'd made a promise to himself yesterday. He'd vowed to treat Corinne with all the respect and caring she deserved, to lead his clan by example, to show them just what he thought of their new lady, his wife.

"Dinnae be nervous," he said, motioning her toward the door leading to the stairs. "Yer skill speaks for itself. And if they willnae listen to that, then they'll listen to me."

She cracked a weak smile and stepped through the door and onto the stairs. He followed her down to the great hall, where another day's worth of complaints, disputes, and rulings awaited him.

The air was already humming with activity as they stepped into the hall. Corinne had lingered in the solar long enough that the morning meal had already been cleared away and the trestle tables and chairs had been moved to the walls. Several dozen people, mainly farmers and villagers, stood waiting for their Laird's arrival so that they could air their grievances.

As he and Corinne made their way toward the raised dais, where his chair was positioned behind the large oak table where he dined, the hall fell quiet.

"What is *she* doing here?" he caught someone whisper.

"Bring Lady Corinne's chair," he ordered loudly, effectively silencing the murmurs rippling in their wake.

A servant hastily dragged the smaller but equally ornately carved companion to Reid's chair onto the dais. Reid helped Corinne up and guided her around the table to her chair, motioning for her to sit. But before lowering himself beside her, he planted his feet and faced the crowd.

"Yer lady is quite accomplished with a quill," he began. "She is also extremely generous, for she has agreed to serve the clan as more than just my wife. She will act as the clan's scribe from here on out. This is to ensure fairness and accuracy in settling all disputes. Lady Corinne is doing us all a great service. If anyone objects" —he stared out at those gathered, narrowing his eyes— "they can leave."

Reid lowered himself into his chair. The faint creak of the wood was nigh deafening in the dead-silent hall. He cleared his throat.

"Let us begin. I believe we left off yesterday with Collum and Dugal."

Hesitantly, the village blacksmith and the stable master edged forward through the crowd.

"This concerns a question over whether a horseshoe was poorly made or improperly shod, is that right?" Reid asked.

Collum, the thick, gnarled blacksmith was the first to speak. "Aye, Laird."

Reid glanced at Corinne. She'd already spread out her supplies, the ledger open and the quill poised above the parchment with a drop of ink darkening its tip.

"Shall we proceed?" he asked her softly.

She lifted her gaze to his, and despite the nervous pinch of her teeth into her plush lower lip, her eyes were bright and clear as a Highland loch.

"Aye," she said, her voice strong and steady.

Though he managed to keep his features stern as he

turned back to Collum and Dugal, he could not deny the pride that filled him to have Corinne seated at his side.

"Verra well," he said to the men before him. "Start from the beginning."

～

"Did ye get that, milady?"

Reid shifted his gaze to Corinne, who was bent over the ledger, the quill practically flying across the parchment.

"Indeed," she replied, not looking up.

She had been like that for hours, only lifting her head in the brief moments between the end of one hearing and the start of the next. Despite the fact that she must be fatigued, she was as focused as ever, her brow knitted in concentration as she worked. Occasionally, she would blow an errant lock of red hair out of her face with a puff of air. Other than that, she remained completely absorbed.

Reid turned his attention back to the two farmers' wives who'd gotten into a dispute over a barter they'd formed while Reid had been away.

"As I was saying," Elsbeth MacRae went on. "I never would have agreed to give ye five dozen bannocks just for milking old Bluebell for me for a month. That would be utter—"

Corinne carefully cleared her throat, frowning at the parchment before her.

Though Reid had begun to grow weary of being

rooted in his chair for so long, he suddenly straightened. "What is it, Corinne?"

She flipped back a page, then gave a single nod.

"Excuse me, mistress Elsbeth, but not long ago you admitted that you and mistress Colleen here agreed that the trade was meant to save each of you time."

Elsbeth's brows drew together. "Aye, milady."

"Well, you mentioned that it took you a good deal longer to milk Bluebell because of the ache in your hands, that it would take you an hour a day, but mistress Colleen could do it in ten minutes."

"Aye," Elsbeth said cautiously.

"And mistress Colleen mentioned that she is known to bake 'the most foul, inedible bannocks'—apologies, Colleen, but I am using your own words for accuracy's sake."

"I cannae deny it, milady," Colleen replied with a shrug. "Everyone in the clan kens I am a God-awful cook."

Corinne tapped the feathery end of the quill on her chin as those gathered in the hall rumbled with laughter. Reid's gaze locked on the quill, and suddenly his mind filled with wicked images of what he'd like to do with Corinne later. First he'd strip her naked, and then he'd drag that feather all over her pale skin until she writhed and moaned, begging for his—

He snapped himself away from his musings, silently cursing himself for succumbing to distraction in the middle of attending to his responsibilities. Still, there was something damned enticing about seeing Corinne so confident and capable.

When the laughter had died down, Corinne went on. "Mistress Elsbeth, you mentioned before that you, on the other hand, bake excellent bannocks, and what's more, that it only takes you an hour to make a batch of them."

Elsbeth puffed up with pride. "Aye, milady, I'm praised by all who taste my bannocks, and I can make them twice as fast as—"

Belatedly, Elsbeth seemed to realize where Corinne was headed. Reid, too, now saw the line of his wife's thought. A slow, admiring smile tugged insistently at his lips.

"With a simple calculation, I notice that mistress Colleen has given you 300 minutes of service this past month by milking Bluebell for you. And it would take you 300 minutes to bake five dozen bannocks at your admirable rate of one batch per hour. It seems that it would make sense, then, that your original agreement with mistress Colleen was for five dozen bannocks."

Colleen grinned widely. "Just as I said, milady."

"Do you dispute what ye said before all here today, Elsbeth, and what Lady Corinne has so diligently recorded?" Reid asked, leveling Elsbeth with a stern look.

"Nay, Laird," she mumbled, dropping her gaze.

"Good. Then see yer agreement honored," he said.

"Thank ye, Laird," Colleen said with a cheerful curtsy to each of them. "Thank ye, milady."

"Thank ye, Laird. Thank ye, milady," Elsbeth grumbled. Though she couldn't be happy about being made to pay Colleen more bannocks than she'd hoped to,

Reid sensed no animosity directed toward Corinne for sussing out the right ruling.

In fact, he could feel a growing warmth in the great hall, and it had naught to do with the fire crackling in the large hearth on the opposite wall. Those gathered applauded the fair judgment as Elsbeth and Colleen stepped back from the dais. Over the course of a dozen disputes, Corinne had proven herself diligent and even-handed—both with the quill and in helping him come to his decisions.

Reminding himself of his commitment to show his clan that Corinne was more than an obligation to him, he reached out and covered her free hand with his own, giving it a squeeze. He let his gaze linger on her face, savoring the pleased blush that rose to her cheeks as he continued to hold her hand before his people.

Murmurs again traveled through the hall, but this time, instead of biting remarks and whispers of displeasure, he saw several nods and grins out of the corner of his eye.

At last letting her go, he straightened in his chair. "Who's next?"

Just as two more clanspeople began making their way through the crowd toward the dais, the hall doors burst open with a blast of frigid air. Alain, who'd been stationed on watch in the eastern tower, strode in. His normally grinning mouth was pulled into a hard line.

"Laird," he said, halting before the dais. "Forgive the intrusion, but the MacDonnell Laird is on the village shores with two dozen warriors. He's demanding to speak with ye."

Shite. Arthur MacDonnell was not the sort of man to leave the comforts of his keep for a social call—especially not with so many men. This could only be about one thing.

"Let him cross to the castle," Reid told Alain. "*Only* him. If his men want to join him, they can swim—though our archers willnae make it pleasant for them."

Alain nodded and strode out of the hall. Reid drummed his fingers on his chair's arm, a knot forming in his stomach. He would have to handle this carefully—more carefully than walking the honed edge of a sword.

"Reid," Corinne murmured softly beside him. He glanced at her to find her creamy brow creased with concern. "What is going on?"

He would give the MacDonnell Laird the benefit of the doubt, he decided, though his gut told him he already knew why the man was here. Still, he would have to meet the Laird's fury with steadfast composure.

"There is naught to fash over," he replied. The words did little to erase the signs of worry from her face, though.

Those gathered in the hall must have sensed their Laird's suddenly tense mood, for they began to shift and murmur in confusion, bound to wait along with Reid to learn what Laird MacDonnell was about.

Only a few moments later, a commotion could be heard in the yard.

"...to pass, for I will have answers from his mouth alone!"

"Cool yer temper, Laird, else I'll be forced to cool it

for ye in Loch Duich," Alain said on the other side of the hall doors.

"Alain!" Reid barked, rising from his chair. "Let the Laird in."

The doors flew open once more, a gust of cold air making the fire flicker. The overcast sky outside was blocked as a rotund figure filled the doorway.

"Laird Mackenzie, ye bastard!" Laird MacDonnell roared, stomping into the hall. "This means war!"

Chapter Twenty-Four

C orinne shivered, only in part from the blast of icy wind blowing in from the open doors.

The barrel of a man charging into the hall could be none other than Laird MacDonnell—the man who could end his clan's alliance with the Mackenzies thanks to Reid and her marriage.

The Laird wore a red plaid slashed with green, his graying hair windblown and his beard twitching with anger. His brown eyes were so wide with rage that Corinne could see the whites all around them.

Alain and a handful of Mackenzie and MacRae guards darted into the great hall behind the Laird, closing the doors against the frigid wind.

"Laird, would ye like me to restrain him?" Alain said even as the MacDonnell Laird continued charging toward the raised dais.

Reid waved Alain and the other warriors off with a gesture, planting his feet and squaring his shoulders to the enraged man approaching.

"Greetings, Laird," he said in a loud, even voice. "I hope this season finds ye well. I'm sure——"

Laird MacDonnell came to a halt directly in front of Reid. Though the dais made Reid more than a head taller, Laird MacDonnell pushed so close that his deep chest nearly bumped Reid.

"Dinnae act as though ye didnae hear me," Laird MacDonnell snapped, pointing an accusing finger right under Reid's nose. "I ken what ye did, and I willnae stand for it."

Corinne held her breath. Judging from the nigh deafening silence that stretched in the great hall, so did everyone else present. Reid stared down at Laird MacDonnell for a long moment. This close, she could see that a muscle ticked in his jaw behind his dark stubble, yet the rest of his demeanor remained controlled.

"I'm glad to welcome ye to Eilean Donan as a friend," Reid said pointedly. "And I am happy to explain aught that ye may have heard."

"Oh, I have *heard* plenty," Laird MacDonnell seethed. His finger swung to where Corinne sat behind the table, and she involuntarily curled back into her chair. "Foremost that ye have replaced my beloved Euna with this English wench!"

Reid's face suddenly dropped into a hard glower, his eyes like sharpened steel. "Kindly lower yer finger from my wife's direction," he ground out.

Laird MacDonnell dropped his hand but rounded on Reid once more. "Ye have disrespected Euna's memory with such an act. Ye've shamed my younger daughter Adelaide by passing her over like some milkless cow. And ye've destroyed my faith in ye—and the alliance along with it. Ye will soon learn what a terrible error ye've made in crossing the MacDonnells, man."

Reid had passed over the Laird's *other* daughter? Confusion swamped Corinne, but before she could puzzle out what Laird MacDonnell meant, he charged on.

"If ye think I will let this pass without—"

"Laird MacDonnell," Reid snapped, cutting the man off. His composure was visibly slipping. Now his hands were clenched so tightly at his sides that his knuckles had turned white. "Do ye wish to have an explanation for the situation we find ourselves in, or do ye wish to shout yerself into an early grave?"

"Is that a threat, Mackenzie?" the Laird growled.

"Nay, man," Reid replied through clenched teeth. "Merely an observation that ye are turning as red as yer plaid."

Reid turned and moved behind the table, taking up his chair at Corinne's side. Into the taut silence now filling the hall, he spoke. "Ye ken that I have been away much of late, for the King has requested that I give him aid in the Borderlands in the fight against the English."

Laird MacDonnell gave a single nod, his face screwed up into a scowl.

"On my most recent mission, he asked that I kidnap a certain Englishwoman," Reid said, slightly inclining his head toward Corinne, "to thwart a marriage alliance that would have united two English border lords against the King. To ensure that Lady Corinne couldnae be taken and forced into a marriage ever again, the King ordered that I wed her."

Corinne stiffened at that. His blunt words stung her pride, just as they had when he'd announced their marriage to his clan upon arriving at Eilean Donan. He'd painted an accurate enough picture, but all that talk of orders and duty made her feel small.

To her shock, though, he reached out and took her hand. "Though I was obliged to marry Lady Corinne at the King's command, I have since come to learn that it is a great privilege to be her husband."

Surprised murmurs rippled through the hall. Corinne felt her face grow warm, but this time it wasn't from embarrassment—nay, it was from a feeling expanding in her heart that she wasn't quite ready to name yet.

"So ye see," Reid went on. "I didnae intend to marry. I didnae plan on endangering our alliance. But now that both have come to pass, I'd like to discuss how we might move forward."

Laird MacDonnell's eyes darted from Corinne to Reid and back again. "Ye cannae expect me to accept that."

Reid's hand tightened on hers.

"Ye've replaced my Euna as if her death meant naught," the Laird continued.

Reid released her hand, his fist coming to rest on the table. "Enough," he bit out.

"Ye broke our agreement that Adelaide would be yer wife when she came of age—"

"We never finalized such an arrangement."

"—and now ye expect me to forgive all just because ye were following orders? Nay, ye cannae just marry some English chit and—"

"Silence!" Reid roared, slamming his fist against the table so hard that Corinne's ink well bounced and tottered precariously before coming back to rest safely. Corinne jumped as well, and several in the hall sucked in a breath.

"Disrespect my wife again, and I'll have ye thrown from the top of the keep into Loch Duich, Laird or nay," Reid growled.

Laird MacDonnell clamped his mouth shut, though he seethed red with anger.

Reid rolled his neck, letting a long breath go. "Clear the hall," he ordered. "And bring us bread and ale. We arenae through here, Laird."

Laird MacDonnell's face flickered with surprise before he hardened his features once more. "I'll make no promises that ye can convince me no' to end the alliance," he said warily.

"Fair enough," Reid replied, his mouth set in a stubborn line. "And I *will* promise to fight tooth and nail for this alliance, just as I did the first time."

As the others began to file out of the hall and a servant brought fresh bread and a pitcher of ale, Corinne tried to rise inconspicuously.

"Nay, wife," Reid said, catching her hand. "Stay. Ye are part of this, too."

Reluctantly, she sank back into her chair, eyeing the disgruntled bear of a Laird across from her.

Reid waited until another servant had brought three

mugs and a chair for Laird MacDonnell before lifting the bread and symbolically tearing it, handing a chunk to the Laird and Corinne before biting into his own piece.

"Now," he said, pouring the ale. "Where would ye like me to begin?"

AS THE AFTERNOON stretched into evening, Reid had to resist the urge to shove back from the table and thrash something. He'd always known Arthur MacDonnell was a stubborn old badger, but the man had put up less of a fight in handing his eldest daughter to a bastard-born Laird in marriage than he did now.

Reid had explained twice more—in detail—his mission from the Bruce to kidnap Corinne and his subsequent order to marry her. He'd assured MacDonnell that he'd argued with the King against such an arrangement for the harm it would do to their clans' alliance.

To his surprise, Corinne spoke up as well, confirming that Reid had fought valiantly against their union, as had she. This seemed to catch MacDonnell off-guard, for his bushy gray eyebrows shot up when Corinne described her own multiple attempts to escape.

"Ye've got a wee bit of fire in ye, dinnae ye, lass?" MacDonnell had said, eyeing Corinne. "Do ye have any Highland blood in yer veins?"

"Nay," she'd replied, flushing. "Only English, as far as I know."

"Hmph. That hair says otherwise."

Though the man seemed open to Corinne's words, he would inevitably turn cold when Reid spoke. As the evening wore on, Reid repeated over and over that his marriage to Corinne was in no way an act of aggression toward the MacDonnells. When those assurances seemed to do little to convince the Laird, Reid reminded him that his own mother, Brinda, was a MacDonnell. Blood already bound their clans together, as did Reid's first marriage to Euna.

"She hasnae been forgotten, nor replaced," Reid said for the third or fourth time, barely containing the desire to toss his hands in the air and give up. Nay, he wouldn't be bested so easily. He would fight for this alliance, for it meant his people's security, and he refused to—

"I have a question," Corinne said, cutting into his frustrated thoughts.

Laird MacDonnell lifted his mug of ale. "Go on with ye then, lass."

Corinne turned to Reid. "You didn't tell me you'd already arranged to marry Laird MacDonnell's other daughter."

Though she was clearly fighting to keep her voice even, a tart edge sharpened the words. The memory of her barging in on him in the bath, demanding to know why he hadn't told her of his previous marriage, rose in his mind.

MacDonnell snorted into his ale. "I like yer spirit, lass," he said. "Dinnae try to convince me ye got that in England, too."

Corinne spared him a glance before turning back to Reid. "Well?"

Christ, if he'd thought it was bad facing Laird MacDonnell in a fit of rage, he didn't stand a chance with Corinne joining the old codger's side.

"We didnae have an official agreement," he said, narrowing his eyes on MacDonnell. "Isnae that right, Arthur?"

The Laird shifted, making his chair groan. "Well, nay, no' exactly an *official* arrangement. More like an understanding."

Corinne still stared at Reid expectantly.

He scrubbed a hand along his bristled jawline. "After Euna passed, Laird MacDonnell suggested that in a few years' time, when his younger daughter Adelaide was of age, we might…renew our clans' commitment to the alliance with another marriage."

"Ah," Corinne said, a frown lingering around her mouth. "And how old is Adelaide?"

"She is seventeen, but we thought to wait a wee bit longer," MacDonnell supplied. He grunted. "Offense no' intended, but I think the lass was rather relieved when news arrived that ye'd wed, Mackenzie. What lass wants to marry her older sister's husband?"

"In any case," Reid said, redirecting the conversation. "Another marriage alliance was merely a suggestion, an idea proposed rather than a solid plan."

One of Corinne's red eyebrows arched and she pinned him with her gaze. "Shall I expect any other bits of news from you? Do you have a third wife, or mayhap another engagement?"

MacDonnell coughed into his ale, but it sounded suspiciously like a bark of laughter.

"Nay, I dinnae have any more surprises," Reid said, shooting a withering look at MacDonnell. He turned back to Corinne. "I ken I havenae been…forthcoming with ye, Corinne, but I vow that I am no' keeping ye in the dark about aught anymore."

He reached out and gently tucked a loose lock of flame-red hair behind her ear, holding her gaze so that she could see the truth of his words in his eyes.

As the moment stretched, he felt MacDonnell eyeing them. At last he broke their look to turn back to the Laird.

"I think I see what ye mean about counting yerself lucky in yer union, Mackenzie," MacDonnell said grudgingly. He planted both hands on the table, his face drawn in contemplation. "I ken now that ye couldnae go against the King's orders. And though ye dinnae ken who yer blood sire is, yer mother was a MacDonnell, as ye say."

Reid stiffened, sensing that the stubborn Laird was about to yield his anger and drop his earlier claim that the alliance was off.

"We need allies now more than ever," the Laird went on, tugging on his graying beard. "The MacVales continue to grow bolder along our eastern border. Just a fortnight ago, we lost more than a dozen sheep to them. My men cannae keep up with their attacks."

This was his opportunity to bring MacDonnell fully back around and seal their alliance.

"Mayhap I can help," Reid said, propping his elbows

on the table. "Ye ken Cedrick is one of my best warriors. Yet without another battle beneath the Bruce's banner in sight, his skills will go to waste behind Eilean Donan's walls."

"Oh, aye?" MacDonnell said, feigning indecision.

"I have a few others I could send as well," Reid went on, thinking of Galen and the men who'd listened to him badmouth Corinne. "Capable warriors, of course, but men who would do well to be away from the clan for a wee while."

MacDonnell pursed his lips. "I suppose that might help." He sighed as if Reid were taxing him greatly. "And I suppose there is naught to do about that fact that ye've married an Englishwoman. But if it must be an Englishwoman, better to have her be as bonny and spirited as this one, eh?"

To Reid's surprise, MacDonnell looked up at Corinne and actually winked at her. Corinne's whole face suffused with red, but she smiled back at the older Laird, lifting her chin. "I seem to have charmed you, Laird MacDonnell, though I confess you haven't seen a fraction of what I am capable of."

"Ha!" MacDonnell roared, slapping his hand on the table top hard enough to make the ale jump in their mugs. "There's that spirit! Now that matters are settled, when will we put aside this bread and weak ale in favor of a real meal and some of that Mackenzie whisky?"

Chapter Twenty-Five

Corinne slipped out the kitchen door, finally letting a broad smile break over her face.

She'd just managed to convince Bitty to let her record several of her most beloved recipes. She'd thought of the idea a sennight ago, not long after Laird MacDonnell had left Eilean Donan, a bit drunk from all the ale and whisky, but happily recommitted to his alliance with the Mackenzies.

Reid had insisted later that night as he'd eased Corinne back into their bed that Laird MacDonnell had been miraculously won over in no small part due to Corinne's charm. Though she still wasn't sure what she'd done to help turn the man off his war path, it had given her an idea for dealing with the others in the clan.

She'd tried to be the perfect lady of the keep before, to be so skilled and competent at running Eilean Donan that she could take over its maintenance completely.

The problem was, she was neither skilled nor competent when it came to managing such a large castle. And in trying to prove herself worthy, she'd undoubtedly stepped on a few toes.

But that night sitting with Reid and Laird MacDonnell, after the initial shock had worn off, she'd simply been herself. She'd spoken up where she'd seen fit instead of holding her tongue, as her father would have demanded.

That had helped her realize that she needn't pretend to be something she was not with the rest of the clan, either. Those who'd witnessed her serving as clan scribe in the great hall were pleased with—even proud of—her abilities with a quill. It had given her the idea to approach Bitty, but not with the aim of taking over the kitchens herself this time.

Bitty had resisted at first, insisting that she knew all her recipes by heart, and therefore there was no need to write them down. But Corinne had gently pointed out that Bitty wouldn't be the castle cook forever—someday she'd have to hand the reins over to one of her undercooks.

That had given the stalwart woman pause. She'd thought on it for several days, and only this morning had agreed to allow Corinne to take down her recipe for baked apple crumble with cream. Tomorrow, Bitty had grudgingly decided, they would move on to her clan-famous roasted pheasant with rosemary and butter sauce.

Corinne clutched the ledger she'd dedicated to

Bitty's recipes to her chest, hugging it with joy as she crossed the great hall.

This had been the happiest sennight of her life. During the days, she'd recorded clan matters at Reid's side. Yesterday, Reid had completed hearing the disputes that had piled up while he'd been away, so today he'd taken to the castle's training grounds despite the cold, rainy weather. Corinne had happily sat in the toasty kitchens with Bitty, jotting down the cook's careful instructions.

And the nights…

Though she knew none of the servants moving through the great hall could read her thoughts, she felt a flush creep into her face as heated memories flooded her. Every night—and sometimes in the afternoon or in the dark, quiet pre-dawn hours—Reid had sent pleasure hammering through her with his lips, his hands, his tongue, his—

She hurried the last few steps into the stairwell, grateful that the cool dimness there hid her blush. Now was not the time to get lost in fancies, she told herself firmly as she climbed the stairs. She had much to do— and she'd have to work swiftly if she hoped to surprise Reid with her new project before he could discover what she was about.

At the first landing, she ducked into the solar and quickly slid the recipe ledger into its place on the wooden shelves. Though she knew Reid was still on the training grounds and the solar was empty, she still darted her gaze around the chamber as she pulled a rolled scroll from behind one of the rows of ledgers.

Carefully carrying the scroll to the desk, she set about paring her quill and readying the ink. She had to get everything just right to ensure that her work was perfect for Reid's surprise.

Just as she was about to dip her quill in the ink, a soft knock came at the door. She jumped, but then she heard Gellis's voice on the landing.

"Milady, may I enter? A missive just arrived for ye."

Corinne felt her brows crease. Who would send her a missive, and why?

"Enter," she called, setting her work aside.

Gellis stepped inside and approached, a folded piece of parchment extended in her hand.

"Father Ewan asked me to bring this to ye," Gellis said.

Corinne's confusion deepened as she took the missive and unfolded it, her eyes scanning the clean, simple text.

DEAR LADY CORINNE,

I am writing to you from Drumleigh Abbey, which lies a two-days' ride from your new home at Eilean Donan. As you are recently arrived, you may not be familiar with our little abbey, though we are quite proud of it. It is a double monastery, where nuns and monks work alongside each other to glorify God and do His humble work.

Word of your remarkable skill as a scribe has reached all the way to us here at Drumleigh. It is also said that you intended to join an order of nuns before your marriage to the Mackenzie Laird.

Pray, do not think me overly bold, for we have never met (I thought it best to pass this missive through Father Ewan's hands, for at least he is familiar to you), but I believe that when a soul such as yours has been touched with a gift to transcribe the most holy of texts, that gift must be put to use in God's service. We have several well-trained scribes at the abbey, and several more students who are learning under them. As you have been called by your gift, I pray that you will join us here and fulfill your most sacred purpose.

Do not fear, for arrangements can be made for your transport, and of course you will be given sanctuary here, which neither the Mackenzie Laird nor the King himself can violate. You will be safe, milady, and looked after, and doing the work you were meant for.

Your humble servant,
Brother Michael

CORINNE RE-READ THE MISSIVE, fingers pressed to her lips in stunned silence.

How could this be? When she'd longed for naught more than to escape Reid and flee to a convent, no help had come. And now that she had finally begun settling into her new life, Brother Michael and those at Drumleigh Abbey were offering her sanctuary to work as a scribe?

She slowly lowered the missive to the desk—the desk where she and Reid had made passionate love a sennight before. The desk where the scrolled paper she'd been working on, Reid's surprise gift, lay unfinished.

She couldn't just abandon it—couldn't abandon Reid. Though she'd never dreamed of such a life for herself, she had already spoken her vows of devotion to Reid and sealed them in the bedchamber next door.

But the truth was, it was more than that. She wasn't merely bound to Reid by marital vows or deeds of the flesh. Her heart did a flip in her chest, a sensation that had become familiar every time she saw Reid, or merely thought of him. Despite their unconventional start, and despite all the reasons she shouldn't, she'd come to care for him.

To love him, a voice whispered in the back of her head. Nay, she couldn't find the courage to speak those words just yet, but the seed of love had already taken root in her heart.

Besides, she'd never truly wanted to be a nun. That had always been the means to an end. What she'd truly longed for deep in her bones was the freedom to use her skills as a scribe, to lose herself in the scratching of the quill over parchment, the sharp smell of ink, the words flowing from her fingertips to be shared and passed on forever.

And didn't she have that here at Eilean Donan, with the Mackenzies—and Reid? She was using her skills to help people, to make their lives better. And when she was done with her project for Reid, she would be able to give him something that would serve the clan long after they'd both turned to dust beneath the Highland soil.

She let a long breath go, her decision made. To her surprise, as she took up a sheet of parchment and lifted her quill, the words came easily, as though a weight had been lifted from her heart.

Dear Brother Michael,

Thank you for your offer, but I must decline. Eilean Donan is my home now, and the Mackenzies my people. I could not betray them, nor my husband, by fleeing to Drumleigh. If I can serve you and the abbey in any other way, however, do not hesitate to ask. I am happy to lend my skills where I can.

Yours,
Lady Corinne Mackenzie

She stared down at her own curving script. It was the first time she'd used the Mackenzie name as her own. It felt…right.

Corinne folded the missive and handed it to Gellis, who stood waiting beside the desk.

"Would you see that this gets to Father Ewan?" she asked. "I assume he has a way of passing it along to Brother Michael at Drumleigh Abbey."

"Aye, milady," Gellis said with a bobbing curtsy. But as Gellis turned to leave, she hesitated. "If I may have yer permission, milady, I would like to visit my sister on MacDonnell lands for the next few days. She is heavy with child, and she's had a hard time managing her other wee ones now that her time approaches."

"Of course," Corinne replied, smiling. "Do send her my well wishes."

"Aye, milady," Gellis said with another quick bob, then slipped out of the solar clutching Corinne's missive.

When the door closed behind her, Corinne turned back to the scroll awaiting her, a soft smile on her face and a growing warmth in her heart.

Chapter Twenty-Six

G ellis sat in silence as Timothy rowed her toward the village, but when she stepped onto the dock, she headed not toward the little kirk at the heart of the town, but straight for the stables.

"Lady Corinne has given me permission to visit my sister," she said to one of the stable lads, who nodded and began saddling a horse for her.

With the Englishwoman's missive securely tucked into the bodice of her gown, she urged the horse northward, toward MacDonnell lands. Yet once she'd reached the fork in the River Elchaig, instead of bearing north toward the MacDonnell clan keep, she guided the horse east. She could cut across the corner of the MacDonnell lands and reach the MacVale keep far faster that way, though if she was recognized, she would be questioned for heading away from her sister's croft.

This was largely empty terrain, however. She likely wouldn't lay eyes on another soul until the MacDonnell-

MacVale border. And by then, she would be under Laird Serlon MacVale's protection. None would be able to stop her then—not even that bitch English mistress of hers.

A DAY and a half of hard riding had left Gellis achy, wet, and chilled to the bone. Heavy rain had chased her all the way to the border, and even now she shivered beneath her woolen cloak. She slipped one hand between the folds and patted her bodice, checking that Corinne's missive was still in place.

Reassured, she blew on her red, wind- and cold-chapped hand, but when she heard a whistle in the dripping trees ahead, she froze. Hastily bringing her chilled fingers to her mouth, she returned the whistle, urging her horse onward.

Mungo, one of the MacVale warriors, emerged from the copse. Despite the fact that she'd seen him several times before, Gellis's heart still leapt. The man was a giant, his massive frame seeming to dwarf the large stallion he rode. His brown head was uncovered, his hair dripping and his deep-set eyes hard as he approached.

"The Laird will be pleased his whore has returned so quickly," Mungo muttered, looking her up and down.

Gellis bit back a retort. Serlon *loved* her. He could warm his bed with any MacVale wench he chose whenever he wanted—and he did—but they shared something far more than that.

Still, Mungo wasn't afraid to smack her face when

he thought she was being too mouthy, so she held her tongue.

"Let us make haste," she replied instead. "The Laird will want what I have."

Mungo grunted, squeezing his beefy knees, which poked out from his green and brown plaid, into his horse's flanks.

By the time they reached the MacVale keep, nervousness coiled in the pit of Gellis's stomach. Serlon might be pleased with her for selling his ruse to the English bitch. Or he could be angry that Corinne hadn't taken the bait. He might praise Gellis for making her way so swiftly back to him with news, or he might go into a rage over the news itself. She could never be sure what mood she would find him in.

Mungo nodded to the guards stationed along the wet, dark battlements topping the small keep. With a groan, the portcullis lifted slowly and the wooden gates behind them creaked open.

Gellis kept her chin level as they rode through the gates, deigning not to look down at the warriors milling aimlessly in the courtyard or the servants scurrying away from them. She was practically mistress of this keep, after all. Serlon had promised to marry her many years ago, and someday this would all be hers. She would send the lazy riff-raff away and sweep out the rubbish collecting in the corners. But until that day, she would serve Serlon loyally.

Mungo dismounted and began striding toward the doors to the great hall without waiting for her. She scrambled from her horse, hurrying after him.

"Gellis MacDonnell has returned, Laird," Mungo said even as Gellis stepped into the great hall, her eyes adapting to the dimness.

A fire burned in the hearth, but the neglected chimney forced some of the smoke back into the hall. The tables and benches had been cleared away, yet Serlon sat at his table atop the dais, eating a roasted pheasant leg by himself.

When his dark eyes fell on Gellis, her heart leapt into her throat, her stomach turning over. She dipped into a curtsy, her skin growing warm despite the chill in the hall.

"Laird," she purred, lifting her gaze beneath her lashes to stare at him.

What a magnificent man he was. Though age had diminished his strength slightly over the years, he was still a powerful man. His black hair was streaked with gray at the temples, his broad shoulders and thick torso visible above the table.

He eyed her with those sharp, dark eyes for a long moment, and all thoughts of running the MacVale keep fled from Gellis's head. He was completely in control— of the clan, of the keep, and of her. It terrified and excited her, knowing he could do anything he wanted with her.

"Did ye deliver the missive?" he demanded, dropping the pheasant leg and slowly licking each finger as he stared her down from the dais.

"Aye, of course, Laird," she replied quickly. "The Englishwoman believed it was from the monk ye invented."

"And?"

Gellis faltered. "She wrote a reply." She dug out the folded piece of parchment from her bodice and stepped onto the dais, extending it toward Serlon.

He snatched it from her fingers, then waved her away. She stepped back, standing before him in silence while her cloak dripped onto the gray-brown rushes.

"Fillan!" Serlon bellowed, eyeing the parchment suspiciously.

From the shadowy stairs in the corner, the Laird's son hobbled forth. His dark head was bowed, his slim shoulders hunched as he awkwardly shuffled toward the dais, using a cane to compensate for his club-foot.

When he'd managed to hoist himself onto the dais, Serlon shoved the missive toward him without looking at him. "Read it," Serlon demanded.

Fillan murmured each word of the missive, his head lowered. When he came to the end, he lifted his gaze at last, his dark eyes, so like his fathers, sharp.

"What is the meaning of this, Father?" he said softly, holding up the piece of parchment. "First ye have me write some nonsensical message from a monk, and now—"

"Silence," Serlon cut in, his gaze forward. "I'll call ye if I have need of yer writing or reading skills again."

Though he was slight due to the deformity to his left leg, Fillan was a man grown at twenty. He stared hard at his father, his eyes flashing with something like hatred. "Ye cannae order me like a dog and use me to—"

Like lightning, Mungo darted forward and snatched

Fillan's cane. With sickening strength, he struck Fillan across his crippled leg.

Fillan cried out in pain and collapsed on the dais.

"I said silence," Serlon said, his voice dangerously low now. Gellis knew what that meant, and so did Fillan. Serlon was close to snapping, and if he did, Fillan would get a great deal more than a single strike with a cane.

Keeping his head lowered, Fillan slowly dragged himself up to standing. In a mock show of consideration, Mungo extended Fillan's cane with a little bow. Taking the cane, Fillan hobbled down from the dais and toward the stairs once more, his shoulders hunched in either pain or impotent fury, Gellis couldn't say.

For her part, she remained silent, her chin tucked and her hands clasped before her in a sign of submission. Serlon liked her that way—at his mercy.

Though she knew he couldn't read, Serlon picked up the missive and eyed it once more, his features hardening with rage.

"The stupid whore," he muttered through clenched teeth. "Now that she's spread her legs for Mackenzie, she'll no' leave him."

His gaze landed on Gellis, and she froze. "Ye said my first missive would be enough to tempt her away from the keep. Ye said she wanted to escape and become a scribe so badly that it would lure her into my trap."

"I-I have done just as ye asked, my love," Gellis replied. "I delivered the missive, I told her it had come by way of Father Ewan, I—"

Serlon slammed his palm against the table, making

Gellis jump. "Come here." His voice was hard but so precariously soft.

On trembling legs, Gellis mounted the dais. Serlon pointed to the ground next to his chair, and she hurried to his side, kneeling beside him.

He captured her chin and she was forced to gaze up at him from her knees.

"Tell me again exactly what happened when the MacDonnell Laird arrived at Eilean Donan."

Gellis hastily repeated what she'd already reported to Mungo nearly a sennight past. She hadn't been able to slip away for the three days it took to get to the MacVale keep and back, so she'd given Mungo the information along the Mackenzie-MacDonnell border.

When she concluded, Serlon released her face and rubbed a hand along his black and silver bristled cheek.

"Fucking hell," he muttered. "Arthur MacDonnell shouldnae have forgiven the Mackenzie for marrying that English bitch so quickly. That *should* have been enough to end their alliance and start a bloody war."

"Their blood is thick," Mungo said, his coarse features contorting with a frown. "Mackenzie is half-MacDonnell, after all."

Serlon's lips twitched into a private smile for a moment before his mouth hardened once more. "The Englishwoman's arrival was supposed to fix that."

"But instead of putting them on the war path," Mungo said, "Mackenzie is giving MacDonnell even more men for his borders."

Gellis kept her mouth shut and remained motionless lest she draw attention to herself. Serlon allowed Mungo far more leeway than was afforded to her. The warrior was practically speaking to the Laird as if he was a counselor or advisor instead of a thick-skulled brute.

"What the bloody hell am I supposed to do with the English chit?" Serlon muttered.

"Ye could wait," Mungo offered. "See if Mackenzie grows tired of her, or if she changes her mind and wants to flee to the abb—"

Serlon once again slammed his hand against the table, cutting Mungo off. Relief flooded Gellis, for while she'd held her tongue, Mungo would now be the recipient of Serlon's anger rather than her.

"Ye fool," Serlon hissed at Mungo. "I cannae *wait*. I've been waiting for thirty-five years! Ever since Brinda MacDonnell was sent to be Murdoch Mackenzie's bride, the MacDonnell-Mackenzie alliance has plagued me. The closer they are allied, the less there is for MacVales to take. Do ye think reiving along the MacDonnell border is going to get *easier* if we simply wait? Do ye think Mackenzie and his clan will grow *weaker* if we wait?"

Serlon smoothed a hand over his hair, visibly trying to regain control over his temper.

"If I am ever to consider replacing my son as my heir and naming ye instead, Mungo, ye must learn to think like a Laird instead of merely a warrior."

Gellis remained crouched and still at Serlon's side, but inside a spike of surprise hit her. It was well-known that Serlon detested the fact that Fillan, his only heir, was a weakling and a cripple. Despite Fillan's sharp mind, Serlon valued strength above all else. Fillan was worthless in his eyes. But could the Laird possibly consider installing Mungo as his successor? Or, a voice whispered in the back of her mind, was the promise Serlon dangled in front of Mungo—that of becoming Laird—no different than the promise of marriage he'd held over Gellis to encourage her obedience?

"Think, man," Serlon continued, fixing Mungo with a hard stare. "The more chaos we create, the less anyone can control what we do—and the more we can take whatever we want. If the MacDonnells and Mackenzies were at war, there wouldnae be any more guards along the border. They wouldnae be able to stop us from reiving—or more. That is why we dinnae need to scrape and beg for alliances—all we have to do to get what we want is ruin others' alliances."

Gellis had heard Serlon say as much before—that the MacVales were in the business of destroying alliances, not making them, for chaos and war bred opportunity. The MacVales could take what they wanted as long as their neighbors were at each other's throats.

She didn't pay any mind to such scheming and strategizing. She would serve Serlon's wishes not because she believed in his mission, but because she believed in *him*—his strength, his power, his terrifying might.

"What will ye do, then, Laird?" Mungo asked cautiously.

Serlon exhaled a frustrated breath. "Brinda's bastard child should have been enough to destroy the union between the MacDonnells and Mackenzies," he muttered. "Euna's death should have been enough. That missive to the English bitch should have been enough."

He drummed his fingers on the table for a long moment. "The Englishwoman hasnae made it easy to get rid of her, but there may yet be a way," he said at last.

He suddenly turned to Gellis, seizing a fistful of her hair. She gasped, rising an inch off her knees to ease his brutal grasp.

"Ye, my dear, are finally going to earn yer keep."

Gellis resisted the urge to remind him of all she'd done for him—becoming Euna's lady's maid, alerting Serlon to the impending pregnancy, slipping the poison into the wine that killed both Euna and the would-be heir that would forever seal the MacDonnells and Mackenzies together.

"It will prove worthwhile that ye stayed on in the Mackenzie clan," he continued, speaking more to himself than to Gellis. "Fillan will write another missive, which ye'll deliver to the English whore. And I'll need ye to secure a bit of MacDonnell plaid."

"Aye," she breathed, staring up at him. "Whatever ye say, my love. But why do ye need a plaid?"

Serlon tsked softly, twisting her hair in his fist until she cried out. "If I am to be the beneficiary of a war between the MacDonnells and the Mackenzies, I must get every detail right."

He eased his grip ever so slightly, allowing Gellis to sink back down onto her knees.

"And that means making the Englishwoman's death look like it came at the hands of a MacDonnell."

Chapter Twenty-Seven

"What's this surprise ye want to show me?" Reid let Corinne tug him by the hand through the great hall despite the curious stares of the servants as they cleared away the midday meal.

Normally, he would have frowned on such a public display—not only of holding hands, but also letting her drag him away from his duties on the training grounds. Yet now he felt an uncharacteristic urge to let everyone in the clan see his wife pulling him up toward their chamber in the middle of the day.

Aye, he would show them his happiness with Corinne, and hers with him. And not simply because it had encouraged them by example to warm to her, to be more accepting and welcoming of her as their mistress. It was more than that. The truth was, Reid doubted he could contain his utter elation if he tried. The fortnight they'd been married had been the best of his life. He was acting a moon-eyed fool, and he didn't care.

"You'll see," she said cryptically over one shoulder, an eager grin curving her mouth.

He felt a smile tug at his own lips. "I thought I left ye so well satisfied this morn that ye wouldnae need to drag me back to bed by midday, but clearly I have underestimated yer hunger for me, wife."

A bonny flush rose to her cheeks. She shot him a chastising look. A short lock of flaming hair fell over her eyes and she distractedly blew it away. "It isn't...*that*," she breathed. "The surprise is...well, you'll see."

They mounted the stairs, but when they reached the first landing, instead of pulling him into their bedchamber, she opened the door to the solar.

When he'd shut the door behind them, she released his hand and strode toward the shelves on the far wall.

"Now close your eyes," she instructed.

"I like where ye're headed with this, lass," he teased, lowering his lids, "but ye ken I like to watch ye undress."

She clucked her tongue from across the room, but then he heard her soft steps approaching once more. "Hold out your hands."

Obediently, he did. A moment later, something light landed in his upturned palms.

"All right," she said, her voice suddenly tight with nerves. "You can open your eyes."

He blinked, staring down at what rested in his hands. It was a parchment scroll, rolled into a tube.

"What is it?"

"Look for yourself," she urged, gnawing at her lower lip.

Carefully, he unfurled the parchment. His eyes

landed on Corinne's elegant, sure script before he realized what the words said.

"This is..." he felt his brows furrow as he read. "This is the Mackenzie clan lineage." He scanned through the names at the top. "Kenneth Mackenzie and Morna MacDougall of Lorn, his wife. They begat Ian Mackenzie, Murdoch's father. And here is Murdoch and Brinda MacDonnell, and—"

His words suddenly caught in his throat at the branch below Murdoch and Brinda.

There, in Corinne's perfect hand, was his name.

Reid Mackenzie, fourth Laird of the Mackenzies of Eilean Donan, Kintail.

His heart seemed to miss a beat, and then it thumped so hard against his ribs that his breath left him.

Beside his name, Euna MacDonnell was written, with her birth and death dates, and a note about their unborn bairn. And Corinne's name appeared on the other side of his.

"I found this," Corinne said, holding up a more aged scroll next to the one in his hands. Reid instantly recognized it as the original record of the clan's Lairds and lineage. That scrap of parchment had brought him a good deal of pain over the years—more than he cared to admit.

"I noticed that your name hadn't been added originally," Corinne went on. She pointed to the spot Reid had stared at many a time. On the original scroll, beneath Murdoch and Brinda, the first entry had been Reid's half-brother Logan, followed by their sister Mairin. Reid's name had been hastily added later, with a line jutting off to the side between Murdoch and Logan.

"And based on what you told me about Logan and Mairin, I changed their entries as well," Corinne said, shifting her finger down over the original record.

When Logan had been thought a murderer, Reid had drawn one heavy, decisive line through his name in ink. And Mairin had been presumed dead after she'd been kidnapped, though instead of a death date, there was only a question mark.

Reid shifted his gaze to the new scroll. Sure enough, below his own name, Logan's entry had been restored, as had Mairin's.

He swallowed against the sudden tightness in his throat, but he could not dislodge the lump of emotion there.

"Corinne…"

She chewed on her lip, looking between the scrolls. "When I found the original records, it didn't seem right to leave them as they were, what with the inaccuracies and changes," she said, her voice faltering. "I thought you might like to see what I've been working on this past sennight. Mayhap it is only of interest to me, but I meant it to be a…to do something kind for…"

Belatedly, he realized she misunderstood his speech-lessness for disapproval. "Corinne," he said again, halting her wavering words. "I love ye."

Her head jerked up, her eyes wide and depthless as the ocean.

He pulled in a breath, just as caught off guard by his words as she was. Still, though he hadn't anticipated them, it didn't make them any less true. His heart thrummed against his ribs as if trying to beat its way toward her. Deep in the pit of his stomach, in the marrow of his bones, and in the expanse of his heart, he knew. He loved her.

"I...I love you, too," she breathed, her eyes suddenly going bright with moisture.

If he'd felt grounded in the knowledge of his love a moment before, now he soared toward heaven with the knowledge of hers.

"Ye do?"

"Aye," she replied, a smile splitting her face. "I do."

Snatching both scrolls in one hand, he pulled her close with the other. When their lips met, there was no need for any more words. A wave of emotion swept across him as they kissed tenderly for a long moment.

With a sigh, she rocked back on her heels, breaking the kiss. She stared up at him, her gaze unguarded and brimming with the love that filled him as well.

"You like it, then?" she asked, tipping her head toward the scrolls.

"Corinne, this is the most amazing thing anyone has ever done for me."

She beamed up at him. "I thought the records should show that you were a wanted child, and a wanted Laird, not some hastily scrawled side note to the clan's history. This denotes your rightful place here."

He looked between the old, marked-up scroll and the new one. There was one piece of information that neither he nor Corinne could add, however.

"I wish I kenned what name to write for my blood father."

Sobering, she captured and held his gaze. "I know your birth weighs heavily on you, Reid. But this—" she held up the newly scribed scroll, "—isn't some fabrication or lie. I've seen with my own eyes how much the clan loves you. You *are* accepted here. You are wanted by your people. And by me."

Corinne dipped her chin, a blush rising to her cheeks. "I…I would also like to think that I've found my rightful place as well." A tentative finger rose and brushed over her name next to his on the parchment. She looked up at him, suddenly shy. "I finally feel that I am wanted, valued—thanks to you."

A new emotion suddenly mingled with love in Reid's belly—desire. He'd never been as good with his words as he was with his actions. He needed to show her just how wanted and valued she truly was to him.

Careful of all her hard work, he set the scrolls down on the desk next to them. But then he couldn't contain the lust roaring to life in his veins any longer. He rounded on her, snatching her up behind the knees and hoisting her so that her legs hitched around his hips. She shrieked in surprise, but her husky chuckle told him she liked being swept off her feet.

Holding her close, he took two swift steps to bring her back against the door to their bedchamber. She locked her arms around his neck and pulled him forward into a searing kiss. Their tongues mated in an erotic imitation of what he intended to do to her.

Heat surged into his cock, making him groan against

her lips. Keeping one hand beneath her bottom, he reached with the other for the doorknob.

But when she circled her hips, grinding her pelvis against his hard cock, he forgot what he'd meant to do. His hand went to his plaid of its own accord, yanking away the folds of wool. When he'd shoved them aside, he fumbled with her skirts, pushing them up her satin thighs.

She gasped as cool air hit her, but just as quickly, the crown of his cock brushed at her entrance, their shared heat sending a jolt through them both. Bloody hell, she was already wet for him. He teased her for a moment, sliding his shaft through her damp folds, but when her head fell back against the oak door and she moaned his name, the last of his patience snapped.

He thrust deep, claiming all of her in one swift stroke. They sucked in a breath in unison. Though it had only been a fortnight since their wedding, there was something familiar, something fundamentally *right* in joining with Corinne. Reid felt like he was home, body and soul.

Home, but in need. He began to move, craving more of her slick tightness. She gasped again as he increased his rhythm. There would be other times for slow exploration, for gentleness. This wasn't one of them. The need to take her, to join their bodies as fiercely as their hearts, was an instinct too powerful to deny.

He drove her into the door with each thrust, uncaring now of how wild and reckless this loving was. Corinne took him with just as much abandon. Her nails clawed his shoulders through his shirt, her legs clamping like a vise around his hips.

Suddenly her breath hitched and he felt her clench around him as her release broke over her. Her pleasure snapped the final thread of his control, triggering his own undoing. He hammered into her once, twice, thrice, the coiled ecstasy unleashing in a fierce torrent.

They rested their foreheads together for a long moment, both struggling to breathe. At last, Corinne's fingers released their grip on his shoulders and her legs loosened around his waist.

Slowly, he lowered her to her feet, though he kept his hands on her hips to steady her when her legs wobbled.

"Damn it all," he murmured. "I wasnae planning for that to happen. I meant to take ye to our bed and make love to ye properly."

"And that certainly wasn't proper," Corinne teased, letting her head fall back against the door with a grin.

He chuckled. God, he loved this woman.

Her hand slid from his shoulder to his chest. His heart hammered wildly beneath her palm. "But really," she said, her smile turning wicked. "Who says we have to choose between the door and the bed?"

With a growl of pleasure, he lifted her off the ground once more, this time throwing her over one shoulder like the barbarian she turned him into with her slightest touch.

She squealed in delight as he shoved open the door. "An excellent point, lass," he said, striding toward their bed. "Now, let's see about doing this the proper way."

Chapter Twenty-Eight

C orinne sat in the solar, her gaze drifting for the hundredth time from the ledgers before her to the door leading to the bedchamber.

Had it only been two days since Reid had taken her there against the hard oak? Warmth bloomed over her skin at the memories. His touch. His words. He loved her. And aye, he'd shown it.

She dragged the feathered end of her quill across her lower lip, her mind wandering. It was early afternoon, and Reid was training with his men outside despite the frigid bite to the air. Iron-colored clouds overhead had threatened snow all day.

She could go to him, make up an excuse to bring him inside from the cold. Or mayhap she wouldn't even bother with a fib, for from the knowing looks Seanad and the other servants had been casting them, all in the keep knew what the two of them were so frequently getting up to.

Her lips tingled where the quill brushed them, heated thoughts of Reid's wicked mouth on her lips, her breasts, between her legs teasing her.

Decided, she set the quill aside and rose from the desk, her pulse thumping in anticipation. She ducked into their chamber for her woolen cloak, but just as she stepped back into the solar, a knock came at the door.

"Another missive for ye, milady," Gellis said from the landing.

Corinne called the lady's maid in. "Good to see you again, Gellis," she said with a smile. "How is your sister? Has her time come already?"

"Nay, milady," Gellis replied, her gaze drifting from Corinne's. "It will be a wee bit longer, but she appreciated my help."

Corinne nodded, accepting the folded parchment Gellis extended toward her.

"When I passed through the village, Father Ewan asked me to deliver another one," Gellis said by way of explanation.

Corinne quickly scanned the writing.

Dear Lady Corinne,

I was sorry to hear of your decision to withhold your gift from God's service, but I understand that you must serve your husband and your new clan.

In your last missive, you offered to be of assistance if you were able. I hope you are able now, for a matter has arisen for which we are in desperate need of your help. Brother Matthew, who was working on a prayer book for one of Drumleigh Abbey's most esteemed benefactors, fell while coming down the stairs. Brother Matthew was most fortunate to escape with only a broken wrist, but he will be unable to complete the prayer book by the date he'd promised our benefactor. He only had a few pages remaining, but our other scribes have been unable to take on his work, as they have tasks of their own.

I have sent the remaining few pages to Father Ewan with the fervent hope that you may be able to steal away for a few hours and complete them. We badly need your help, Lady Corinne, and time is of the essence, so I can only pray that you are able to reach Father Ewan when you receive this.

Godspeed,
Brother Michael

CORINNE PLACED a hand over her heart when she was done reading. "Poor Brother Matthew—and poor Brother Michael," she murmured to herself. She looked up to find Gellis's wide brown eyes fixed on her.

"Is there something the matter, milady?" she asked.

Corinne tapped a finger on her lips as she considered. She'd already dressed to go outside, though if she went to the village church to work on Brother Matthew's prayer book, it meant her tryst with Reid would have to wait. Heat climbed up her neck at that—she'd once thought to commit herself to life as a nun, and now she was contemplating ways to get out of serving the church to have an erotic encounter with her husband.

Corinne yanked her mind back to the matter at

hand. Though only a few hours of gray daylight remained, it might be enough to complete the last remaining pages of a prayer book. Besides, Reid was busy training, and the ledgers she'd been working on could wait.

"I think I had better go to Father Ewan," she replied, folding the missive and tucking it into a pocket in her cloak.

"I'll go with ye," Gellis blurted. She ducked her brown head. "Ye shouldnae leave the castle alone, milady."

At Corinne's nod of acquiescence, Gellis went to fetch her own cloak, then the two of them descended to the great hall. As they stepped outside, Corinne pinched the front of her cloak closed. The air was sharp with cold and heavy with the smell of impending snow. She shivered, her breath coming in a white puff before her face.

As they crossed to the sea gate, Corinne strained to see across the yard to the training grounds on the opposite side of the keep. Though she made out a group of men sparring, a cloud of steam rising from the heat of their exertions, she couldn't spot Reid.

Seeming to sense the direction of her thoughts, Gellis said, "I'm sure ye'll be done with Brother Matthew's prayer book and back to the castle long before the Laird calls an end to the training for the day, milady."

"You're probably right," Corinne said, continuing on.

At the sea gate, they found that Timothy was already

on the island's small beach, so they didn't have to wait for him to be signaled from the village docks. As always, he rowed in silence, his breaths making a frosty plume with each of the oar's strokes.

When they reached the docks, Gellis helped her up. "Come, milady," she said, her pace quick as she made her way toward the village church.

Corinne hurried after her, for though it seemed strange for Gellis to take the lead, walking faster did help warm her a bit.

Corinne followed the widest street in the village, which she'd taken on her wedding day to get from the docks to the church, but when the little spire came into view, Gellis turned down a narrow alley.

"Father Ewan will likely be in his private chambers at this hour," Gellis said over her shoulder. "I ken a back entrance that will be faster."

Corinne frowned as they wound their way deeper into the dim alley. As she stared at Gellis's back, a realization struck her. Gellis had said that Corinne would be able to finish Brother Matthew's prayer book quickly and get back to the castle, but Corinne had never mentioned why she was going to the church.

Unease slithered up her spine. Mayhap Gellis had read the missive before delivering it. It hadn't been sealed, for it didn't contain anything worth hiding. Nonetheless, it would be impertinent of Gellis to read it.

Could Gellis even read, though? Corinne had only rarely known of servants who could.

Something wasn't right.

"Gellis, I think we should—"

Just then, they rounded a corner—into a dead end.

An enormous shadow pushed off from the stone wall sealing the end of the alley. The shadow loomed forth, materializing into a giant of a man.

A scream rose in Corinne's throat, but before it left her mouth, the giant's hand closed around her neck and he lifted her clear off the ground. Corinne's feet kicked wildly, looking for purchase on something. Blessedly, a heartbeat later the giant released her. But instead of simply dropping her, he flung her against the stone wall he'd been leaning against a moment before.

Pain and light exploded through her as she slammed into the stones and crumpled to the ground. Blinding stars danced before her eyes as she struggled to draw a breath into her battered body.

Through the ringing in her ears, she heard Gellis's voice, but instead of a scream of panic or pain, the lady's maid whispered. "Don't kill her yet, ye fool!" she hissed.

"Shut yer mouth, woman," was the deep-voiced reply. "I'm only making sure she willnae be able to struggle overmuch."

Bile and vomit rose in the back of Corinne's throat. She'd walked into a trap—that Gellis had conspired to set.

A hard boot nudged her. Though she couldn't find her limbs through the throbbing pain, she blinked, the white edges of her vision receding until she could make out both Gellis and her attacker's shadows looming over her.

"Ye see," the man commented. "She's fine, only stunned."

"Just do as we planned, Mungo," Gellis whispered, glancing nervously over her shoulder.

The man, Mungo, closed in on her. Corinne shied back, sucking in a breath to scream for help. But Mungo's enormous hand clamped around her throat once more, squeezing until Corinne sputtered.

Taking advantage of her wheezing, he released her and swiftly gagged her with a length of cloth. Then he jerked her limp hands up and bound her wrists with a rope.

"Hurry," Gellis hissed, watching the empty alleyway.

Mungo unsheathed a dagger from his boot and lifted it toward Corinne's face. She screamed against the gag, not caring that it muffled her cry. But instead of drawing the blade across her throat, Mungo pinched a lock of her hair and held it up.

"Isnae much here to cut," he grumbled, eyeing her already-shorn locks. "But they'll ken by the color that it's hers."

With that, he slid the dagger along the strands and dropped the two-inch-long lock onto the ground. Then he pulled a scrap of red and green plaid from the pouch on his belt and dropped it alongside the little clump of hair.

Through the numb shock clouding her mind, recognition dawned. She'd seen that plaid before. Laird MacDonnell had worn those colors when he'd visited— or rather, descended upon—Eilean Donan. Her gaze shot to Mungo. Beneath his cloak, he wore a different plaid of green and brown checked wool.

Comprehension turned her blood to ice. This wasn't just a trap for her—it was a trap for Reid as well. Whoever Gellis was working with, they meant to not only kidnap Corinne, but to frame the MacDonnells for it.

They meant to start a war.

Mungo suddenly yanked her to her feet by her elbow. He lowered his brown head until his cold, hard gaze was even with hers. Giving her a sickening grin, he reached around and pulled up her hood.

"Cannae have that bonny hair giving us away," he said. "No' until we're onto MacDonnell land, that is."

"Let's go," Gellis whispered. "I cannae be recognized either."

Mungo snorted as he dragged Corinne out of the dead end and into the alley. "Too late for ye, anyway," he muttered. "Ye will be the last one seen with the English bitch. When they find the MacDonnell plaid, they'll believe ye were in on her kidnapping."

"Laird MacVale will protect me," Gellis murmured.

Despite the pain and terror radiating through her, Corinne's mind latched onto Gellis's words.

MacVale.

Of course. The clan had been causing trouble for the MacDonnells. They would benefit from driving a wedge between their neighbors and the Mackenzies, who were aiding them.

They turned another corner to find two saddled

horses waiting. Clearly everything had been arranged, planned out to ensure a war.

Mungo mounted one of the horses and dragged Corinne into the saddle in front of him. Gellis took the other horse, carefully raising her hood as the first flakes of snow began to fall.

As Mungo kicked the horse into motion, sending them swiftly out of the village, a new thought struck her. It stole her breath just as sure as when she'd slammed into the stone wall.

She knew their plans. She knew their names and their faces. They hadn't attempted to hide aught from her once they'd subdued her.

Which meant that sooner or later, they planned to kill her.

Chapter Twenty-Nine

Despite the cold edge to the air and the fact that the sun had set nearly an hour past, Reid wiped sweat from his brow with his shirt sleeve.

He lifted his fingers to his mouth and whistled, halting his warriors' sparring.

Bluish gray gloaming had allowed them to continue training even as the snow had begun to fall lightly, but now it was getting dark enough that they risked injuring each other with an inaccurate jab of the pike or swing of the sword. Besides, the flakes were coming thicker, coating the training grounds with a dusting of slippery white snow.

"We'll resume in the morning, unless the snow has other ideas," he said to the men.

As they began filing into the great hall, good-naturedly ribbing each other over this or that defeat or victory in practice, Reid fell in behind them with a smile.

Aye, he was glad to go inside for a warm meal with the men, but more than that, he was eager to see Corinne.

The servants were just placing steaming trenchers on the trestle tables when he stepped into the hall. His gaze went to the dais, but Corinne's seat was empty. She must be hard at work in the solar yet again. Reid's blood coursed warmly. He was more than happy to join her there—and mayhap enjoy a different sort of feast.

Grinning, he climbed the stairs, but when he entered the solar, it was empty, as was their chamber. Disappointed, he returned to the hall. Seanad passed him on her way to a seat at one of the tables.

"Have ye seen Corinne?" he asked.

Seanad's dark blonde brows drew together. "No' for a few hours, Laird," she replied. "She was in the solar, I believe, and then I saw her pass through the hall with Gellis."

Where could she have been headed? Besides her tour of the castle with Wallace, Corinne hadn't spent any time in the other watch towers—she'd had no reason to.

As if conjured by his thoughts, Reid's gaze landed on Wallace, who sat at one of the tables with Hamond, Alain, and a few others.

"Wallace," Reid said, approaching the table. "Did ye happen to see Corinne go into one of the other towers this afternoon?"

Wallace stood formally, his tall, thin frame unfolding from the bench. "She didnae go into the towers, Laird, but I did see her cross the yard to the sea gate. She and Gellis went to the village a few hours past."

"What?" Despite his best efforts to remain calm, unease pricked along the back of Reid's neck. She hadn't left the castle since their wedding day.

A terrible thought drifted up from a dark corner of his mind. What if she'd slipped away with the intention of escaping him?

Nay, he told himself firmly, discarding the idea. He would have believed before they spoke their vows that she might try to flee, but not now. They'd shared too much. She'd told him she loved him.

"Forgive me, Laird," Wallace said, his chin drawing back in mortification at the edge in Reid's tone. "I watched her go from the northwest tower, but I didnae try to stop her. I didnae realize I was no' to allow her to—"

"Nay, Wallace," he said, distractedly trying to soothe his proud seneschal's ruffled feathers. "Ye did naught wrong. Corinne is free to come and go as she pleases. I am only surprised she hasnae returned yet."

The truth was, he couldn't fathom why she would go to the village in the first place, let alone why she hadn't come back before nightfall—especially now that the weather had broken and snow fell steadily. Mayhap he was overreacting. Still, he wouldn't take any chances with her wellbeing.

"I'm going to the village."

"I'll go with ye," Alain said, rising from the bench.

"And I," Leith said.

"And I," Hamond added, rising a bit slower than the younger men.

Reid wished he hadn't already sent Cedrick to the

MacDonnell border, for he wouldn't mind having another warrior with him. Then again, he didn't need a war party to descend on the village and cause alarm when Corinne was likely just visiting the shops.

With a nod to his men, he hurried upstairs to sling a cloak around his shoulders. When he returned to the hall, the three stood ready and waiting for him with their cloaks—and their swords belted to their waists. Though he wore his as well, he prayed he wouldn't need it. Still, his men could no doubt sense his unease and had prepared accordingly.

Timothy was waiting outside the sea gate, just as much a guard on duty against boats approaching the island as he was an oarsman. The normally stoic man blinked in surprise as Reid and the others strode toward him through the snow.

"Did ye transport my wife and her lady's maid to the shore, Timothy?" Reid asked as they shoved off from the little beach.

"Aye, Laird," Timothy replied.

"And did they say where they were going?"

"Nay, Laird."

Reid let out a frustrated breath. "Did aught seem…amiss?"

Timothy thought for a moment. One of the reasons Reid had assigned the man to be the castle oarsman was because he was just as watchful as he was quiet. As the rower of the sole sanctioned transport between the village and the castle, Timothy had a great responsibility. He was always alert for suspicious behavior, and he likely knew quite a bit more about his charges than they realized.

"Lady Corinne was at ease, Laird," Timothy said at last. "Though Gellis was sweating despite the cold."

Sharp apprehension stabbed Reid in the gut. Something wasn't right.

"Did ye see which direction they went when they got to the village?"

"Aye, Laird," Timothy said as he rowed faster, clearly sensing Reid's fear. "Down the main road, toward the kirk."

The moment they bumped into the dock, Reid leapt from the boat, the others close behind him. "We'll check the kirk first," he said, striding over the snow-dusted planks.

But when they reached the modest church, it was dark and quiet inside, with no sign of Corinne. Reid found Father Ewan taking a simple meal in his private chambers attached to the back of the chapel.

"Did Corinne come here, Father?" he demanded, no longer able to muster a polite tone.

Father Ewan blinked at the four warriors filling his wee chamber.

"Nay, Laird," he replied, shaking his head. "I havenae seen Lady Corinne since yer wedding day."

With a muttered apology, Reid stormed out of the church and into the cold night.

"Fan out," he snapped. "Sweep each street leading to or from the kirk. If we dinnae find her, we'll start knocking on doors."

With curt nods, Alain, Leith, and Hamond each took a direction and began moving away from the church. Reid ducked into a nearby alley, his hand resting on the hilt of his sword as he strode through the narrow, dim pathway.

All too soon, he reached a dead end. Muttering a curse under his breath, Reid turned to retrace his steps, but something on the ground caught his eye. He bent down, lifting a strip of red and green plaid from the snow.

A MacDonnell plaid.

It could be naught, for a few MacDonnells lived on Mackenzie land—Gellis, for one. Yet Reid's instincts told him something was amiss, and this was part of it.

He whistled, and in a moment, his men came running around the corner.

"Did ye find her?" Alain panted, his breath puffing white.

"Nay," Reid said, holding up the torn plaid. "But I found this."

The men came closer. "What the hell is a MacDonnell plaid doing lying around next to the kirk?" Hamond asked. "And why would—"

Glancing down, Hamond knocked snow off his boot. And froze.

Reid's gaze followed Hamond's. Though it was dark in the alley, he could make out something bright lying in the snow next to Hamond's boot.

Reid crouched, scooping up the snow to eye the little red slash across it.

As realization hit him, it was as if the ground had

opened up and Reid was falling, falling straight into the mouth of hell.

There was no mistaking that color.

"This is…" he began, his throat so tight that he had to swallow before continuing. "This is a lock of Corinne's hair."

Reid stood slowly, the blood roaring in his ears and his vision narrowing to the two objects in his hands—a scrap of MacDonnell plaid and a piece of Corinne's hair. Someone had hurt her. Someone might be hurting her now.

His lips curled back into an involuntary snarl as his hands closed into fists.

"To the stables," he hissed. "We ride for MacDonnell land."

"Laird," Alain said, his voice a warning. When Reid pushed past him, Alain caught his arm and spun him around. "Reid!"

He drew himself out of the storm breaking inside him long enough to meet Alain's gaze. His friend's eyes were clouded with worry, his light brown brows lowered.

"This could be a trap," Alain said, keeping his voice even.

"I dinnae fucking care!" Reid roared. "I'm going after her."

"And we are going with ye," Alain said, gripping Reid's arm tighter. "But try to think, man. We are at peace with the MacDonnells. Why would they take Corinne? And what kind of kidnapper leaves a lock of hair and a scrap of kilt to be found after he's gone?"

"How the bloody hell should I ken," Reid snapped.

"Ye're wasting time. Every moment we stand here talking, Corinne could be—" He choked on his next words, all rational thought shattering at the idea of her being in danger—or dead already.

"We should contact Laird MacDonnell," Hamond said. "Or at least gather more men."

Reid barely managed to repress another bellow of frustration. "There isnae time," he rasped. "Even now the snow is covering any tracks or other signs there may be."

Leith at last spoke up. "Then we need to ride now," he said, his young face hard-set.

"Aye," Reid said, jerking free of Alain's hold. "Do what ye like, but I'm going."

Only the briefest hesitation flickered in Alain's eyes before he set his jaw and nodded to Reid. "Trap or nay, I'm with ye."

Without waiting another moment, Reid bolted in the direction of the stables. He burst inside, the other three close behind him, making the sleepy stable lad watching the animals start awake.

At Reid's sharp orders, the lad hurried to help the men saddle and bridle their horses, then held the stable door open for them as they rode out into the night.

When they reached the northern edge of the village, Reid reined in his horse. Though the clouds were thick overhead, the moon was nearly full behind them, casting a diffuse silver-blue light across the sparkling blanket of snow stretching before them.

"There," Alain said, pointing ahead. Reid squinted,

just making out a trailing row of divots beneath the fresh snow.

Without hesitation, Reid spurred his horse into motion, plunging them into the night.

He would find Corinne, and he would make whoever had taken her pay. He vowed it.

Chapter Thirty

Despite the biting cold, Corinne hunched as far forward as she could in the saddle, away from the heat that radiated from Mungo's thick body.

She clutched the saddle's pommel with hands that had long ago lost sensation. As they'd ridden though the outskirts of the village, Mungo had wrapped a heavy arm around her, preventing her from being able to yank down the gag. When he'd released his grip at last, she'd removed the gag, but he'd only snorted. "No' a soul to hear ye scream anyway, wee one," he'd muttered in her ear.

Darkness stretched all around them like a nightmare. Time seemed to bend and twist freakishly. The snow muffled their horses' hoof falls, and the black trees surrounding them toyed with her mind. At every moment she thought she saw Reid's shadow, or the silhouette of another soul who could help her. But inevitably the outlines would turn to drooping pines or bare-limbed oaks.

Part of her prayed that Reid would come for her, that even now he was running her captors to the ground, hunting them down just as he'd hunted her every time she'd tried to escape him.

Ye willnae defeat me.

His voice, low and rough, filled her mind.

Yield. I willnae fail.

Reid's determination to see his mission through had been solid as stone. Back then, it had nigh crushed Corinne, for no matter how hard she struggled, how fiercely she fought, he could not be bested or deterred.

Deep in her heart, she knew that once he discovered her missing, he would use that same steely force of will to find her.

Yet that thought sent terror stabbing her chest, for he would be plowing right into a trap.

Mungo had made no effort to cover their tracks, despite the fact that the two horses left a clear trail through the snow. Flakes continued to fall softly, yet it would be hours—mayhap a full day—before their tracks were covered by the light snow. It only confirmed Corinne's worst fear—they were baiting Reid. With her.

Sometime in the darkest hours of night, Mungo reined in his horse within a copse of pines. Gellis did the same, sagging in the saddle. No doubt the woman wasn't used to such hard riding.

Gellis puffed a frosty breath. "Surely we can rest a moment."

Mungo grunted. "Only as long as it takes the horses

to drink." He flicked a hand toward a stream that trickled through the trees, its banks lined with snow.

Mungo dismounted, then dragged Corinne after him. Her feet felt like blocks of ice, yet she managed to stay upright due to Mungo's grip on her elbow.

"See to yer needs," he said. "But try aught, and I willnae hesitate to mark yer bonny face."

She swallowed, but then she forced herself to meet his beady eyes and stare him down defiantly.

He gave her a shove toward a large tree a few paces away, nearly sending her face-down into the snow. She stumbled toward the tree on wooden feet, holding her cloak tight around her.

If Mungo and Gellis hadn't already made a clear path behind them, she could have dragged her boots through the snow, or broken a few branches as she made her way to the tree. But that only played into Mungo's hand—and apparently into the MacVales' plan.

Aye, they wanted Reid to follow them. But mayhap there was some way she could warn him, alert him that he was walking into a trap.

As she ducked behind the wide tree, an idea sparked then kindled to life. Out of Gellis and Mungo's line of sight now, she dove her trembling, bound hands into the pocket of her cloak. Parchment crinkled against her fingers. She snatched the missive Gellis had given her— the one she'd used to lure Corinne away from the castle —from her cloak pocket.

But the missive itself wouldn't be enough. Her gaze darted around, landing on naught but a blanket of snow at her feet and the thick tree behind her. As her eyes rested on the thick pine bark, another idea struck.

Her fingers burned with cold, but she forced them to pry free a chunk of bark. Then she crouched in the snow, turning the folded missive so that the blank side faced her.

Knowing her time was running out, she wracked her mind wildly. What could she say to warn Reid? She began to scratch the most important word onto the parchment with the piece of bark, praying it would be enough.

"Just a little longer," Gellis pleaded a few paces away. Corinne's heart leapt to her throat as she hastily finished the last letter.

"Quit yer whining," Mungo snapped. "Else I'll leave ye behind. Ye arenae needed for this plan."

"Laird MacVale will skin ye alive if ye abandon me," Gellis replied, though her voice wavered with uncertainty.

Mungo apparently ignored her, for suddenly she heard the crunch of his boots in the snow as he approached.

Blood roaring in her ears, she crumpled the missive and shoved the ball of parchment into the divot where she'd pried off the hunk of bark. She threw the piece of bark into the snow just as Mungo rounded the edge of the tree.

"What are ye about?" he demanded, grabbing her by the arm.

"Naught," she cried as he dragged her out from behind the tree.

He eyed her for a moment, then without preamble, he backhanded her across the face. Stars exploded behind her eyes and she tasted blood in her mouth.

"I warned ye no' to try aught."

"I…I didn't," she breathed, her jaw aching and her lip burning where his knuckle had split it. Her mouth filling with the taste of metal, she bent and spat. The snow at her feet turned red with several drops of blood.

He grunted, but she couldn't tell if she'd convinced him or not. When he pulled her toward his waiting horse rather than investigating the back side of the tree, she let a shaking breath go.

Gellis mounted slowly, grumbling as she did. Mungo lifted Corinne into the saddle and swung up behind her. As they set off again, Corinne fought against the pain and fear that threatened to turn her numb. If she gave over to her terror, to the throbbing in her face and the ache in her hands and feet, she would fail Reid. She had to be strong for him, to do everything she could to warn him.

The hours became a blur of snow and darkness and pain. At last, a gray dawn began to break behind the iron clouds overhead and the snow let up.

From the direction of the diffuse light, Corinne could tell they still rode north. They crossed an open expanse blanketed in white, but then when they reached a wide, forking river, Mungo reined in once more.

"Why are ye stopping?" Gellis demanded, her face pulled into a scowl.

"We need to ensure that the Mackenzies will take the bait," Mungo snapped. "We'll continue deeper into

MacDonnell land, but then we'll double back through the river to be sure they follow our tracks north."

"Well, I'm resting then." Gellis dismounted with a groan and hobbled toward the slow-moving river.

"Five minutes," Mungo grumbled, dismounting as well.

Corinne's thoughts whirled to life once more despite the deadening cold and exhaustion encasing her mind. "I have to relieve my bladder again," she said as Mungo drew her down from the horse.

"Be quick about it," he muttered, releasing her and pointing to a large boulder next to the river.

Corinne shuffled to the far side of the snow-dusted rock. As soon as she was out of sight, however, she forced her limbs to move faster. She didn't have another piece of parchment to write on, so the ground would have to do.

She hastily scraped off the layer of snow covering the ground with her boot, then kicked away the loose rocks until she'd reached hard-packed dirt. Crouching, she grabbed one of the rocks in her bound hands and began scratching it against the frozen ground.

Her progress was painfully slow, with each line taking precious seconds as she struggled to mark the hard earth. An image of Reid being harmed or, God forbid, killed, kept her working furiously. She had to make sure he didn't follow their tracks farther north, had to warn him who was behind this scheme.

As she moved on to yet another letter, Gellis and Mungo's voices drifted to her.

"...have to waste time doubling back with her?"

Gellis was saying, her tone sour. "If we are dumping her body anyway, why no' just do it now and make haste back to MacVale land?"

Corinne sucked in a hard breath, the cold air stabbing her lungs. They didn't just mean to kill her—they meant to leave her body out in this desolate, frozen landscape. Now.

The rock fell from her shaking hands. Her warning to Reid would mean little if she were already dead when he found her. She was out of time. She had to run.

Lifting her skirts and cloak, she bolted from behind the boulder, headed away from the river. A clump of trees lay in the distance. If she could run fast enough… if she could just reach them…

She heard the muted footfalls in the snow behind her a heartbeat before someone slammed into her, taking her down. The air whooshed painfully from her lungs as a heavy body landed on top of her, crushing her into the snow.

"What did I tell ye, bitch?" Mungo hissed, rising above her with a snarl on his thick features. He yanked the dagger from his boot and pressed the tip just below her eye, the cold blade flush against her cheek.

A scream rose in her throat as the pressure increased.

"Mungo!" Gellis shouted behind him. "No' her face. The Mackenzie Laird needs to be able to recognize her."

Though the blade eased slightly, sickness rose in Corinne's throat. *Oh God! Please, nay!*

Then the dagger vanished completely and Mungo

stood. "I've had enough of yer interference, whore," he spat at Gellis. "I wasnae going to kill her yet, only scare her. And we cannae just dump her before we ensure that the Mackenzies will ride straight to the MacDonnell keep ready to go to war."

He dragged Corinne's crumpled body from the snow. "*Then* we can drop her anywhere we please on MacDonnell land. But if we dinnae do this right, Laird MacVale will have our heads."

Gellis cast a glance around, though the landscape was bare and silent. "I dinnae like it," she muttered, sparing a distasteful look at Corinne. "The longer she's alive, the more that can go wrong."

"Then quit yer pissing and moaning. Ye're slowing me down."

Gellis huffed, but she spun on her heels and made her way back to her waiting horse.

As Mungo strode to his own animal with Corinne in tow, he bent his head to her ear. "Try something foolish again and Gellis will have her way," he rasped.

Corinne nodded numbly, too terrified to speak. She was safe for now, she told herself over and over. They still had to ride north, as Mungo had said, then back down through the river. She had a few more hours to live—that might be all.

Through the stomach-churning fear, she held on to one last hope. Reid would find her message. She had to believe that.

Otherwise all would be lost.

Chapter Thirty-One

Reid dragged a hand over his face, willing his eyes to remain focused on the trail of horse hooves through the snow. The tracks looked fresher than they had an hour past. They were gaining ground, which meant he was closer to Corinne. And closer to whoever had taken her.

Ahead between the trees, the snow appeared disturbed. He leaned forward, squinting through the dark woods.

"Hold," he ordered as they came upon the churned snow. "They appear to have stopped here."

He swung down from his horse's back and searched the stirred ground, looking for any sign to give him hope that Corinne was unharmed. His gaze landed on a smattering of red in the snow nearby. *Blood.* He swore on all that was holy that if it was Corinne's, he would make her kidnappers pay one hundred-fold.

"The tracks continue north," Alain said from atop his horse, his gaze locked on the ground ahead of them.

Reid should have mounted then and pushed them all after the trail. He was closing in, he was sure of it. Yet something made him hesitate. Some instinct drew his gaze from the spots of blood to the two pairs of boot prints leading to a large pine tree. One set of prints was large and wide—a man's tracks. But the other was slim like a woman's.

Reid followed the prints to the tree. He scanned the area, but the tracks turned back the way they'd come. Naught seemed amiss.

Just as he turned away, his gaze caught on something off-white stuck into the tree's bark. He reached for it, and when he pulled it free, his heart leapt into his throat.

"I found something!" he called to the others. They dismounted and hurried to his side as he held up the bit of parchment.

With shaking hands, he unfolded the parchment and angled it to capture what weak light there was to be had amongst the night-dark trees. A knot of dread tightened in his stomach. It was addressed to Corinne.

"'I was sorry to hear of your decision to withhold your gift from God's service, but I understand that you must serve your husband and your new clan,'" Reid read aloud. This wasn't the first time someone had written to her? Inferring from the words, the writer had offered her a position as a scribe—which she'd turned down. For him.

He continued reading, but after a few more sentences, ice stole through his veins. Reid knew this area. He'd lived on Mackenzie land all his life and had traveled a great deal throughout Scotland in service of the Bruce.

There was no such place as Drumleigh Abbey.

He glanced up to find that the others had realized the same thing, for their faces were set in grim lines.

Reid hurriedly finished the missive, then lowered it. "This was a trap for Corinne," he rasped. "This is what they used to draw her away from the castle."

"Do ye suspect Father Ewan?" Alain asked softly.

"Nay," Reid replied without hesitation. "I imagine whoever arranged this simply used his name because they kenned Corinne would trust Father Ewan."

"Lady Corinne trusted Gellis, too," Hamond murmured. "That MacDonnell lady's maid was the last person seen with her."

That, paired with the scrap of MacDonnell plaid next to the lock of Corinne's hair, made it seem all the more likely that the MacDonnells had something to do with this. It made no sense, just as Alain had said, but Reid couldn't think rationally knowing that Corinne was in danger.

He crushed the sheet of parchment in his fist, but as it crinkled, a marking on the other side caught his eye. He turned the parchment over, and the air in his lungs froze.

Though the script was coarse, he would recognize Corinne's hand anywhere. Only a single word had been scratched onto the parchment.

Trap.

The others must have followed his gaze, for Hamond

let out a slow breath and Alain and Leith each muttered a curse.

"It still doesnae make sense for the MacDonnells to kidnap Corinne," Alain said, clearly attempting to level all of their heads. "But even if they did, they are only leading us deeper into MacDonnell land." He nodded toward the tracks that continued northward. "If this is some sort of trap, we'll be riding right into it, with four men against however many they'll have."

A distant voice whispered that Alain was right, but Reid didn't care. There would be no stopping him now. The parchment was proof that Corinne was still alive—or at least that she'd been alive a few hours past. He would ride straight into Lucifer's mouth to save her.

"We'll stay on the alert," Reid said, striding back toward his horse. "But we'll follow the tracks."

Even if Alain and the others had doubts, none of them hesitated. They mounted up swiftly and set out once more. Their loyalty to him, and their dedication to saving Corinne, was one sliver of light cutting through the black fears that consumed Reid as they rode through the night.

WHEN DAWN BROKE and the snow stopped falling, Reid pushed them even harder. But it was two more hours until he saw another sign that had him reining in his horse.

The River Elchaig cut across the flat, white-coated plain over which they'd been riding. Where it forked, the trail of hoof prints was muddled once more, indicating that Corinne's kidnappers had stopped again.

He and the others dismounted, scanning the ground for clues.

"It looks like there was a scuffle here," Leith called a dozen paces away. At his feet, the snow had been flattened.

Reid swallowed hard, keeping a tight leash on his thoughts lest he spiral into a rage over what the churned snow might indicate. He followed the same woman's footprints to a large rock near the river. He found more disturbed ground, but this time the snow had been pushed away completely from a little patch of dirt.

"Someone must have cleared that since the snow stopped falling," Alain said, joining his side. "That was...two hours past."

Reid's heart surged. They were still gaining ground. He crouched, looking closer at the hard-packed dirt.

"What in..."

Ever so faintly, something had been carved into the frozen ground.

"M. A. C..."

Alain leaned closer, squinting at the lettering.

Confusion swamped Reid as he stared at the final marking. "What is that?" It should have been a D for MacDonnell, yet only the downward slash of the letter had been made, and it was at an angle, cutting away from the first three letters.

"It isnae the MacDonnells," Alain said, his eyes going wide. "That is half of a V—for MacVale."

Realization slammed so hard into Reid that he felt like he'd been punched in the gut.

"Of course," he breathed.

He'd been a fool, blinded by fear and rage at the thought of Corrine being hurt. But just as Alain had said, everything pointed too obviously toward the MacDonnells when there was no cause for them to take Corinne.

The MacVales, on the other hand, had everything to gain from the situation. Though Reid had never met the MacVale Laird, Arthur MacDonnell had spoken vehemently against Serlon MacVale many a time. The man was manipulative, deceitful, and most of all greedy, according to MacDonnell.

If he chose, Laird MacVale could ransom Corinne back to Reid, thus hobbling the Mackenzie clan in terms of coin and supplies, which would force Reid to withdraw his aid to the MacDonnells. Some instinct told him that MacVale likely wouldn't stop there, however. He had sown discontent along his border with the MacDonnells for decades now. He would undoubtedly seek to strike his enemies—and their allies—with a far greater blow.

"If he wants a war, he'll have one," Reid bit out, staring at the ground.

Just then, Hamond and Leith arrived at his side. Alain quickly explained what they'd found—another message from Corinne that just might save an alliance, not to mention many men's lives.

"But the trail continues north, right toward the MacDonnell keep," Leith said, pointing to the fork of the river that wound northward. Sure enough, two sets of tracks edged the river.

Yet instinct told Reid that the MacVales who'd kidnapped Corinne wouldn't risk going farther into MacDonnell land in broad daylight. To the east lay MacVale land—and Corinne, he was certain.

"Leith, ye and Hamond ride north," Reid ordered. "Get to the MacDonnell keep as fast as ye can and tell the Laird what is afoot. The MacVales have Corinne and are trying to incite a war between the MacDonnells and Mackenzies."

Leith and Hamond nodded and hustled to their horses.

"And what of ye and I?" Alain asked, his voice low.

"We ride for MacVale land."

Chapter Thirty-Two

"Shite," Mungo growled behind Corinne.

He'd halted their horses in a clump of trees at the top of a rise overlooking the valley where the river forked. In the distance, Corinne could see two horses riding hard northward, where Mungo had laid a trail and then doubled back through the wide, slow river.

And another two riders headed east. Right toward where they hid in the trees.

Corinne's heart soared. Even from this distance, she could see the blue and green Mackenzie plaid flashing beneath the men's cloaks. They were coming after her. And they must have found her messages, for they weren't duped by Mungo's false tracks.

"How could they ken to ride east?" Gellis hissed, her gaze fixed on the riders. She rounded on Corinne. "Ye did something, didnae ye, ye little bitch! Ye've put us all in danger, and Laird MacVale as well."

She lashed out at Corinne, her fingers curled into claws, but Mungo caught her wrist.

"Stop wasting time," he snapped.

"We should finish her," Gellis retorted, twisting her hand away. "Leave her body here. We are still on MacDonnell land, and—"

"If I have to tell ye again no' to interfere, I'll cut yer tongue from your mouth, whore," Mungo said. "Ye overstep yerself. It isnae yer place to make decisions."

"And it is yers?" Gellis breathed frostily. "Just because the Laird made ye a few promises and gave ye a wee taste of power doesnae mean ye are—"

Mungo hit Gellis across the face, nearly sending her toppling out of the saddle.

"Ye need to learn yer place," he said. "For I ken mine." He shifted behind Corinne, glancing once more in the distance at the approaching riders. "This is Laird MacVale's decision to make, no' ours. He can do with the English bitch as he likes—and those two Mackenzies as well. We best no' keep him waiting at the border."

Without acknowledging Gellis again, he urged his horse into motion, leaving the lady's maid to scramble to right herself and hurry after them.

THOUGH THE TREES surrounding them looked the same to Corinne, Mungo must have been able to see an imperceptible difference. He brought his fingers to his lips and whistled. In the distance, an answering whistle sounded.

Corinne clutched the pommel frantically as Mungo kicked his horse into a gallop over the slippery snow. Ahead, a clearing appeared—a clearing filled with half a dozen mounted men.

"What took ye so long?" the man at the front of the group snapped testily as Mungo and Gellis's horses approached. But when his dark, cold eyes landed on Corinne, his annoyance turned to rage.

"Why the bloody hell did ye bring her to me?" he roared at Mungo. "Ye were supposed to make it look like the MacDonnells killed her, no' leave a trail right to my lands!"

Corinne felt her eyes go wide on the large, broad-chested man wearing a brown and green plaid beneath his cloak. He must be Laird MacVale himself.

Mungo reined in a few paces away, with Gellis lingering at the edge of the group.

"They didnae take the bait," Mungo replied tersely. "Two Mackenzies followed us east."

"What?" the Laird hissed. He huffed a frosty breath, dragging a hand across his silver-slashed black hair, visibly trying to regain control.

This close, Corinne could see every weathered line of the Laird's hard-set face. Unease slithered up her spine and pricked at the nape of her neck. There was something… disconcertingly familiar about the Laird.

His downturned mouth was a firm line across his face. A shadow of dark stubble covered his angular jaw. Though his eyes were nigh black, they were a similar shape as…

Nay. Corinne swayed in the saddle as the world seemed to tilt on its side. Nay, it couldn't be.

Laird MacVale's voice, deep and rough, dragged her from her spinning thoughts.

"How could they have kenned to ride east?" he demanded, staring hard at Mungo.

"*She* may have done something, my love," Gellis interjected from the fringes.

"Dinnae deign to be so familiar with me, woman," the Laird snapped.

Gellis blinked, her brown eyes filling with tears. "I-I am sorry, Laird."

Laird MacVale swiveled to Corinne, fixing her with a look.

"What am I to do with her?"

"I wasnae sure, Laird," Mungo said. "But if naught else, ye can use her to lay a trap for the approaching Mackenzies."

Laird MacVale's dark eyes sparked at that. "Now ye are thinking like a Laird, Mungo."

"Nay!" Corinne cried, unable to hold back any longer. For a fleeting moment, she'd believed that fate had turned in her favor. Her messages had reached the Mackenzies pursuing her. Help was on the way.

Her hopes shattered to a thousand pieces as a slow smile broke over Laird MacVale's face.

"Oh aye," he said. "She'll make excellent bait."

WHEN REID and Alain had discovered the tracks at the

286

top of the rise overlooking the river valley, they urged their horses as fast as they dared over the snowy ground. Someone had gone to a great deal of trouble creating a trail to the north, doubling back, and circling to the top of the ridge. And the fact that the tracks led due east, the shortest distance to the MacVale border, only confirmed Corinne's message.

Reid fought to control his emotions, but the rage boiling inside him at what the MacVales were about—kidnapping Corinne, framing the MacDonnells, attempting to incite a war—left him nigh blinded.

He told himself over and over as they rode that Corinne was alive, that her bravery and courage would keep her strong. And that she'd maintained her wits enough in an undoubtedly terrifying situation to send him not one, but two messages. He could only pray that he had half her strength and level-headedness when he caught up to her kidnappers.

Strength, aye. But, he amended, no amount of praying would keep him calm when he faced her abductors.

Ahead, something caught his eye in a small clearing between the trees. Was it a stump? He stared hard. Nay, it was a crouched figure—a figure who was lifting her flame-red head.

"Corinne!" He kicked his horse faster for another dozen paces, but then he flung himself from the animal's back and scrambled across the remaining distance.

"Reid!" she cried, reaching for him. "It's a—"

Behind him, Alain's pained bellow cut her off. Reid

turned to find his friend sliding from his horse, an arrow protruding from his chest.

The clearing was suddenly swarming with men, swords drawn and descending on Reid. He counted six as he lurched to his feet, yanking his sword from its sheath. Another man appeared from the woods with a drawn arrow poised in his bow.

Reid placed himself between Corinne and the archer, but the others with swords circled them, closing in.

Corinne's scream behind him had him whirling, sword raised. But what he saw froze him in his tracks.

A giant of a man had dragged Corinne to her feet, a dagger held at her throat.

"Drop yer sword," a commanding voice boomed from the trees. A man stepped forward, his dark head tilted as he assessed Reid.

When Reid didn't move, the man nodded toward the giant holding Corinne. The giant pressed the blade into her skin, making her cry out.

Desperation clawing at him, Reid released the sword. It fell with a muted thump in the snow.

"The Laird of the Mackenzies himself has come after his English bride," the dark-headed man said, approaching slowly. "I am impressed—by yer foolishness if naught else. On yer knees."

Grudgingly, Reid bent a knee and knelt down.

"Bind him," the man commanded one of his warriors. Reid's hands were roughly pulled behind him and tied with coarse rope. All the while, he kept his gaze fixed on the apparent leader.

"Ye MacVales," Reid ground out. "All ye do is steal, dinnae ye? Steal MacDonnell sheep, steal from the King's cause by refusing to join him, and now ye steal my wife."

The leader came to a halt in front of Reid, looming over him. The man tipped his gray-tinged head as if considering Reid's words, but his dark eyes glittered with venom.

"Come now, Laird," he said softly. "Is that any way to speak to yer father?"

Chapter Thirty-Three

Reid felt as though the ground had opened beneath him and he was spiraling into an endless pit.

"Ye…" His own voice sounded distant to his ears. "Ye arenae my father."

But even as he said it, he knew deep in his bones that the man spoke the truth. Reid's eyes were like his mother's, the same steely gray Brinda had given to Logan and Mairin. Yet the man before him had Reid's coloring, his mouth, his jawline…it was like looking at a warped likeness of himself, a reflection seen on the rippling surface of a loch.

"We meet at last," the man said, staring down at Reid where he knelt in the snow. "I had always wondered if ye took more after me or Brinda. It is a miracle ye didnae realize it sooner, but as I said, ye seem a fool."

"How?" Reid breathed, hardly registering the man's cruel words.

The man lifted one shoulder. "It was easy enough to snatch yer mother during one of her beloved rides in the months before her wedding to Murdoch Mackenzie. Her family's farm was close to my border, ye ken."

His border? The wheels in Reid's mind turned slowly. Could this man be...?

"Laird Serlon MacVale."

Serlon paused at the interruption, but tilted his head in acknowledgement. "Ye should be proud," he said coolly. "Though ye were bastard-born, ye are still the son of a Laird."

Reid surged to his feet, struggling against the rope holding his hands behind his back. "What did ye do to my mother?" he bellowed, spit flying in Serlon's face.

Two of Serlon's warriors took him by the elbows and kicked his knees out from under him, forcing him to the ground once more.

"I fucked her a few times, hoping that sullying her would be enough to end the alliance between the Mackenzies and the MacDonnells," Serlon said evenly. "But when I released her, the bitch didnae open her mouth and confess to Murdoch that she had been ruined. Her pregnancy should have done the trick even with her continued silence, yet for some reason Murdoch accepted ye as his own."

Reid wanted to vomit. He wanted to scream. He wanted to tear Serlon MacVale apart bit by bit with naught but his hands and teeth.

He tried to bolt to his feet once more, but the MacVale warriors held him fast.

"And Euna..." Serlon clucked his tongue. "Her death should have thwarted yer alliance as well. Gellis here was sent with the express task of putting an end to it." He motioned to the trees, and for the first time Reid noticed the lady's maid huddling next to a horse.

She took a few cautious steps forward. "I did everything ye asked, Laird," she said. "I waited until she was pregnant, I put the poison in her wine——"

Reid felt bile rising in the back of his throat. Harmless, innocent Euna and their unborn bairn had been poisoned at his own father's command.

"Enough," Serlon snapped, cutting Gellis off. "Ye were supposed to break the alliance, but ye didnae, did ye?"

Gellis shrank back, hunching into her shoulders.

"And then I got word that ye'd married some English chit," Serlon went on, waving over his shoulder at Corinne. She stood stiff as a board with the knife to her throat, her eyes round and wet with terrified tears.

"I drank to yer marriage," Serlon continued, "for I couldnae have planned things better myself. But ye somehow managed to convince that old fool MacDonnell to remain allied with ye. I realized I needed to take matters into my own hands. So ye see," he said, fixing Reid with a hard look. "I am no' some petty thief. I didnae just steal yer mother's innocence, nor yer wife and bairn, nor yer new bride. I have *worked* for this year after year, decade after decade."

His dark eyes glittered. "And now at last I'll have what I've worked so hard for. I'll have my war."

"Why?" Reid demanded.

Serlon lifted one brow. "Chaos breeds opportunity," he replied with a grim quirk of his lips.

Of course. If Serlon could set the MacDonnells and Mackenzies at each other's throats, no one would pay attention to the MacVales. He could reive and poach as much as he wanted.

Serlon's words were disturbingly similar to something the Bruce had told Reid. *It's what I'm good at*, the Bruce had said. *Creating a stir and then making the most of it.* Yet the Bruce was fighting for the freedom of all Scottish people from English tyranny. Serlon MacVale fought only for himself.

"Aye, ye'll have yer war," Reid rasped. "For I willnae stop until every last MacVale is wiped from this land for what ye've done. As will the MacDonnells. I sent two of my men to the MacDonnell keep to tell them what ye are about. No doubt they'll arrive shortly, and I imagine they'll be eager to gut ye for attempting to frame them."

For the first time, Serlon's gaze faltered. He shot a look to the giant holding Corinne.

"Is that true?" he demanded.

The giant lifted one shoulder, dropping his eyes. "When Mackenzie and the other rode east, two more headed north."

"Ye fool, Mungo!" Serlon hissed. "Why didnae ye tell me before? I wouldnae have stood here blathering if I'd kenned that—"

"Laird," the archer said, jogging toward them

through the trees. Reid hadn't noticed the man slip away, but now that he returned, his face was red from exertion and cold. "From the ridge to the west I saw a band of MacDonnells approaching. They are mayhap an hour away."

"How many?" Serlon snapped.

"Two score, mayhap more."

"*Shite.*"

"Ye wanted war," Reid said, glowering up at Serlon. "Now ye'll have it."

"Shut yer mouth," Serlon barked. "I need to think."

Taking advantage of Serlon's sudden agitation, Reid continued. "Everyone kens what ye did, MacVale. The ruse is up. Ye cannae face two score MacDonnell warriors, let alone the might of the Mackenzie clan when I bring my wrath upon ye."

"I said shut yer mouth!"

Serlon drove his fist into Reid's jaw, making his head snap back. Reid spat blood and let a low, harsh laugh rise from his throat.

"Ye're as good as dead." Though Reid wasn't as certain as his words, he had to keep Serlon off-balance until he could find a way to get Corinne to safety.

Ignoring Reid, Serlon's eyes searched the surrounding trees in thought. "We'll lay a trap for them," he said, the wheels of his mind turning behind his dark eyes. "Just as we did for Mackenzie here. We'll draw them farther onto MacVale land using Mackenzie as bait. But when we reach the keep, we'll outnumber them four to one."

"What of that one?" the giant called Mungo said, nodding behind Reid.

Reid twisted his head, his gaze landing on Alain. Blessedly, his friend's chest still rose and fell shallowly. The arrow protruding from his torso hadn't killed him—yet.

"Leave him," Serlon answered. "He can tell the MacDonnells that we have Mackenzie on MacVale land —if he lives."

"Laird," Gellis said tentatively. "This is a dangerous plan. If ye make all-out war with the MacDonnells—"

"I didnae ask for yer opinion, woman," Serlon cut in.

Gellis's gaze darted around the clearing. "But the MacDonnells—"

"Are ye loyal to yer precious MacDonnells, or are ye loyal to me?" Serlon roared.

"Ye, Laird," Gellis said quickly, her brown eyes rounding.

"Come here, then."

Gellis cautiously moved forward, ducking her chin but watching Serlon like a beggar watched a wealthy man reaching for his coin.

When she halted before him, he took hold of her chin, leveling her with a hard look. Suddenly he yanked a dagger from his belt and slashed it across Gellis's throat.

A bright red ribbon of blood shot from Gellis's neck. Her eyes bulged and she made a gurgling noise as she sank to her knees in the snow.

"S-Serlon," she hissed with her last breath, staring up at him in horror.

"I warned ye no' to be so familiar with me," he murmured, pushing her the rest of the way down with his boot.

As her blood darkened the snow and her eyes glassed over in death, Serlon stood over her for a moment. "Worthless whore," he said flatly, turning back to Reid.

Reid met his gaze unflinchingly, but sickness once again crashed over him, threatening to tear asunder the last of Reid's control. He bore no sympathy for Gellis, for she'd done evil in Serlon's name, yet Serlon was the true monster.

His father.

How long had he yearned to know the man who had given him life, who shared the same blood as Reid? He'd once thought that knowing his blood sire would close some door that had been left ajar deep in his heart. He'd thought it would end the nagging anxiety he felt about his legitimacy, his origins.

But instead of closing a door, it was as if it had been thrown open to reveal a world of nightmarish horrors. Instead of soothing his anxiety and laying to rest his doubts, he was cast into the heart of a storm, no longer knowing up from down.

Reid had this man's jaw, his dark hair, the shape of his eyes. What else had he inherited from this demon? Did he hold the capacity for such hatred, such destruction and greed, in his own soul?

Serlon stared down at Reid, his hard features unreadable. Mayhap he was contemplating the same thing—what sort of man was his son, whom he'd never met, yet who shared his blood?

"Laird," the archer murmured urgently, dragging Serlon's attention away at last. "We must move if we hope to make it back to the keep before the MacDonnells reach us."

Serlon drew the sword on his hip and turned back to Reid. For a terrible heartbeat, Reid thought Serlon had changed his mind about using Reid as bait. His gaze sought Corinne's. If naught else, Reid had done one good thing that Serlon's darkness could never touch—he'd loved Corinne.

But then Serlon turned his sword and brought down the hilt instead of the blade. The hilt made contact with Reid's head, and the world turned black.

Chapter Thirty-Four

A s they rode, the clouds scuttled away and the sun burst forth over the white-blanketed land. The snow glittered like a million diamonds. It was nigh blinding in its beauty, yet Corinne could stare at naught but Reid, terror filling her.

He sat slumped forward in the saddle. His head, which drooped nearly to the horse's neck, bobbed loosely with the animal's steps. His hands remained bound behind his back, and one of Serlon's men had lashed his legs together with a length of rope underneath the horse's belly.

Corinne prayed that he did not slip from the saddle, for if he did, he would be dragged along the ground, tied as he was. She prayed that he would wake soon, that his head would stop bleeding where Serlon had hit him with his sword.

But most of all, she prayed that no matter what happened, she be granted another look into Reid's stormy gray eyes. That she be able to tell him she loved him one more time. That he would enfold her in his arms and she'd know they would be safe.

The sun marked the passage of morning to midday, its cheerful progression across the blue sky a cruel contrast to the darkness squeezing Corinne's heart as she watched Reid.

At last, he stirred, groaning.

"Reid!" she breathed.

"Quiet," Mungo snapped behind her.

The MacVale warrior holding Reid's horse's reins looked at him, then rose his voice to Serlon. "He's awakening, Laird."

Serlon guided his horse closer to Reid's. "Ye are a strong one, arenae ye?" he muttered. "I wish my other son was more like ye."

Reid lifted his head, his eyes clouded and bleary, a muscle jumping in his jaw. "Ye have another son?" he asked tightly. No doubt he was in a great deal of pain from the blow he'd received.

"Aye," Serlon replied, his gaze traveling over the sparkling landscape. "Ye'll meet him soon enough."

He kicked his horse into a trot, and the others hastened after him. Corinne's gaze followed the direction he rode, her eyes landing on a dark smudge against the white plain. A tower rose in the distance. It must be the MacVale keep.

Heart leaping to her throat, she turned to Reid once more. He squeezed his horse tight with his knees, managing to keep his seat in the saddle even as he grimaced with each jarring step.

The chance of a miracle, some way to break free and escape, had dwindled to nearly naught. There was no more time to plot a getaway, to plan a daring flight. There was only the two of them, Reid bleeding and hurt, and she held immobile in Mungo's crushing grip. All this time, she'd survived on little more than hope, but now she had to face the truth.

Once they reached the MacVale keep, the MacDonnells couldn't save them. No one could.

REID CLENCHED his teeth against the agony that jolted through his skull like a hammer strike with each of the horse's steps. He forced his eyes to remain focused on the keep they drew toward, for if he looked at Corinne again, he would see the fear in her eyes, the bruise darkening her cheek, and the split in her lip, and rage would consume what little of his wits he had left.

He had another brother somewhere behind those towering stone walls. It had been nigh two days of panic, pain, and shock, yet that revelation was mayhap the most staggering of all.

He'd sworn to Serlon that he would wipe out the MacVales once and for all for his actions. Could he stand not only against his father, but against a brother he didn't know?

Reid cursed silently, squeezing his eyes shut against the pain for a long moment. For all that he'd threatened Serlon, he was completely at the man's mercy. If it was only himself, he might have tried to escape, to spook his horse and make a break for it. But he had no doubt that Serlon would hurt Corinne to punish him.

The MacVale keep now loomed before them. It was a single tower, dark and severe against the sharp blue sky, surrounded by a circular stone curtain wall. Along the wall, Reid could make out several men in the green and brown MacVale plaid watching their approach across the snowy moor.

The MacVales inside the keep continued to stare down at them, but to Reid's surprise, the portcullis hadn't begun to rise by the time they'd halted before the gates.

"Open up!" Serlon bellowed, glaring at the battlements overhead.

A strange silence was the only response.

"I am yer Laird!" Serlon shouted. His horse danced sideways at his angry tone, but still the portcullis didn't move.

"Nay," came a loud, clear voice from the wall. "Ye arenae. No' anymore."

A ripple of confusion traveled through the half dozen MacVales surrounding Serlon. Reid felt his aching jaw slacken. What in...

"Fillan," Serlon hissed, his gaze fixed on the spot where the voice had come from. "Ye sniveling wee cripple, what have ye done?"

A dark brown head appeared on the battlements. Even from this distance, Reid knew.

It was his brother.

He pulled in a hard breath as their gazes connected

and he saw recognition mirrored in the young man's keen eyes.

Fillan's gaze shifted to Corinne, his features hardening before returning to Serlon.

"I have done what ye should have long ago, Father," he said, his voice steady and cold. "I recognized that our people have been starving—for food, aye, but for leadership as well."

"Open the gate," Serlon roared, "else I'll rip off that club leg of yers and beat ye to hell with it!"

"Nay," Fillan snapped icily. "Ye willnae hurt me—or our people—anymore. Ye've nearly destroyed the clan in yer quest for war and chaos. But while ye have been scheming against the MacDonnells and Mackenzies, I've been plotting as well."

Fillan tilted his head to the left, then the right. "These arenae yer men anymore. This isnae yer keep, nor yer land. And ye are no' our Laird."

A chorus of shouts rose from the battlements and inside the wall, drowning out Serlon's enraged reply. The man's face was beginning to turn deep red.

"This is treason," Serlon spat. "I am the Laird. Ye cannae—"

"*Ye* are the treasonous one," Fillan cut in. "Ye've starved us, beaten us into submission, and taken our honor. The clan willnae stand for yer warmongering any longer."

Sensing an opportunity, Reid raised his voice. "I am Laird Reid Mackenzie. Serlon MacVale kidnapped my wife and attempted to frame the MacDonnells for it." Even before the murmurs of discontent subsided from within the keep, he went on. "He failed, for the MacDonnells now ken what he was about. A war party is riding toward the keep even as we speak, ready to bring down the hammer on the MacVales for what Serlon has done."

The rumble of displeasure turned to shock as the MacVales learned just how much harm Serlon had done.

Serlon reined his horse toward Reid, drawing his sword as he went. "I told ye to shut yer mouth!"

With no hope of defending himself, all Reid could do was lurch to the side. He would have toppled from the saddle, but the rope that bound his legs under the horse's middle held him suspended, forcing him to dangle sideways.

Serlon's blade slashed across his exposed calf. Reid only had a moment to feel the burn of the cut when suddenly his legs were freed and he fell the rest of the way to the ground. Though Serlon's sword had opened his flesh, it had also cut the rope binding him.

Bellowing a curse, Serlon yanked on his reins, trying to wheel his horse around to where Reid lay in the snow.

"Halt!" Fillan shouted from the battlements. "Ye've already set the MacDonnells against us. Ye willnae harm the Mackenzie Laird also."

"Try and stop me, ye ungrateful—"

"This is an act of war against the MacVales," Fillan called. "Put up yer sword or die where ye stand."

Serlon froze, his sword raised over Reid. His dark eyes blazed with fury as he turned to his men. "Attack the keep!" he cried.

His warriors stared at him, stunned.

"How, Laird?" the archer said, his eyes wide.

"Ye fools!" Serlon snapped, turning away from Reid. He kicked his horse to the archer's side. "Draw yer weapons! Use yer bow, Paider. Attack! They threatened yer Laird!"

"Dinnae," Fillan boomed in warning.

Sensing that the situation was about to explode in disaster, Reid shoved himself upright, his gaze locking on Corinne. She still sat perched in the saddle, one of Mungo's thick arms wrapped around her and her hands bound before her.

"Corinne," he said, willing his voice to be steady.

Her gaze snapped to him, her eyes so wide he could see the whites all around their blue-green depths. He flashed his teeth at her, then jutted his chin toward Mungo.

Just as Paider hesitantly lifted his bow toward the keep, he gave Corinne a single nod.

And then all hell broke loose.

Chapter Thirty-Five

Time seemed to stand still as Corinne's eyes met Reid's. She understood what he intended for her to do, yet her heart screamed that she couldn't.

He meant for her to break free, to get herself to safety somehow—without making a plan for himself. He was sacrificing himself for her.

Just as time had ground to a halt, suddenly it leapt forward and everything raced at a terrifying speed.

Out of the corner of her eye, she saw the MacVale archer lift his bow. On the wall, Fillan raised his arm, and all at once the battlements bristled with more than a score of arrows—all drawn and aimed at their little group at the base of the keep.

"Now!" Reid's shout tore through her mind. There was no more time to think, to fear. Only to act.

She sank her teeth into Mungo's arm so hard that her mouth filled with his blood. He roared in pain, swatting her away with such force that she went sailing from the horse's back.

She landed several feet away, the air slamming from her lungs at the impact. The layer of snow had likely saved her from a broken neck, yet her body screamed in agony as she struggled to draw a breath.

"Run, Corinne!" Reid shouted somewhere behind her.

Just then, she heard the thunk of bowstrings snapping, and the whir of nearly two dozen arrows slicing through the air—right at her.

She staggered to her feet as the arrows began to rain down all around them. Several made contact with the MacVale warriors loyal to Serlon, while others sank into the snow.

But when she scanned the chaos for Reid, her heart squeezed as if crushed by a fist.

He'd dragged himself to his feet, his hands still tied behind him. Arrows hailed all around him, blackening the air as they fell with deadly impact.

Part of her mind screamed at her to run, to do as Reid had said and get herself away. Yet another part irrationally tried to tug her through the storm of arrows toward Reid.

"Corinne!" he shouted again, and then he was running for her.

Heedless of the falling arrows, he bolted straight at her. Blood poured from his left calf where Serlon had cut him, but he didn't seem to notice. He didn't slow as he drew nearer. Instead, he plowed right into her, bringing them both to the ground and sending the air from her lungs once more.

He hunched over her, using his body as a shield as the arrows continued to shower down all around them, driving with muffled thumps into the snow. Distantly, she heard men's screams as they were hit, then the muted thuds of their bodies hitting the ground.

Slowly, the arrows stopped and an eerie silence fell, broken only by Reid's breath in her ear. Even when she heard the creak of the keep's gates and the groan of the portcullis being raised, Reid remained motionless above her, protecting her with naught but his unarmored back.

"Laird Mackenzie." Distantly, she recognized Fillan's voice as he approached slowly from behind them.

At last, Reid lifted his head and rose to his knees, but he still positioned himself between Corinne and the MacVales that approached from the keep.

Fillan limped before a group of a dozen warriors, his foot dragging in the snow. He gripped a wooden cane in one hand, but when Reid stood before Corinne, Fillan held up his other hand to show that he bore no weapon.

"Free their hands," he ordered one of the men behind him.

A MacVale approached cautiously, holding a dagger with its tip upward to show he meant no harm.

Grudgingly, Reid turned his shoulders but kept his narrowed gaze on the MacVale as he sawed through the rope binding his hands behind his back. When he was free, he snatched the dagger and cut Corinne's bindings himself.

"I ken ye dinnae trust us, and rightly so," Fillan said,

coming to a halt several paces away. "But we mean ye no harm. In fact, I plan to work hard to undo the sins of my father. And it begins here."

To Corinne's shock, Fillan awkwardly lowered himself to his knees before them, clutching his cane to steady himself.

"I must beg yer forgiveness, Lady Corinne. I was the one who wrote ye those missives, pretending to be Brother Michael to lure ye from safety."

Corinne sucked in a breath. "Why?"

Fillan bowed his dark head. "My father forced me to copy down his words. That isnae an excuse for all he did to ye, though—and my part in it."

This close, Corinne now saw the shadow of bruises on Fillan's youthful face. Some had faded to yellow, while others were dark purple.

She knew what it meant to be hurt by someone who was supposed to love her, what it was like to be bent to another's will by pain and force. Her father had terrorized her just as surely as Serlon had apparently terrorized Fillan.

"I forgive you," she said, meeting Fillan's surprised eyes when he lifted his head.

"My forgiveness willnae be so easily won," Reid bit out, staring at Fillan. "Explain yerself."

Fillan pulled himself to standing by his cane. "It is as I told my father. He let his quest for war blind him to the hardships his people struggled under. Many of our men have ceased farming over the years, relying on reiving for sheep and cattle or stealing MacDonnell grain. But when they could not steal, we starved."

Several of the men behind Fillan nodded.

"Besides the few warriors that my father favored, our people grew weak—and no' just from lack of food. We have been isolated these long years, without an ally or friend, and no' even loyal to the King. My father believed that might made right, that only our warriors' strength mattered. He forgot that a clan needs more than swords to live on—it needs hope, and pride, and honor."

"Aye," the MacVale warriors murmured.

"While my father turned a blind eye to his people, I have worked to sow new seeds—that the MacVale name can be carried proudly in the future, but only if we change." Fillan lifted one slim shoulder. "While he was away reaping war and hurting innocents," he said, nodding toward Corinne, "I told the clan the time to act was now. They agreed."

He leveled Reid with his keen, intelligent gaze. "Now I can only hope to convince ye of the same, Laird Mackenzie. What my father did should by rights put the Mackenzies at war with the MacVales. Yet I would beg ye to give us a chance to prove that we dinnae have to follow the path Serlon MacVale set us on."

Reid opened his mouth, but just as he was about to speak, Corinne felt the ground begin to rumble beneath her boots.

A voice rose from the battlements. "MacDonnells approach!"

Chapter Thirty-Six

R eid spun around, ignoring the screaming pain in his leg, then pulled Corinne behind him. With a curse, he squared himself to the band of MacDonnells barreling down on the MacVale keep.

"Inside, everyone!" Fillan shouted.

"Nay!" Reid barked, making Fillan freeze. "We'll face them without a stone wall between us. This must end now if there can ever be peace."

A shadow fell over Fillan's eyes. Clearly, he was unsure if Reid meant to let the MacDonnells cut the MacVales down for what Serlon had done, or allow the MacVales another chance.

In truth, Reid wasn't sure either, but he could only hope that the right decision would become clear before something irreversible happened.

The MacDonnells approached in a flurry of snow kicked up by their galloping horses' hooves. To Reid's surprise, he made out Laird MacDonnell himself at the lead, his sword already drawn as they closed in.

"Hold!" Reid bellowed, raising both hands at the MacDonnells.

The Laird and the others reined in, their horses' breaths puffing white in the chilly air.

"Thank God ye are alive, Mackenzie," MacDonnell said, his gray beard quivering with rage. "Now move aside. The MacVales have made their last mistake."

"Aye, we have," Fillan said. "I can assure ye that without Serlon as our Laird, we willnae wrong ye or yer people again."

Laird MacDonnell's eyes rounded as they fell on Fillan. "What in the—"

Fillan repeated what he'd told Reid—of Serlon's cruelty and blindness, the MacVales' suffering, and the hope for a new direction under Fillan's leadership.

MacDonnell turned a disbelieving stare on Reid. "Dinnae tell me ye are buying this rubbish. Yer men Hamond and Leith told me about MacVale's skullduggery in kidnapping yer bride."

He waved toward the back of his retinue, and Reid's gaze landed on Leith and Hamond. They each gave him a nod of reassurance.

MacDonnell turned back to Reid and seemed to notice Corinne behind him for the first time. "Praise Heaven she is well."

"Did ye come across my man Alain?" Reid said, his gut twisting in fear for his friend.

"Aye, aye," MacDonnell replied quickly. "He was alive when we found him. I sent him back to my keep with two of my men so that he could be seen by a healer." The Laird's mouth turned down even more behind his beard. "We also found the body of Gellis MacDonnell, whom I am ashamed to call a former clanswoman. But yer man is in good hands now."

Reid let a breath go, but the moment of relief was short-lived.

"Enough talk, Mackenzie," MacDonnell ground out, his gaze shifting to Fillan and the MacVales outside the keep. "Stand aside so that I can finish what these bloody MacVales started."

At MacDonnell's words, several of the MacVales reached for their swords, but Fillan held up a hand to stay them.

"Yer anger is justified, Laird," he said. "But the men responsible for the majority of the trouble lie dead before ye."

Fillan swept a hand over the arrow-pocked snow surrounding them, and at last Reid let himself truly look at the destruction.

The ground bristled with arrows—and bodies. Mungo lay on his back, an arrow through his eye. The other MacVales who had followed Serlon lay crumpled and bloody in the snow. Most of the horses had fled in terror when their riders had been picked off, but a few lingered, one with a wound to his shoulder.

When Reid's gaze landed on Serlon, he went taut. His father lay face-up, his eyes wide and unseeing. A snarl twisted his features, so like Reid's, in an eternal grimace. Five arrows protruded from his chest, pinning him in the blood-churned snow beneath the keep he'd once called his own.

A hush fell over all those gathered as they surveyed the carnage and ruin Serlon had brought to himself and his men. At last, Reid felt Corinne's soft hand on his shoulder, and he pulled his gaze away.

For the first time since he'd arrived, a shadow of doubt crossed Laird MacDonnell's weathered features. "What say ye, Mackenzie? The MacVales have wronged ye as much as they have me."

Reid felt the eyes of both the MacDonnells and the MacVales shift to him. The only sound was his own heartbeat in his ears—his MacDonnell and MacVale blood coursing through his veins.

And Murdoch Mackenzie's voice in the back of his head. Murdoch had taught him the meaning of honor, of leadership.

Do right by our people, son.

Murdoch's words rose in Reid's mind, bringing forth a tight knot of emotion to his throat.

Aye, Father.

Reid drew in a lungful of air. "I say," he said, his voice echoing off the stone wall, "that we have had enough of war."

MacDonnell blinked in surprise, and the MacVales began to murmur their agreement. Reid lifted his voice to be heard over them.

"Those who are guilty have paid the highest price," he continued, nodding toward the dead MacVales. "There is still much to atone for, much to make right."

At that, the MacDonnells grunted and muttered, eyeing the MacVales.

"But," Reid went on, "we must start somewhere. What say ye, MacVale?" He turned to Fillan, pinning him with a look.

"I want peace for my people," Fillan said, his gaze unflinching. "And that begins with making peace with our neighbors. The MacVales will rebuild the crofts we've destroyed over the years, and work the MacDonnell soil to help yer farmers recoup what we took. It is time we got back to hard work."

"Aye," his men said, nodding somberly.

"And ye, MacDonnell?" Reid asked, turning toward the older man.

The Laird shifted in his saddle, remaining silent for a long moment. Reid began to fear that the man wouldn't yield an inch of goodwill, but at last he spoke.

"I'll accept such a gesture," he said slowly. "But I'll be watching yer every move, MacVale. Betray my trust, and ye willnae get a second chance."

"My father's blood runs through my veins," Fillan replied. "But that is all we shared. I willnae follow his path."

Fillan's words were like a lance to Reid's heart. He pulled in a breath, taking Corinne's small hand in his. "And for my part," he said, drawing Fillan and Laird MacDonnell's gazes back to him, "My mother's MacDonnell blood flows in my veins." He nodded to MacDonnell, then fixed Fillan with a penetrating look. "And Serlon MacVale's blood as well."

Gasps rose from both the MacDonnells and the

MacVales. Fillan's dark eyes rounded. He staggered back a half-step, barely managing to catch himself with his cane.

"Ye are…my brother?"

"Aye," Reid murmured.

"I-I never kenned. I thought I was alone."

"I only learned this morn." He glanced down at Corinne, whose eyes were filled with sadness—and love. She squeezed his hand, then released it, urging him toward Fillan.

Reid strode forward until a pace separated them.

"Serlon raped my mother in an attempt to sow discord—through me."

Fillan's dark eyes hardened with pain. "I am truly sorry. I never kenned my mother, for she died giving birth to me, yet many murmured that it was a blessing, for it allowed her to escape my father."

Slowly, Reid extended his hand toward the younger man. "As ye say, we dinnae have to follow his path."

His eyes glistening, Fillan took hold of Reid's hand. "To the future."

"To the future!" the MacVales behind him echoed. The MacDonnells remained quiet, though Reid saw many of them nodding in approval.

Reluctantly, Fillan released their grasp. "I hope we can come to ken each other no' only as allies, but as brothers, Laird Mackenzie."

"Call me Reid," he replied. "And aye, I'd like that, too. But for now…" He turned to Corinne, his heart swelling with more love than it could contain. "I am taking my wife home."

Chapter Thirty-Seven

Their journey home took a full sennight, for Reid wanted to go to the MacDonnell keep first to check on Alain. Corinne didn't mind the delay, though, for as long as she could stay by Reid's side, she was happy.

The MacDonnell healer stitched Reid's calf and checked on their other injuries, but none required more than rest and time to heal.

Alain had been lucky. The arrow had hit him more in the shoulder than the chest, and after only a few days in the healer's care, he was ready to return to Eilean Donan, his arm in a sling but his usual smile once more on his face.

Reid had sent Leith and Hamond ahead to the castle to alert the clan that all was well, but that Reid, Corinne, and Alain wouldn't arrive for several days. Despite his men's reassurances, though, the three of them were met with a sea of concerned faces when they rode into the village.

"Welcome back, Laird!" the villagers shouted, parting for their horses. "God be praised!"

In a strange way, this reception echoed Corinne's first time facing the clan. Just as before, people swelled all around them, showering blessings and greetings on their Laird.

But this time, instead of curious or downright stony stares, she was met with the same warm smiles and kind words that greeted Reid and Alain.

"Milady, are ye well?"

"Welcome back, milady!"

"Lady Corinne, blessings on ye!"

Tears burned her eyes as she scanned the people's upturned faces—*her* people. She waved and met their smiles, touching their hands when they reached for her and assuring them as best she could as they rode on that she was all right.

When they reached the docks and dismounted, the questions came fast and urgent from the crowd.

"Laird, what happened?"

"Is all well?"

"What of the MacVales?"

Reid held up a hand for silence.

"Those responsible for attempting to harm my lady wife and reap war with our allies have faced the ultimate punishment—and their souls are no doubt writhing in hell."

A murmur of sober approval traveled through those gathered.

"As for the MacVales," Reid continued, pausing.

Corinne watched him as he searched for the right words. "They have a new Laird who is committed to a different direction moving forward. I have chosen to stand by him and give him a chance."

A ripple of surprise passed over Corinne, mirroring the astonished whispers from the crowd. The Mackenzie villagers were no doubt shocked at their newfound peace with the MacVales, yet Corinne was more startled by what Reid *didn't* say—namely that Fillan MacVale was his half-brother.

Reid remained quiet as they crossed to the castle in Timothy's boat. Inside Eilean Donan's walls, he repeated what he'd said in the village to the castle's inhabitants.

To celebrate the Laird and lady's safe return, Bitty insisted on throwing a feast. Alain was more than happy to be the center of several lasses' attention during the meal. They fawned over him, refilling his ale mug, piling his trencher high, and cooing over his injured shoulder.

Reid, on the other hand, sat beside Corinne on the dais in silence, his flinty gray eyes distant in thought.

Seanad approached and pulled Corinne into a warm hug. "Welcome home, milady," she said, giving Corinne another squeeze. Even Wallace came before the dais and bowed deeply to them both in his formal way. Despite the clan's joy, Reid remained reserved.

Sensing the storm brewing behind his eyes, Corinne rose from her chair and took his hand. Without speaking, she led him across the hall and to the stairs. When they reached their chamber, she closed the door softly behind them and faced him.

"Tell me what troubles you."

He let a weary breath go. "Am I so easily read, wife?"

"Only by someone who knows and loves you," she replied, stepping closer.

One dark brow rose. "Ye are too clever by half. Which reminds me." He moved to the hearth and stoked the fire which Seanad had thoughtfully lit. Winter was nigh upon them now. Though the bright, crisp sun had peeked through the clouds several times over the last sennight, snow still lingered in the shadows and the air held a sharp edge of cold.

"The missive ye left me—the one ye wrote yer message on," he said, setting aside the fire poker. "It wasnae the first, was it?"

Corinne stilled. "Are you upset with me?"

In two strides he was before her, pulling her against his hard, warm chest. "Nay, lass." His deep voice rumbled through her bones. "Never. It is only that I dinnae want ye to feel that ye ever have to keep things from me."

She nestled into him, drawing strength from the corded arms holding her tight. "Gellis delivered another missive before that one. Brother Michael—or rather, Serlon MacVale pretending to be Brother Michael—offered to give me sanctuary and a place to work as a scribe if I left you. Now I know Serlon made Fillan write it in an attempt to lure me to him."

"But ye didnae go."

Corinne pulled back slightly so that she could look up at Reid. "Nay," she replied. "Of course not."

"But before ye kenned it was a trap, ye were offered everything ye ever wanted."

She felt her brows draw together. "Nay," she repeated, more fervently this time. "I had already found what I wanted—here, serving the clan. With you."

The tension eased from his hard features and his steely eyes softened.

"The only reason I went with Gellis after the second missive was because I thought I could help someone in need while keeping the life I had come to love," she continued. "Not because I wished to run away."

Emotion burned in his stormy gaze. Slowly, he dipped his head and kissed her softly.

When at last he pulled back, she had to take a moment to catch her breath.

"Is that what has been troubling you?" she asked. "You thought I was still trying to escape?"

Reluctantly, he released her and dragged a hand through his dark hair. "No' truly, nay," he said, turning back to the fire. His broad shoulders cast her in shadow, his voice coming low and tight. "I trust in yer love for me, Corinne, just as I hope ye trust in mine."

"Then what is it?" she murmured.

"I have been thinking on the scroll ye transcribed. The clan history."

She waited, staring at the outline of his bristled jaw, where a muscle ticked as he searched for his words.

"It is a shame to think of ye having to redo it," he said at last. "But now that I ken who my real father is, it seems that he must be added."

Understanding washed over her, followed by pain for

all that Reid had endured. She knew how much he'd longed for the knowledge of his blood sire, and what a blow it had been to learn the truth.

She slipped a gentle hand around his middle, pulling herself flush with his broad, strong back.

"I see no need to re-transcribe the clan records," she said softly.

"But it willnae do to hastily add lines, as we did before. If the records are to show my real father—"

"They already do," she cut in. "Reid, your *real* father already appears above your name—Murdoch Mackenzie."

He stilled against her. "A question has plagued me ever since I learned that Serlon was my blood sire. Am I like him? I share his features, his blood—what else might I have in common with that monster?"

Corinne's heart broke for Reid in that moment, but she couldn't simply comfort him and let his words go unchallenged.

She planted herself in front of him, placing a hand over his heart. Even as she kept her touch gentle, her voice came out firm.

"Look at me, Reid. Though their blood runs in my veins, I couldn't be any more different than my parents. My mother has shrunk into practically naught, and my father is a tyrant. I had to *learn* how to be strong and brave. I didn't inherit that."

A light of comprehension kindled in his eyes, but she went on.

"Speaking of learning, take my scribing, for instance. I wasn't born knowing how to do it. I was taught. I worked at it. I practiced. It is the same with your honor, your goodness, your devotion to your people. You weren't born knowing how to be a fair and just Laird, or a good man. You learned it—from Murdoch. Serlon's sins can never change that."

His gaze clouded with emotion, then turned molten. "God, how I love ye."

Warmth crept from her neck into her face under his heated stare.

"Ye are the most incredible woman I've ever kenned," he rasped, closing his hand over hers where it rested on his heart. She felt the strong, steady thrum there and knew it beat for her.

He lowered his head, claiming her mouth in another kiss. This time, though, his lips weren't gentle. He showed her wordlessly just how deep and fierce his love for her was.

When at last he broke the contact, they were both left panting.

"There is...something else I need to tell you," she breathed.

Reid stilled, his eyes searching her face. "What is it?"

This time, the heat in her cheeks wasn't just from desire. "It is...a woman's matter. My courses were supposed to come two weeks past, but they didn't."

He stood frozen for a long moment, and then his jaw loosened. "Do ye mean to say..."

"It is early yet," she added hurriedly. "But..." A soft smile pulled at her lips. "But I feel different. I think I am pregnant."

He enfolded her in a crushing embrace, burying his

face in her hair. "My love. My heart," he rasped, sending shivers racing over her skin. "Ye undo me."

Tears pricking her eyes and heart swelling against her ribs, she let him hold her for a long moment, savoring his strength, his passion, his love.

At last, she eased back so that she could look up at him once more.

"You know what this means, don't you?" she murmured, her mouth twitching as she fought against a grin. "You'll have to admit to King Robert the Bruce that he was right. It seems your English bride has proven to be a boon after all."

He leveled her with a look, but his lips quirked in barely-contained mirth as well. "I am no' above putting aside my pride and admitting I was wrong," he said. "If it pleases ye, I'll shout it from the top of Eilean Donan —I am the luckiest man in all of Scotland."

And when he dipped his head and kissed her fiercely, Corinne knew she was the luckiest woman, too.

Epilogue

❦

April, 1320
Six months later
Eilean Donan Castle, Scottish Highlands

"Jerome Munro asks admittance to the castle, Laird."

Reid lifted his gaze to Alain, who stood in the great hall's doorway, a broad grin on his face.

A ripple of excitement moved through those gathered in the hall. They all knew what this meant.

Peace.

He turned to the two farmers who were airing their dispute before him. "Do ye mind if we continue this later, men?"

Both nodded eagerly. They were no doubt counting themselves fortunate to have happened to be in the castle for this monumental day.

Reid glanced over to find Corinne nigh bouncing out of her chair with excitement, no small feat considering she was round with their bairn. The quill in her hands, which she'd been using to record the settling of disputes, was all but forgotten as she met his gaze, elation brimming in her eyes.

Corinne was mayhap the most excited out of everyone in the clan. Of course, she was as happy as they all were about what would shortly take place, but she had extra reason for her delight.

Robert the Bruce had officially accepted Edward II's request for a truce before Christmas a few months past. It meant a blessed break in the seemingly endless war against the English, yet the Bruce wasn't content to sit on his heels and wile away all he'd accomplished.

Nay, the Bruce had decided that it was time to extract another truce of sorts—this time from the Pope himself. The Pope had excommunicated the Bruce nearly fifteen years earlier for killing on holy ground. It had meant that the Church didn't recognize him as a legitimate King—or Scotland as a sovereign nation, but rather the property of England.

With Edward II's truce secured, however, the Bruce had pushed to petition the Pope to acknowledge that Scotland was its own country, and he its rightful King.

Murmurs of the document declaring Scotland's independence had swirled through the Highlands as winter had turned to spring. Then Reid had gotten word that the Bruce was asking his Lairds and noblemen to add their seals to the document, showing the Pope that

Scotland's leaders—and the people they represented—were behind the Bruce's cause.

The document had been completed earlier that month at Arbroath Abbey in the east by an Abbot. Some had begun calling it the Declaration of Arbroath.

While a few Lairds had been able to travel to the abbey to append their seals to the document, many, including Reid, had too many duties to see to at home. So the Bruce had selected a warrior, Jerome Munro, to travel to every corner of Scotland collecting Lairds' seals and spreading the word about the bold declaration the Bruce intended to send to the Pope.

Corinne had been thrilled at the news, along with everyone else in the clan, for it meant the chance of true freedom once and for all for Scotland.

Yet Reid knew what had her springing from her chair now was the significance of participating, even in a small way, in such an important document. She was convinced that the Declaration of Arbroath would forever change Scottish history, and to be a part of that sent her nigh into an elated frenzy that Reid guessed only another scribe could fully appreciate.

"I'll fetch your sealing wax and the clan signet ring," Corinne said, popping to her feet with remarkable alacrity. "And the clan records—this moment must be recorded!"

Just as she was about to fly from the dais, he caught her arm and pulled her into his lap. "Send Seanad for it," he murmured, "and save yer feet the trip."

Though her pregnancy had been relatively smooth

so far, Corinne was round enough now that moving about overmuch made her feet ache and swell.

She sighed, some of the wind taken out of her sails, yet she seemed more than happy to remain in his lap until Seanad returned with the retrieved items.

When the double doors to the hall opened at last, those gathered were nigh abuzz with anticipation.

"Jerome Munro, Laird," Alain said, stepping aside.

A dark-haired man strode in, his red plaid, which was slashed with yellow and green lines, a stark contrast to the Mackenzie blue and green all around.

"Laird Mackenzie," Jerome said when he reached the dais, dipping his head in respect.

"Munro. I hear ye've paid visits to the MacVales and the MacDonnells already," Reid said, nodding back. "How fare our neighbors?"

"Verra well," Jerome replied. "Both Arthur MacDonnell and Fillan MacVale contributed their seals to the Declaration." He lifted a dark brow. "And I have been instructed by our King to thank ye especially, for he heard ye had a hand in encouraging the MacVales to put an end to their lawlessness and join his cause."

Reid waved a hand, but inside he warmed with pride. A slow but steadily building trust had begun to grow between the MacVales and the MacDonnells. And for his part, Reid was coming to know his smart, capable younger half-brother as both a Laird and a friend. "Credit goes to Fillan," he said, "though I am happy to call the MacVales allies at last."

Jerome nodded, then drew a rolled piece of parchment from the pouch on his belt. "Shall I proceed?"

With Reid's assent, Jerome lifted his voice so that it traveled throughout the hall. "These are the sentiments our King, Robert the Bruce, sends to the Pope, and which he asks Laird Mackenzie to co-sign." He raised the scroll and began reading. "To the most Holy Father and Lord in Christ, the Lord John, by divine providence Supreme Pontiff of the Holy Roman and Universal Church..."

Though Reid knew the declaration had been written in Latin to respect the Pope's authority, Jerome read in Gaelic for the benefit of the people gathered. He recited the atrocities committed by the English against the Scots, and of the Bruce's noble fight for freedom. But the document also asserted that if the Bruce should ever fail the people of Scotland, it was their right as a sovereign nation to replace him with someone who would fight on their behalf.

Reid had never heard aught like it. It took a brave and confident King to make such a bold declaration to the Pope himself, and yet to acknowledge the limits of his power as a servant of the Scottish people. But Reid had to agree—a good leader, a good *man*, was made, not born. Reid, like the Bruce, was only as strong as the people he served.

"This declaration was given at the monastery of Arbroath in Scotland on the sixth day of the month of April in the year of grace thirteen hundred and twenty and the fifteenth year of the reign of our King afore-said," Jerome concluded. "Directed to our Lord the Supreme Pontiff by the community of Scotland, and endorsed by all who freely give their seal."

He lowered the scroll, his dark eyes landing on Reid. All in the hall seemed to hold their breath, but then someone began stamping their feet. Another joined him, and another clapped until the hall was filled with the roar of voices, the pounding of hands, and the stomping of feet.

Reid held up his hand for silence, and the hall stilled.

"I, Reid Mackenzie, fourth Laird of the Mackenzies of Eilean Donan, Kintail, do freely give my seal," he said loudly.

The crowd erupted once more into revelry. Jerome's stony features remained unchanged, though Reid did notice a flicker of pride in his dark eyes. He tucked the scroll away and withdrew two strips of thick vellum.

Holding up both parchment strips, he stepped onto the dais. "One for the Pope's copy, and one for the King's," he said, placing the slips on the table before Reid.

Carefully, Reid warmed the stick of red sealing wax in a nearby candle's flame, then lowered the melting tip to the tab of parchment. As the glob of wax began to cool onto the parchment, he lifted the Mackenzie clan signet ring and pressed it into the wax.

He moved to do the same with the other vellum strip, but then his gaze landed on Corinne, who watched the ceremony beside him, rapt.

Reid extended the stick of wax to her. "Ye do the other," he urged softly.

Her eyes widened so much that he feared he would drown in their sea-green depths. "Truly?"

"Aye."

With trembling fingers, she took the wax and held it to the candle. As he had done, she dripped a blob onto the piece of parchment, then imprinted the Mackenzie seal into it.

When she raised her head, the crowd broke out into cheers again, bringing a bonny blush to her cheeks.

Jerome nodded approvingly, lifting both sealed pieces of vellum and tucking them safely into his pouch.

As the revelry died down, Reid turned to the dark-headed man. "Where are ye headed next, Munro?"

"To the Lowlands and Borderlands," he replied. "The Bruce wants all the seals collected in the next month, though I dinnae think he realizes I cannae sprout wings and simply fly from clan to clan." He lifted one dark brow, and Reid got the impression that this was as close to humor as the serious warrior ever got.

"Ye're welcome to stay the night and sample our Mackenzie whisky if ye can afford the time," Reid offered.

"Ye had me as whisky," Jerome replied, the faintest hint of a smile touching his lips. "Many thanks."

As Jerome stepped off the dais, Corinne's hand slipped into Reid's. He found her eyes, which shone with emotion. "Thank you for that."

"Nay, lass," he replied, pulling her onto his lap once more, uncaring that his people looked on and murmured good-natured teases for their lovesick Laird. "Thank ye—for allowing me to be the one to make ye happy."

He coiled a finger in her flame-red hair, which had grown out past her shoulders now. "I love ye," he murmured, gently pulling her closer by the lock of hair. "And I'm determined never to let ye forget it."

She chuckled, low and soft. "I love you, too."

And then there was no more need for words, for their lips sealed in a kiss.

The End

Author's Note

As always, part of the joy of getting to write historical romance is sharing not only a happily-ever-after with you, but also the historical context that makes the story possible! *The Bastard Laird's Bride* was particularly rich with historical detail, so there's lots of fun tidbits to share!

The book opens on my retelling of the Battle of Myton, which took place outside of York, England on September 20, 1319. Back in April of 1318, Berwick Castle was wrested from English control by the Scottish (which I touch on in two other books, *Claimed by the Bounty Hunter* and *A Highland Betrothal*). King Edward II of England was furious to have lost such an important Borderland stronghold, so in the summer of 1319, he decided to attempt to take it back.

Edward had been feuding with his noblemen, many of whom thought he was doing a terrible job as King— including Thomas, Earl of Lancaster. You'll remember

Lancaster from *The Lady's Protector* and other books in the Highland Bodyguard series—he was arguably as rich and powerful as the King himself, and the two, though cousins, did not get along. But for the sake of reclaiming Berwick, they entered a truce and joined forces to lay siege to the castle.

The Scots defended Berwick nobly, but Robert the Bruce soon realized that they couldn't hold out against the siege indefinitely. So the Bruce, keen tactician and master of distractions that he was, came up with a diversionary attack on York to draw off the siege.

The Bruce had learned that Isabella, the Queen of England and Edward's wife, had accompanied her husband and Lancaster as far north as York to reside for the summer while the English sieged Berwick. Rumors began to swirl that the purpose of the Bruce's sudden advance on York was to kidnap the Queen and hold her for ransom. The Queen was whisked to safety in Nottingham, but York was almost completely defenseless, leaving the Scots free to attack the city at will.

The Scots won the encounter decisively, but the victory was actually three-fold. In addition to winning the battle, the attack on York had the desired effect of drawing Edward and the siegers away from Berwick, leaving the important stronghold safely in the Scots' hands.

Perhaps most important, though, it pitted Lancaster and Edward against each other once more. With the end of the siege, Lancaster and Edward's alliance crumbled. Worse, rumors began to spread that Lancaster had been the one to inform the Bruce that the Queen was in

York. Suspicions of Lancaster's treason were heightened when the Bruce's army, which was returning through Northern England back to Scotland after the successful battle, didn't raid, raze, or otherwise touch Lancaster's lands.

Whether Lancaster actually helped the Bruce or the clever King of Scotland simply saw an opportunity to sow discord between two of his enemies, we do not know. Whatever the case, the Scots' raids into Northern England, and their attack all the way to York, proved that Edward could no longer contain them. He was forced to ask the Bruce for a truce, which the Bruce granted just before Christmas of 1319.

For his part, the Bruce realized that with the Borderlands now secure, it was time he attended to governance. He began to spend more time at Scone Abbey in Perth, where the Scottish Parliament gathered. He also had a home built in Cardross so that he could spend time with his family. But he wasn't done fighting for Scottish freedom—more on that in a moment.

There were indeed female scribes in the medieval era—in fact, there is evidence that women worked as scribes all the way back to ancient Greek and Roman times! Scribing largely took place in holy houses, for the work mainly involved copying bibles and prayer books for wealthy patrons of the church (though there are examples of non-religious professional scribes as well).

The work was grueling—sitting bent over a piece of parchment, eyes straining in the low light, attempting to keep warm in a drafty stone building. But it was also a high-skill, high-value trade—in the time before the printing press was invented, transcription done by hand (usually by monks or nuns) was the *only* way to duplicate a text.

For Benedictine nuns and monks, the Rule of St. Benedict dictated that transcribing religious manuscripts was a requirement, for it helped spread Christianity. This allowed some women (whose education would normally be very limited) to learn to read and write, and to work as scribes within nunneries. Because of this, joining a nunnery became a viable path for many women as an alternative to marriage—it gave women the chance to study, be creative, and excel at a craft in a time when many weren't given such freedoms.

When a woman entered a nunnery, she was required to relinquish her worldly possessions—including her hair. Novices had their hair cut or tonsured, often by the Abbess, to show a complete renunciation of the outside world. This was symbolically significant because a woman's hair in the medieval period was a sign of marital and social status, as well as an indicator of her purity. Long, flowing hair was a sign of maidenhood, so the cutting of nuns' hair was considered a sign of sexual renunciation—it meant the nun was abandoning the secular world in favor of devotion to God. (This is why I included a few knuckleheads questioning Corinne's virginity—her short hair would have been highly suspect to them.)

Speaking of virgins, I had fun including some of the lore surrounding the Five Sisters mountain range into the story. According to legend, the five sisters used to actually be seven, but two brothers sailed into Loch

Duich (the sea loch on which Eilean Donan castle sits) from far away (some say Ireland, some say Norway) and fell in love with the youngest two sisters. The lasses' father refused to allow the couples to marry until the older five sisters had wed as well. The two sailors swore they had five other eligible brothers and promised to fetch them. Instead, they snatched the two youngest daughters and sailed away, never to return. The five older sisters waited so long for the sailors to return that they turned to stone, with their feet in the lochs and rivers and their heads in the clouds.

Now the Five Sisters mountains overlook the Kintail region, whose crown jewel is Eilean Donan Castle. It is considered one of the most photographed places in all of Scotland, and for good reason. It sits on the tidal sea lochs of Loch Duich, Loch Long, and Loch Alsh on the western coast of Scotland. What we see today of Eilean Donan Castle was actually an early-twentieth-century restoration (including the arched bridge connecting it to land), but remnants of the medieval castle give histo-rians clues about what the original structure looked like.

Eilean Donan simply means "Island of Donnán," named after a seventh-century Celtic saint (though there may have been Picts on the island even before Donnán). Donnán is thought to have established a church on the island upon which the castle now sits, though no trace of it remains.

The medieval version of the castle was first built in the early thirteenth century and became a stronghold for Clan Mackenzie and their close allies, Clan MacRae. In its first iteration, the castle took up nearly the entire small island on which it sits. A curtain wall with several watch towers enclosed the main keep, which was likely about four storeys tall. There was a sea gate below the largest of the towers, which was accessed by a small sandy beach on the back side of the island. All the towers, including the keep, were rectangular, with walls nearly ten feet thick. It was a defensive stronghold to rival all of its era, yet the island-castle was also large enough to contain an orchard, an archery range, a smithy, and other amenities to make life in the castle more comfortable.

The castle was destroyed in one of the Jacobite uprisings of the eighteenth century, and it remained in ruins after that for over two centuries. In the 1930s, the MacRaes, who were traditionally the hereditary constables of the castle on the Mackenzies' behalf, took up the project of restoring the castle. Interestingly, because the MacRaes had served so long as bodyguards and soldiers amongst the Mackenzie clan, they were dubbed "the Mackenzies' shirt of mail"—I sense another story here!

In their own right, the Mackenzie clan was one of the largest and most powerful Highland clans in the medieval era. Their unwavering support of Robert the Bruce played an important role in the King's success. As far as I know, there are no tales of an illegitimate Laird in the clan history, though I did lightly draw on historical records to describe the clan's lineage. Kenneth was indeed the first Laird of the clan, followed by Ian, and Murdoch was a historically significant name, appearing twice in the records of fourteenth-century Lairds' names.

Lastly, a quick note on the Declaration of Arbroath —but I don't want to say too much, because it (and Jerome Munro!) will be featured in the next book in the Highland Bodyguards series, entitled *Surrender to the Scot*.

The declaration was another of Robert the Bruce's moves to secure freedom for Scotland. It petitioned the Pope, who had excommunicated the Bruce and viewed Scotland as belonging to England, to recognize Scotland's sovereignty, and the Bruce as its King. It was revolutionary in its day, for it implied that the will of the people could override a King's—the Bruce declared himself King of Scotland, but he also believed that if he failed to serve the people as they saw fit, he could be removed in favor of a different leader.

Many consider the Declaration of Arbroath a precursor of—and even an inspiration for—the United States Declaration of Independence. With its emphasis on the will of the people, some historians believe it is also an indication of proto-democracy—in early fourteenth-century Scotland!

There are thought to be about fifty names of the Bruce's supporters added to the declaration, including signatures and appended seals—literally seals of approval. Many of the seals have fallen off over the centuries, and the Mackenzie clan seal is not among those that remain, but given their unwavering support of the Bruce, I imagine they would have backed the declaration.

There's so much more to say about the Declaration of Arbroath (and all these other wonderful historical tidbits), but for now, thank you for journeying back to the medieval Highlands with me!

Make sure to sign up for my newsletter to hear about all my sales, giveaways, and new releases. Plus, get exclusive content like stories, excerpts, cover reveals, and more. Sign up at www.EmmaPrinceBooks.com

Thank You!

Thank you for taking the time to read *The Bastard Laird's Bride* (Highland Bodyguards, Book 6)!

And thank you in advance for sharing your enjoyment of this book (or my other books) with fellow readers by leaving a review on Amazon. Long or short, detailed or to the point, I read all reviews and greatly appreciate you for writing one!

I love connecting with readers! Sign up for my newsletter and be the first to hear about my latest book news, flash sales, giveaways, and more—signing up is free and easy at www.EmmaPrinceBooks.com.

You also can join me on Twitter at @EmmaPrinceBooks. Or keep up on Facebook at https://www.facebook.com/EmmaPrinceBooks.

TEASERS FOR EMMA
PRINCE'S BOOKS

Highland Bodyguards Series

The Lady's Protector, the thrilling start to the Highland Bodyguards series, is available now on Amazon!

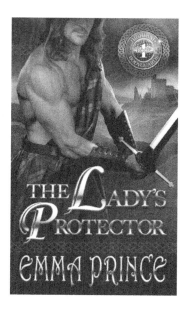

The Battle of Bannockburn may be over, but the war is far from won.

Her Protector...

Ansel Sutherland is charged with a mission from King

Robert the Bruce to protect the illegitimate son of a powerful English Earl. Though Ansel bristles at aiding an Englishman, the nature of the war for Scottish independence is changing, and he is honor-bound to serve as a bodyguard. He arrives in England to fulfill his assignment, only to meet the beautiful but secretive Lady Isolda, who refuses to tell him where his ward is. When a mysterious attacker threatens Isolda's life, Ansel realizes he is the only thing standing between her and deadly peril.

His Lady…

Lady Isolda harbors dark secrets—secrets she refuses to reveal to the rugged Highland rogue who arrives at her castle demanding answers. But Ansel's dark eyes cut through all her defenses, threatening to undo her resolve. To protect her past, she cannot submit to the white-hot desire that burns between them. As the threat to her life spirals out of control, she has no choice but to trust Ansel to whisk her to safety deep in the heart of the Highlands…

Don't miss the story of Reid's brother Logan in **The Promise of a Highlander** (**Highland Bodyguards, Book 5**). Available now on Amazon.

He is no man of honor...

To help his sister heal from a traumatic captivity, Logan Mackenzie reluctantly seeks the Bodyguard Corps' protection. After so many years as a mercenary, he is resistant to live by their code—until he rescues a beautiful Englishwoman from a snowstorm. He vows to protect Helena, even though she kindles a desire that threatens to expose his shameful past. Now he must fight

to regain the honor he thought destroyed years before—
or risk losing Helena forever.

She is fleeing for her life...

When a foreboding vision warns Helena that her life is
in danger, she escapes from her Borderland castle to the
Highland wilds. Under Logan's care, Helena begins to
hope she can trust the scarred warrior with the secret of
her curse. When forced to confront the past she abandoned, Helena must choose between surrendering to
fate or having the courage to forge her own path with
Logan. But will their love be enough to overcome the
hidden truths threatening to tear them apart?

The Sinclair Brothers Trilogy

Go back to where it all began—with Robert and Alwin's story in *Highlander's Ransom*, Book One of the Sinclair Brothers Trilogy. Available now on Amazon!

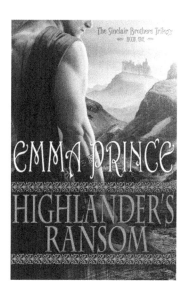

He was out for revenge...

Laird Robert Sinclair will stop at nothing to exact revenge on Lord Raef Warren, the English scoundrel who brought war to his doorstep and razed his lands and people. Leaving his clan in the Highlands to conduct covert attacks in the Borderlands, Robert lives to be a thorn in Warren's side. So when he finds a beautiful English lass on her way to marry Warren, he whisks her away to the Highlands with a plan to ransom her back to her dastardly fiancé.

She would not be controlled...

Lady Alwin Hewett had no idea when she left her father's manor to marry a man she'd never met that she would instead be kidnapped by a Highland rogue out for vengeance. But she refuses to be a pawn in any man's game. So when she learns that Robert has had them secretly wed, she will stop at nothing to regain her freedom. But her heart may have other plans...

Viking Lore Series

Step into the lush, daring world of the Vikings with *Enthralled* (**Viking Lore, Book 1**)!

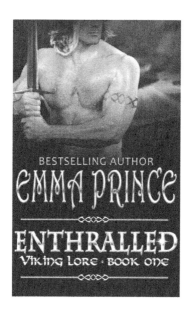

He is bound by honor...

Eirik is eager to plunder the treasures of the fabled lands to the west in order to secure the future of his village. The one thing he swears never to do is claim possession over another human being. But when he journeys across the North Sea to raid the holy houses of Northumbria, he encounters a dark-haired beauty, Laurel, who stirs him like no other. When his cruel cousin tries to take Laurel for himself, Eirik breaks his oath in an attempt to protect her. He claims her as his thrall. But can he claim her heart, or will Laurel fall prey to the devious schemes of his enemies?

She has the heart of a warrior...

Life as an orphan at Whitby Abbey hasn't been easy, but Laurel refuses to be bested by the backbreaking work and lecherous advances she must endure. When Viking raiders storm the abbey and take her captive, her strength may finally fail her—especially when she must face her fear of water at every turn. But under Eirik's gentle protection, she discovers a deeper bravery within herself—and a yearning for her golden-haired captor that she shouldn't harbor. Torn between securing her freedom or giving herself to her Viking master, will fate decide for her—and rip them apart forever?

About the Author

Emma Prince is the Bestselling and Amazon All-Star Author of steamy historical romances jam-packed with adventure, conflict, and of course love!

Emma grew up in drizzly Seattle, but traded her rain boots for sunglasses when she and her husband moved to the eastern slopes of the Sierra Nevada. Emma spent several years in academia, both as a graduate student and an instructor of college-level English and Humanities courses. She always savored her "fun books"—normally historical romances—on breaks or vacations. But as she began looking for the next chapter in her life, she wondered if perhaps her passion could turn into a career. Ever since then, she's been reading and writing books that celebrate happily ever afters!

Visit Emma's website, www.EmmaPrinceBooks.com, for updates on new books, future projects, her newsletter sign-up, book extras, and more!

You can follow Emma on Twitter at: @Emma-PrinceBooks.

Or join her on Facebook at: www.facebook.com/EmmaPrinceBooks.